THE LITTLE GIRL IN THE WINDOW

A Psychological Thriller

C.G. TWILES

HURACÁN PUBLISHING

Chapter One

12 Years Ago

The summer she was fourteen years old, she fell in love.

And she killed two people.

In mid-June, about a week after her freshman school year ended, Romy Renskler was trying to shrink inconspicuously into the farthest, shadiest corner of the Glass Town Country Club pool area when the lifeguard casually loped his way over to her.

Heath Asher.

He was eighteen years old, gloriously tanned, with a lanky, muscular body slipped inside neon-orange lifeguard shorts, and mussed, dark chestnut hair that grew longer and blonder as the endless (to a fourteen-year-old girl) summer wore on.

Seeing him approach, Romy froze with apprehension, as she was certain he was about to kick her out.

The Glass Town Country Club pool was members only. But she'd found a spot in the metal fence where two bars were kinked out just enough that the resulting space could accommodate her scrawny body.

As Heath Asher closed in, something about his expression set her marginally at ease—it didn't seem like a *get the hell out* look.

"Whatcha writing?" he asked.

Romy wasn't writing, she was drawing. Warily, she held out her sketchbook, showing him her pencil sketch of a winged dragon with a young girl riding on its back, hoping this would act as a talisman that would ward off being booted out of the pool. But perhaps it would do the opposite. Depended on if he liked dragons, she supposed.

"That's awesome." He flipped his sunglasses to his head and looked down at her as if she'd only then truly appeared.

He had magnificent eyes that were a dark, soulful blue—indigo. The bridge of his nose had an infinitesimal thickness to it, which saved him from being "too pretty."

Of course, she'd seen him before.

Romy's freshman year at Glass Town High had just come to an uneventful close, and Heath had been a senior during that time. Freshmen and seniors generally only crossed paths in the hallways. But Romy was aware of him because she'd heard girls her age tittering hormonally as he slouched by them, usually in distressed jeans and a dark hoodie. *Heaaaathhh Asssshhuurrrr. Hessogurguss.*

"You're super talented," he said, handing the sketch-book back.

Romy smiled and reflexively covered her mouth with one hand because she had a slightly outward-turned incisor that embarrassed her.

The only people who'd ever told her she was talented were her grandmother and her art teacher, Mr. Sands. To have someone like Heath Asher tell her this was a revelation because she knew he wouldn't say it unless it was true—he had no reason to otherwise.

She felt her cheeks burning and hoped if he noticed, he'd attribute it to the blazing sun—the sun she wasn't in. She considered taking off her five-dollar plastic sunglasses so he could see her eyes. They were toffee-colored and fringed with sparse but long lashes, and she'd begun using mascara. She thought her eyes were her nicest feature.

But she worried the look in them would blast out everything she was feeling. Her feelings weren't anything she could articulate even in her mind but she knew they were powerful and potentially very humiliating.

"Miss Talent," he said, in a way that wasn't sarcastic. "That's what I'll call you, but what's your name?"

"Romy."

"Like that movie, *Romy and Michelle's High School Reunion?*"

"No, like Romy-some-French-actress, engaged to a guy my mom was obsessed with. A French actor, supposed to be the most handsome man in the world. I looked him up. He's not bad."

She couldn't believe she was speaking so much but

his demeanor was nonjudgmental and encouraging. He stared blankly at her for a moment, then a slow-burn smile spread across his face.

"So, Romy, are you a member here?" He asked in a way that made it clear he already knew she wasn't.

"No. I live up the hill." She hoped her proximity to the pool would somehow grant her membership privileges. "I just moved here from the south side and didn't know it was private, and, um..."

She trailed off, rubbing one bony knee and fidgeting, feeling abysmally awkward in her black and red one-piece bathing suit that was frayed along the pelvis' hem.

"How are you getting in?"

She shamefully pointed to the space in the bars, partly hidden by tree branches.

"Ohh. You must be skinny to get through there."

"Sorry," she mumbled. "I can leave." She made a half-hearted grab for her sketch bag.

"No, it's okay. As long as you stay out here, no one should notice. But don't use the changing rooms. And don't cause trouble."

He stared down at her until it sunk in that he was joking and she could feel her cheeks start to warm again.

"I won't," she said. "Thanks."

"Better not. See ya, Miss Talent."

He loped off back to his lifeguard station, swinging up to the top perch in one fluid motion, like a jungle animal.

* * *

She spent the rest of the summer staring at him from behind her sunglasses, hyperattuned to his every movement. Sometimes he did nothing but twirl the lanyard of his whistle around and around his finger as he surveilled his charges, the people he would have to save from drowning.

Every gesture—an elbow on a knee, chin in a palm, a wipe of his forehead, a wave to someone he knew—captivated her. There was a hint of danger to his lazy movements, like a snake coiled in the grass.

She anticipated those minutes he would come over and speak with her, which he always did, usually in the early afternoon, after his lunch break.

"Maybe one day I can write a book, and you can illustrate it," he said, in a way that made her think he was serious, not teasing her.

"Sure."

"I'll be prelaw." He shrugged his tanned, sinewy shoulders. "But I'd rather write books."

"You definitely should." She had no idea whether he had the capacity to write books but wanted to encourage him nonetheless. "Prelaw" sounded boring and she felt sorry for him, doomed to that kind of bone-dry life.

Their chats only lasted five, maybe ten, occasionally fifteen minutes, over too fast. She thought about secretly recording them so she could replay them at her leisure but couldn't figure out how to set up a microcassette recorder and get it working before he came over to her. She did not yet have a cell phone and all its accompanying apps. She'd been promised one for her fifteenth birthday, which wasn't for another four months.

One day, he brought over a notebook with a story he was writing. He left the pages with her and she consumed them as if they contained the answers to the universe's grandest mysteries—and in a way they did, because this summer, her universe consisted of only drawing, her grandmother, her pool life, and Heath Asher.

Several months ago, her parents had decided to sell their company. It produced a face goop (Steffie's Fountain of Youth) that was inexplicably popular, millions of women believing it kept them eternally young. Then they retired on the Hawaiian island of Maui.

Romy didn't want to go with them. In particular, she didn't want to leave her art teacher, Mr. Sands. He was mentoring her for admission to one of the better art schools—hopefully, The Rhode Island School of Design. (She did not get in but did get into The New School, in Manhattan.) She'd met him when, in junior high, she'd taken a high school level art class for extra credit.

Additionally, Romy couldn't move so far away from her grandmother, Nana. She wondered how her mother could do it. Nana, whose real name was Ella, was in her seventies now. She wouldn't be around forever.

So, after some legalities which Romy barely understood but that involved a lawyer and giving Nana temporary guardianship, her parents had moved, with the understanding that Romy could always change her mind.

She tried not to think too much about what—deep down—this all meant. That she and her parents simply didn't care that much about each other. Or at least not enough to want to live together.

When she saw families on TV who ate each other up, she felt a vague shame about her situation. But she would grow up to feel she had a reservoir of resilience that people her age who'd had hovering parents—always anxious to safeguard their children from any and all discomfort—didn't have. And that reservoir would come in handy.

Romy read Heath's story. It was about a young boy who woke up one morning with the power to control the weather.

She could tell Heath wasn't what anyone would call a profoundly talented writer. But he wasn't terrible. The sentences were constructed properly. The characters, if not compelling, at least made a degree of impact. She didn't get the feeling he would ever be a famous writer but his musings weren't atrocious either.

He also had nice handwriting for a boy, and she was surprised he handwrote.

"Well?" he asked, returning an hour or so later, during the adults-only swim.

"It's not bad," she said. "The lead guy is fun but I don't really like the girl. She's too…"

"Girly?"

"Yeah, maybe."

Even that young, she was incapable of the kind of fakery that stroking his ego would have required. Intuition told her he didn't want that anyway—didn't want her to act like those depraved girls at school who fell into swoons if he glanced in their direction.

"You should keep going," she said. "I'm curious about what happens. Especially with the tornado."

"Are you really?" he asked, sounding dubious.

"Well, I mean, not *dying*. But curious."

"Where are you on the curious scale? From one to ten."

"Um. Six and a half."

"Okay then," he laughed. "Thanks for being honest. I know I have a lot of work to do. I read Tolkien and it's like, who am I kidding?"

When he smiled at her again, she felt like one of those girls at school, almost faint. With her being fourteen and him being nearly in college, there was no chance of them dating. But she'd be old enough for him in a year or two, wouldn't she?

The mellow yet pleasantly eager tone of his voice, his genuine smile, the way he sought her out in her corner… it all conveyed something that she felt on a molecular level. She was more than a precocious child to him.

Wasn't she?

When she left the pool, filled with his image, she became disoriented inside of the woods and walked straight into a low-hanging tree branch, sending a long scratch along her cheek.

Chapter Two

*R*omy instantly noticed when Heath's attention shifted to Misty Glass, the town's prettiest girl. Not only beautiful but from the Glass family, which had founded the town—her ancestors had owned the former tobacco plant that had once employed most of the locals, both men and women.

Misty was an incoming senior, and Romy hadn't seen her at the pool much before but suddenly she was there every day with a friend or two.

Everyone knew she was "going with" Jonathan Dugan, who—as cliché would have it—was a football player, and, as ultra-cliché would have it, was the quarterback. Misty, to her credit, was not a cheerleader.

When Misty began regularly showing up at the country club pool without Jonathan, Romy realized they must have broken up.

There she was in all her glory—the girl you can't look away from. Blue-black hair with sinuous waves to the middle of her back, a nose that could have been the model for Barbie's, the kind of lips women pay hard-earned cash for, and sky-blue eyes.

Her curves weren't the fledgling, striving curves of a typical sixteen-year-old girl, but the ripe curves of a woman in her prime. Put all that in a barely-there white bikini and the magnetic pull around her was palpable.

Sometimes Romy observed the males—old and young alike—as they watched Misty, in awe at the power she had over the opposite sex. Then Misty turned that power on the one male that Romy was fervently hoping she wouldn't.

Day by day over the course of a week, Romy watched as Misty moved her towel with the big sunflower on it closer and closer to Heath's lifeguard station. Watched as she tilted her face up and talked to him, and how he began looking down at her, at first only responding to her flirtation, then—inevitably, Romy supposed—initiating it.

He began twisting to peer over his shoulder towards the main building, where people emerged from the changing and showering area.

He'd sit flinging the cord of his whistle around his finger, waiting for her arrival. She usually got there with her friend shortly after noon.

By now, Misty would spread her sunflower towel directly under Heath's station so they could easily inter-act. When he climbed down to smear suntan lotion on her back, Romy knew they'd become a couple. With his attention fully consumed elsewhere, he stopped coming over to speak with Romy. She'd vanished from his awareness.

A sore lump of dejection sprouted in her chest and stayed there. She'd forget about the sore lump when she slept, but upon awakening, it was only a few minutes before it swelled up again.

She was surprised by the physicality of it. She'd heard the term "heartbreak" but didn't know this was actually what it felt like, as if her heart had been pierced with a spike.

How unfair life was! Of course, he'd want to be with a girl closer to his own age. Of course, he'd want to be with Misty Glass, with her full breasts and woman's ass, with her golden-tanned skin, and glossy, wavy blue-black hair.

Besides, you couldn't even hate Misty. She smiled constantly. You'd smile too if you were her. No one ever said a bad word about her. She was friendly—even to a nobody like Romy.

"Hi, Romy!" she'd chirp if they passed each other in the school's hallways. She was saying hello because she knew Romy was friends with her next-door neighbor, Gillian Frenetti, whom Misty used to babysit.

Still. A girl like Misty didn't *have* to say hello to a girl like Romy. Hell, the town was named after her family. Not only the town but the high school, the hardware store, the diner, the library, and the cemetery, which was dominated by gravestones carved GLASS. Not to mention all the living and breathing residents with Glass blood in their veins.

Despite being a member of the town's unofficial aristocracy, Misty dwelled not in a castle but in a regular-looking, two-story, gray-shingled house at the end of

Shane Road. Not Glass Road, but don't worry, that was only a few streets over. (There was also Glass Hill, Glass Lane, Glass Overlook, and Glass Drive.)

It made complete and despairing sense that Misty would, after parting ways with Jonathan Dugan for whatever reason, get together with Heath Asher, because Misty was special, and Heath was special. And special people find each other.

Chapter Three

That night.

That night, Romy's budding conscience knew what she was about to do was wrong. But she was consumed by something she didn't comprehend.

She stealthily swung out of bed and arranged two pillows horizontally on her mattress, and tucked her sheet around them. Then she opened her window screen, sliding it up slowly. One long, gangly leg stuck out, heel resting on the banged-up lid of a metal garbage can. Maneuvering her way onto the can, she carefully lowered herself to the outdoor patio.

Closing the screen behind her, she took care to leave a half-inch of space at the bottom so she could slide it back up upon her return.

In jeans cutoffs, a sleeveless black T-shirt, and sneakers with no socks, she hustled down the sloping backyard of her grandmother's house toward the woods that buttressed the acre-large property.

She plucked her little Lumen flashlight out of her

back pocket, shining it along the trodden path of brush that led to the country club pool.

She knew these woods so well she probably didn't need a flashlight but didn't want to trip over a raised root. She also hoped the flashlight would ward off any wild animals.

In these parts roamed mammoth raccoons, fisher cats, wild turkeys, snakes both harmless and deadly, and more and more black bears were making appearances. If she stumbled upon one and scared it, she could end up shredded.

It took her about five minutes to get to the pool. The path was rusty-red with fallen pine needles, and they were slippery, hence her sneakers. She had to dig her feet sideways so she wouldn't slide down the mountainous, almost vertical trail. The path was illuminated with the ghostly poles of white birch trees reflecting the glow of the moon.

Almost every night, as her grandmother slept, Romy found herself sneaking out of her house and scampering down the night woods. Taking up a spying spot behind a massive poplar tree, she'd watch Heath and Misty inside the pool area. Heath must have a set of keys. It was obviously their assignation spot.

A few weeks ago, their voices and laughter had started wafting all the way up the hillside into Romy's open bedroom window. She'd sneaked down to investigate, as she was certain it was them. Even though she couldn't make out any words, she recognized the timbre of Heath's voice—it called to her as plainly as one songbird calls to another through a forest of trees.

Romy would spy with a sour churning in her belly as Heath chased Misty around the pool, slapping her shapely ass with his bright orange lifeguard towel. Then they'd get on the pool's thick blue tarp and slip and slide around for a while.

By the time they'd snuggle together on one of the long pool chairs, kissing and murmuring and gliding their hands all over each other's perfect bodies, Romy was too disgusted to continue watching.

She'd traipse sullenly back up the hillside, woozy with jealousy—even anger. It felt as if a thing that was rightfully hers had been stolen from her. The first time she'd watched them, she had a good, hard cry under her sheets, bewildered by the force and newness of her feelings.

Romy couldn't quite remember when the idea came into her head. But she'd spent at least two weeks grappling with it, stamping it down, and when she couldn't wrestle it into submission, starting the justification process, getting all the details lined up.

It gave her something to concentrate on besides watching them at the pool, watching how Heath swept the tendrils of Misty's blue-black hair to one side as he sensuously applied lotion to her golden back while she closed her eyes and smiled dreamily.

Romy couldn't stop watching them during the day, couldn't stop sneaking down to the pool to watch them at night. Because if she stopped watching them, then all hope was lost. Plus, he would be leaving for college soon. It was better to see him with Misty than to not see him at all.

Yes, what she was about to do was wrong. She was old enough to know that. But it was a small thing, a prank. It would be a memory Romy would have, something to savor and privately grin about.

That's all.

Chapter Four

*R*omy skidded down through the woods about nine-thirty p.m. The pool closed at eight p.m. during the summer. She knew Heath and Misty usually arrived about ten p.m.

Whether they were sneaking out of their homes or not, she didn't know. At sixteen and eighteen, she assumed the pair had much more freedom than she did. Amazing the difference a year or two can make when you're young.

It was a risk leaving earlier than she normally did, as her grandmother was still awake, watching television in the living room, one of her cop shows. Nana loved cop shows. They gave her a sense of safety and order in the world—the bad guys always rounded up in the end, the cops always unequivocally good.

But that night, Romy feigned a stomachache, saying she wanted to go to bed early. If her grandmother decided to check on her by opening the bedroom door, she would see a body shape under the sheet and (hopefully) assume the mound was a sleeping Romy.

It never occurred to Romy what she would say if her grandmother caught on. She was too young for that kind of predetermined fabrication.

Tonight, it was silent when she arrived at the pool. She crouched behind the wide poplar and reconnoitered. A few of the pool house lights were on and between that and the nearly full moon, Romy had a decent view of the surroundings.

The pair wasn't there yet but would arrive any minute. She had to be quick.

Slipping through the kinked metal bars as she normally did, she scampered to the first corner of the pool, her heart pounding in her chest.

She crouched down and grasped the thick steel hook fastening one corner of the tarp to a bolt in the platform, and flicked the lever back. The tarp was heavy and, at first, she wasn't sure she would be able to get the hook off the bolt but after yanking hard, so hard her shoulder popped slightly, she released it and watched as one corner of the tarp sank a few inches below the water.

She ran back to the opening in the fence, turned sideways, and slithered out. She wended through the trees to the first curve of the hillside, her usual spying spot. Then she sat, breathing heavily, not from the effort, but from nerves.

In fact, she was so nervous, she couldn't comprehend why she'd set her mind upon this, why the thought of seeing them plummet into the water had fixed in her brain until it had become something she had to accomplish or go mad. How this idea had gone from distant and amorphous to banging insistently on the interior of her skull. *Do it, do it, do it, do it.*

Heath was a swimmer. He was a human fish. Getting dumped in the pool wouldn't bother him in the slightest but Romy had never seen Misty in the water except on the shallow end, where she'd delicately swish around, the water never rising above her thighs. She never joined her friends, who were making noisy cannonballs off the diving board.

Romy suspected that Misty didn't want to get her beautiful wavy blue-black hair wet, didn't want to get her perfect face wet, with that shiny pink gloss on her juicy lips. Maybe she wouldn't be so pretty all wet— those glossy waves would turn scraggly or even frizzy. Would Heath love Misty as much if she didn't look so perfect?

Romy heard Heath's hormonal arrival hoot. Then Misty's delighted feminine cawing. The couple did not drive to the pool, they biked from their nearby homes. Romy knew there was no way they could see her in the gloom of the forest but her heart pounded and she crept farther behind the poplar, tall and wide as a sequoia. She grasped her bare knees, smelling her own earthy child-skin.

"I can't believe it!" Heath shouted, thrusting his arms up in the air. He twirled, kind of a victory twirl.

"You're not mad?" Misty asked as she walked towards the woods-side of the pool. Her melodious voice was closer and clearer than Romy had ever heard it.

"Of course not," he said.

He took off his white, glowing T-shirt, chucked it onto a nearby chair, then merged with Misty, spinning her a couple of times. She laughed loudly, and Heath hushed her.

"We should be quieter," he said.

The couple sat on pool chairs, undressing. Romy had the urgent need to hear everything they were saying. Biting her lower lip, she edged stealthily down the sloped hill and ducked behind another wide tree. She couldn't have been more than fifty feet from them.

"What about Georgetown?" Misty asked.

"Well, everything is paid for. The dorm, books, deposit. Everything. Orientation is next week."

"Oh, no. What do we do?"

"We have to make it work. Either you come with me or stay here and I come up every weekend."

"There are options. I could get an abortion. I don't want to, though."

Romy felt her eyes go large and wide. She froze with her fingers pressed up to her mouth, trying not to breathe loudly.

Heath bent over to kiss Misty. "No, neither do I. I mean, I'd thought we were careful…"

"It happens. It's not one hundred percent."

"Yeah. I guess I didn't know that."

"Me neither. Mom is going to kill me. Dad, he'll understand, I think. Nothing gets him upset. It's Mom… ugh."

He looked out over the pool, then back at her. "Nah. Your mom likes me. Besides, I'm going to be a lawyer, I'll be making piles of money."

Romy felt a stab of disappointment. Why, with her, had he acted like he didn't want to go to law school? That he was creative and wanted to write books... with her? That money didn't mean anything to him?

This was her first real indication that people could have distinct and opposing sides to them—an awakening she didn't welcome.

Heath disappeared and Romy realized he'd gone down to the pool's platform. Was he... on his knees?

"Will you marry me, Misty Glass?"

"Yes!" she squeaked without any hesitation, and the silhouettes of their bodies merged into one.

Romy was sickened, devastated. He was lost to her. The couple was going to get married. He would be a lawyer, making piles of money, working in a skyscraper. He and Misty would live in a McMansion, have a horde of children.

Vague and dreamlike as Romy's imagined artistic future with Heath had been, it had also been sharply real and specific. She felt the loss of that imagined future as keenly as if it had been promised to her.

But how foolish, how infantile she'd been. He was a man, with a man's needs and wants. Romy had to admit she couldn't fulfill those needs and wants. She barely understood what sex was. Of course, she knew what it *was*, she wasn't completely stupid, but she also knew she wasn't ready to have it, not even with Heath.

The pair moved towards the pool. Romy remembered why she was crouched in the moonlit woods, what she'd stolen down here to do. How she'd unlatched one corner of the tarp and the couple was about to slide on it as they normally did and...

Misty was pregnant.

Suddenly, it didn't seem funny to send a pregnant woman plunging into the cold depths of the pool. An ominous sensation rippled through her. She thought about calling out to them. She could pretend she was taking a walk and happened to see them.

But who would believe that? She was a child down in the woods past bedtime. They'd know she'd sneaked out; they'd know she was the one who'd untethered the tarp.

In Romy's adolescent imagination, that meant they'd know what a stupid and mortifying crush she had on Heath—and they would laugh about it in private, make fun of her. Maybe they'd even hate her and spread rumors about her around town. She had a hard enough time fitting in.

So, she did nothing but watch. Her hope was that Heath would go first on the tarp and, upon realizing one side was unlatched, alert Misty not to step on it.

But instead, Romy heard a faint jingle. Heath said, "Hold up" and ambled to the small outdoor changing station. It appeared to Romy as if he moved in slow motion.

Misty stood looking after him as he disappeared into the wooden, white-painted changing station. She stood, with her head turned, for what seemed a long time.

Then she quickly turned back around and stepped off the side of the pool.

Romy couldn't see what was happening. Misty had gone down behind the pool rim, below Romy's line of vision. Her breath quickened and she felt queasy and cold. She heard what sounded like several small splashes in quick succession.

Where was Heath? Where had he gone? What was happening? Romy wanted to yell out, to call for Heath, but she couldn't speak or move.

Then Heath was sprinting towards the pool, fast as a panther, his bare feet *slap slap slapping* on the pavement. It knifed Romy dead in the heart that Misty couldn't swim and she was in the deep end. Romy knew it with a certainty that was ancient and primal.

Romy was moving, moving as if in the water herself but being continually tugged back, and back, and back into danger. It all started to dissolve—the crunch of her shoes on the trail, her heavy breathing, the air coursing into her open mouth and down into her heaving lungs—everything became quieter and quieter, fading out like the end of a song.

Only one sound remained—animal-like wails chasing her up the hill, the otherworldly cries at her back as Heath tried to save Misty who, Romy knew, had become entangled in the tarp and drowned.

Chapter Five

Now

"If it isn't Miss Talent."

His smile was warm. All of him was more attractive than she remembered even in her fevered imagination and in the photos on social media she'd failed to stop checking out over the years.

Those eyes she remembered so well, the blue you'd see on old china patterns, a rare, sublime kind of blue. And they looked at her approvingly, in a way they had not looked at her when she was a child.

She wasn't *completely* surprised at his look. She'd grown pretty over the years. Not gorgeous, but an elfin pretty that certain types of men, especially artistic ones, responded to. But she hadn't been certain Heath would look at her like that, as she knew she wasn't *his type*.

"Hello yourself, Heath Asher. Congratulations on the book."

She held out her copy for him, unabashedly examining him as he kept his head down, signing. At thirty years old, he'd grown into his lankiness and exuded the casual magnetism of a man who knew he appealed to both sexes, a man to be bedded or befriended or both.

He had no idea he'd been sporadically conversing via email with Romy for three years, as she was his cover designer. He had a three-book romance series called *For the Love of Missy* published by a small—microscopic, really, with only a handful of authors—press. So small that Heath had to retain his own cover designer.

Thanks to Heath's PayPal information, Romy—whose design service was known as Golden-Eye—had quickly deduced that romance author "Helen Asher" was actually Heath Asher.

She'd been dumbfounded at the coincidence and couldn't bring herself to tell him who she was, though it was astonishing that his teenage declaration that they should collaborate on a book had come true.

Heath also had no idea that Romy had then started buying copies of his books, keeping his rank afloat. (The copies went into free little libraries all over the city.) Until she walked into the Court Street bookshop in Brooklyn, she had no idea how *much* she'd been keeping his rank afloat, because there were only about a dozen people scattered in the metal folding chairs in front of the dais. The sizable number of empty chairs gawping at her made her feel uncomfortable for him.

After his reading and question-and-answer session, about half the audience—all of six women—lined up for him to sign their books, Romy bringing up the rear.

The women, all forty and up, didn't seem to mind that "Helen" was a man. Given that he was a young, attractive man, the starry look in their eyes and eager lilt in their voices as they received his John Hancock indicated they preferred it.

He signed Romy's inside cover of *Missy's Wedding* (following *Missy's Courtship* and *Missy's Engagement*), "To Romy—Here's to escaping Glass Town!" Then he closed the book and looked up at her. She tried not to blush but felt heat pulsing under her skin.

"Thanks for coming," he said, grinning wryly. "You and the other two people."

"Oh no. There were more than that. At least three." She grinned back. "Well..." She hesitated. "Maybe it's that virus thing."

All winter the virus had been something happening in far-off countries, one of those things that had nothing to do with being in current-day America, like mass famine or civil war. But then it had started to roll towards the country like a giant wave, first engulfing Asia, and last she'd heard, washing up on the West Coast.

So far as anyone knew, it wasn't in New York, but people were getting jittery, conversation turning to the virus. If it was on the West Coast, how long before it was here, on the East Coast? No one said, *Maybe it's here now.* But perhaps Heath's poor turnout wasn't merely a sign that Helen Asher's romance series was dismally unpopular.

"Yeah, maybe," he said, seeming both doubtful and grateful for her attempt to soothe his ego. "This is my first signing, so... My publisher thought Helen should come out of the shadows, that it might perk up sales. Besides, I felt weird letting people think I was a woman."

"I can't wait to read it."

Not true. She couldn't bring herself to read his books, as she'd quickly realized that "Missy" was a surrogate for Misty Glass. The fact that Heath had emailed Golden-Eye an actual photo of Misty and requested that she use a cover model who resembled his dead high school girlfriend was more than enough to clue her in.

"Well..." Romy said, looking around awkwardly. The bookstore was empty except for an employee who was eyeing them impatiently. "It was nice seeing you again."

"Come on, Miss Talent, you're not going to bail on me, are you? Want to grab a drink?"

* * *

THE IRISH PUB across the street from the bookstore was packed. So much for the theory that people were staying home because of the virus. Perhaps everyone thought alcohol consumption was the best way to deal with the surreal turn the world had taken.

Heath paid for Romy's glass of bitter white wine and his pint of ale, and they headed to a back table. The bar was dark and stale-smelling.

"Again, thanks for coming," he said.

A couple of weeks ago, he'd out-of-the-blue sent her a friend request on social media. She'd stared and stared at the request, not acknowledging it for several days. Then, all of a sudden, her curiosity became insatiable and she accepted.

She then did what she'd feared she'd do—spent hours and hours obsessively combing through his every post. She wanted evidence, definitive proof, that he was in a good place and was happy—his writing romance novels about Misty Glass notwithstanding.

"Of course," she said. "Thanks for inviting me."

At first, the idea of coming to his book signing was repugnant to her. She was genuinely afraid he would take one look at her, point, and scream, "Murderer!"

But eventually, as with his friend request, curiosity got the better of her.

He took a sip of beer and examined her. "Interesting to see you all grown up. I forgot that would happen. I half-expected a young girl to walk in. You hardly have any pictures on your social."

"Once you get the millionth unsolicited come-on from a supposed Swedish pilot who looks like a stripper, you kind of go incognito."

"Same old Romy." He smiled. "I remember that drollness. Is that a word? Drollness? Drollity?" He laughed. "Some writer, eh?"

She could only give a weak smile. "What are the odds we'd both end up in Brooklyn?"

"Yeahhhh," he drawled, staring down into his glass. "Kind of a cliché, writer living in Brooklyn. But I only do this on the side, a hobby. There's no money in it. Full time, I restore furniture."

"What happened to law school?" she asked and

cringed, as her question gave away that she'd committed to memory something he'd told her twelve years ago.

"I went for a year after college but it wasn't for me. I'd been restoring furniture with my roommate to make extra cash. When he moved here and opened up a place, I followed. What about you? Please tell me you did something with art."

Romy's chest tightened as she tried to decide whether to reveal that she was Golden-Eye. "Yeah, I—I have a freelance operation. Design a lot of stuff, logos, ad campaigns, merch."

"Oh, great. If I didn't have an amazing cover designer, I'd ask you to take a look at them. Maybe you know the place? Golden-Eye."

She sat nervously tapping her finger on her wine glass, acting as if she was preoccupied with the oil painting above his head of a dog sitting on a throne.

Why couldn't she tell him that she was Golden-Eye? It would be so strange to admit she'd been keeping it from him for three years. And why *had* she kept it from him?

She supposed she'd worried about the very thing that was happening—that she'd be unable to resist getting sucked into his orbit and being constantly reminded of the thing she'd done. The thing she'd succeeded in pushing so far into the corners of her mind that she could go long periods wondering if she'd only imagined it.

Misty's smiling face on the cover of the local newspaper delivered to her grandmother's house, every day for several weeks. Gossip Romy had absorbed that

Heath had been questioned by the police. Theories that his teen girlfriend's pregnancy had caused him to react violently, drowning her.

But that suspicion had turned to town-wide sympathy when poor-quality, grainy surveillance camera footage of him dashing from the changing station had come to light. And more grainy footage of him struggling to get Misty out of the pool, giving her CPR, calling 911, and wailing in grief as he was unable to revive her.

Heath must have been erasing the footage during his working hours, hiding his and Misty's nightly clandestine meetings.

Romy had had no knowledge that there was a camera down at the pool. For weeks, months even, she'd lived in stark terror, barely eating, hardly able to think, only sure that any moment a police officer would knock on her grandmother's door, or come to school, snatch her out of class, and parade her down the hallway as a killer.

But no one ever came. Whatever angle she'd been at when she'd unhooked the tarp hadn't been picked up by the pool's one and only camera.

"That poor boy," Romy's grandmother had said, reading snippets of the newspaper articles aloud. "That poor girl. And poor Delta, that was her only daughter. Such a pretty girl too. And pregnant. What a pity. Such a tragedy. What were they doing on that tarp? Thank God, Romy, you never did anything like that. You have too much common sense."

Nothing evinces more horror and outrage than a

young, fertile—and attractive, that's very important—woman dying tragically. Human beings are wired to breed, and losing an attractive breeder (proven by her pregnancy!) is virtually intolerable. So, the local newspaper—which had only passingly and obligingly covered the death in a fire of a grandmother of five, the death of a middle-aged man in a motorcycle accident, and the death of a ten-year-old boy from brain cancer—was morbidly consumed with the death of Misty Glass.

The more the town and her grandmother mourned and parsed and outraged over the death of Misty Glass, the more and more impossible it became for Romy to consider telling anyone what had happened. She would be the town plague, the town degenerate. Her grandmother would be forever tainted to have given birth to someone who gave birth to someone who drowned Misty Glass.

And it seemed patently obvious that Misty couldn't swim. Hadn't Romy sat there day after day watching her never venture to the deep end, never jump off the diving board with her friends?

Who would believe Romy didn't know? Who would believe she hadn't deviously, wickedly plotted to drown Misty in a misguided and pitiful attempt to have Heath Asher—a young man who hardly acknowledged her, mind you, only spoke to her here and there to be nice, look what *that* got him—to herself?

At what point Romy learned about the subconscious she couldn't say but from the time she learned about it, she was tortured by the notion that *subconsciously* she knew. She knew Misty couldn't swim.

Romy and her grandmother had gone to Misty's funeral. So had the entire town. So had what seemed like every town around them. Hundreds of people. In Romy's young mind, it was thousands, maybe millions. Maybe more than had watched Princess Diana's wedding. She hadn't seen Princess Diana's wedding but Nana had and she'd periodically say something like, "There are more ants in that hill than people who watched Princess Diana's wedding."

There were television cameras at the funeral. *Television cameras.* Romy had never seen a television camera. Newscasters (she'd never seen them in real life either) in black suits stood outside the church interviewing locals who said things like, "It's a complete tragedy. Misty was so nice, so sweet, so pretty. None of us can believe this happened. That pool needs to take off that tarp!"

Romy and her grandmother couldn't even get inside the Methodist Church, so they'd waited in the stifling early September heat, listening to the deep, eerie drone of the organ playing inside.

She didn't see Heath at the funeral and wasn't sure he'd attended. For that, she was thankful, as she felt certain if she saw his anguished face, she'd scream out what she'd done, scream it out to the sea of mourners. Let them turn on her and rip her to pieces.

At the hoppy-smelling Irish bar, Romy made a forceful effort to drag her mind back to the present. "Your covers are great," she told Heath, deciding to keep her identity a secret for now. "Hold on to that designer."

"Please tell me about you. Dating anyone?"

"Um, you know," she said, vaguely. "What about you?"

The question was absurd. His fiancée was all over his social media page. A Misty lookalike, no less. Her name was Tara, she was a physical therapist, and she had shoulder-length, wavy black hair and turquoise eyes. She wasn't the stunner that Misty had been, more like the slightly-less-attractive cousin. But Romy thought it a bit creepy nonetheless.

"I was engaged," he said, sipping more beer.

"*Was?*"

"Yeah... I'm not anymore."

She remained silent, her heart cracking. She'd at least been able to console herself that he'd found his Misty lookalike and was happy.

"It was me," he said, forlornly shrugging. "I started to think... Maybe you're the only person I can tell this to. I started to think..." In the dark of the bar, Romy thought she saw him shudder. "Well, Tara, my fiancée —*ex*-fiancée—it dawned on me how much she looked like..." He paused, clearly struggling. "You remember Misty, don't you? And everything that..."

"Yeah, yeah. Of course."

"I realized, truly realized, that I was trying to replace her. That's why I always felt so empty with Tara, despite her being an awesome girl. She deserves someone without all this baggage."

Romy regretted coming here tonight. Now she knew that he was, like her, stuck in an excruciating limbo, stuck in the past. She took a sip of wine to obscure the discomfort she was certain was radiating out from her face.

"Maybe," Romy murmured, staring at the slick table, which no one had bothered to wipe, "you weren't trying to *replace* her. Just trying to bring her back."

She glanced up at him and he seemed lost to another world. He tapped his beautifully defined jawline with two of his long, tapered fingers. "I hadn't thought of it like that. Either way, Tara deserves better. Here's something really crazy."

She waited.

"My romance series. It's about Misty. I named my heroine Missy. I even sent my designer a picture of Misty and wanted a girl who looked like her on the covers."

Romy parted her lips slightly, trying to look surprised and concerned with this news.

"I thought I was giving Misty the life she deserved, the one she should have had. I mean, she marries a prince. A fucking *prince*. Prince Holden! Who's *me*! It's all so twisted."

"It's not twisted, Heath. You just—"

"No, it is. Last year, I started seeing someone. A therapist. She doesn't think it's healthy. I've *got* to move on."

They said nothing for what seemed a squirm-inducing eternity. Why, oh why, had she come here?

"I'm sorry," she mumbled.

"You don't need to be sorry." He tipped his glass toward her. "Not like it was your fault."

* * *

"HERE'S MY NUMBER," Heath said on the sidewalk, handing her a business card. "If I didn't bum you out completely, let's do this again. I work so much that I never really made friends." Pause. "The few friends I do have, they're Tara's friends, too. Can't bear to look them in the eye right now."

"Okay, um. Sure."

Phone in hand, he stood staring expectedly at her until she surrendered her own phone number.

"If that virus doesn't get us," he added, raising his brows in a joshing manner.

"Yeah," Romy tittered. "Starting to sound kind of out there, isn't it? Like a sci-fi movie."

"I'm sure we'll be fine. They always exaggerate these things. The news. Gets ratings, you know."

"Bye then," she said, and despite his dismissive proclamation, neither one could bring themselves to move in for a handshake or cheek kiss. Instead, they bumped fists, then nervously laughed.

"Goodbye, Miss Talent."

She watched him as he ambled down the lamp-lit sidewalk, partly hoping she would never see him again, partly wishing to run after him and keep talking, about anything, so long as she was near him.

Chapter Six

*T*he dog had been barking intermittently for two days, but on the third day, it kept up an escalating stream of yips and yowls.

Romy's neighbor—a man (forties? fifties?) she'd only seen a handful of times, and who was so nondescript she couldn't have picked him out of a lineup—wasn't exactly Mr. Garrulous. She was reluctant to knock on his door and ask him to direct his dog to pipe down. She had no idea how dog owners managed that task but there must be a way, right? But by the late afternoon, she couldn't take it anymore, she needed to get work done.

Besides, dark thoughts were starting to roll like cumulus clouds in the back of her mind. Reported rising virus cases in the city meant that people had already begun to leave.

She'd walked by several moving vans on the surrounding streets, seen determined-looking neighbors loading their belongings into them, and had even witnessed one person in her building strapping a mattress to the roof of his car as his wife piled their three bewildered-eyed kids into the backseat. There was a *frisson* in the air—the stirrings of human panic.

It seemed paranoid to Romy. Perhaps two dozen positive cases had been identified in a city of over ten million people. One stood a much better chance of getting hit by a car while crossing the street than catching the virus. But a part of her wondered if she was being obtuse. Did these fleeing people know something she didn't?

She walked out of her apartment, to her neighbor's door. The hallway was dim and musty-smelling. It was a decent building but not exactly a luxurious one, and despite living here since right after college, five years, she only knew one neighbor, Suzie, a woman in her early thirties who lived on the top floor and was trying to make it as an actress and comedian.

Last year, Romy had gone to one of Suzie's open mic nights in the East Village. She didn't think her neighbor was very funny but laughed obligingly at her forgettable jokes.

The neighbor's dog, sensing Romy's presence behind the door, grew quiet before bursting out with a torrent of barks and a flurry of scratches on the floor as if trying to dig its way out.

Romy instinctively backed away, then called out, "Sir?! Hello?!" She didn't know the man's name.

There was no noise except the low, gruff barking of

the dog, interspersed with what could be growls. The barking sounded like *Wroah Wroah*.

She remembered seeing the man and his dog a few times and recalled that the dog wasn't little. Definitely large enough to tear out her throat if it was so inclined. And now the thought she'd only vaguely entertained came rushing on her—had the man fled the city and abandoned his animal?

"Hello?!" she called out. The dog went silent, though she could still hear its claws clapping on the wood beams underneath the doorway as if it was frantically pacing. "Are you home?"

No answer.

She waited, then went back to her apartment, stymied. The dog was silent for several minutes and she got her hopes up that the problem had resolved itself. Then the barking once more pierced the walls. Inside her bedroom, she pounded on the wall separating the two apartments.

"Hellooooooo!!!!"

Nothing.

Hand on hip, she looked around, wondering if she should call the police. Then it occurred to her that if she got onto the fire escape, she could lean forward far enough to see into the window catty-corner to her kitchen window. The two windows were so close together that she could sometimes smell her neighbor cooking and even hear him if he was on the phone in that area.

She slipped on her moccasins and a light jacket and

opened the window. It was the beginning of March and cold outside. She crawled out to the rickety, rusty-red fire escape, the chill air hitting her face, and leaned over the railing, worried it was ancient enough that it might give way underneath her.

Peering through the window, she saw the kitchen was empty but realized there was a narrow window next to it and she could see a shower curtain—the bathroom.

"Hello?! Sir?! Are you home?!" she called loudly towards both windows.

Then she heard it—deep and guttural. Unmistakable. A groan. Not an animal groan either but a man-groan. Her heart kicked up nervously and she had the distinct feeling that the man was in trouble. He had fallen, maybe broken a bone.

"Hi!" she yelled. "Are you okay? Do you need help?"

The dog was still yelping but the barks were muffled through the rooms between them.

The groan got louder. Then stopped.

Then she heard something that made her insides liquify in fear.

Coughing.

Deep, racking, agonized coughing.

Instinctively, Romy covered her mouth with her hand and backed away from his windows. She quickly clambered back through her window and shut it. Shut it hard.

What to do, what to do?

Should she call 911?

She decided to call Suzie, who thankfully answered.

"Hey, it's me," Romy said. "Listen, I have a dilemma here. The guy who lives next to me, he's got a dog who's been barking for three days straight. Right now I heard the guy in his apartment moaning. He was coughing and—"

"Coughing?"

"Yeah, a coughing fit. He's not answering me when I knock or call out to him."

"Oh my God, Romy!" Suzie burst out. "He's probably got it! The virus!"

"How do you know?"

"Seriously? It's all over the news. They're finding more cases by the day. Like hundreds!"

Romy had been working intensely nonstop, and she always tried to tune out all distractions when she worked. No surfing the internet. No social media. She didn't own a television, so she hadn't watched the news.

She'd known the virus was proliferating in one of those wealthy, suburban areas directly north of the city, and New Jersey too, come to think of it—but hadn't known it was multiplying inside the boroughs like rabbits in a field.

"What do I do?" she asked. "Should I call an ambulance?"

"No, no!" Suzie scolded. "They might bring him to the hospital."

"What's wrong with that?"

"You don't understand. He'll die in there. There will be more people in there who have it. It's better he stay home and recuperate. They can't treat it, you know."

"What about his dog? It sounds like he isn't feeding it. Besides, the barking is driving me nuts. I can't concentrate. I need to figure out what's going on."

"Check his mat," Suzie said. "Sometimes he keeps a key there. I've walked Mack a few times when he's been away."

"You *know* this guy?"

"Barely. His name is Bill. He's really weird and quiet. But he saw me walking Shorty and asked me if I walked dogs. I only did it a few times but that's where he told me he leaves a key."

"Then please come down here and help. He and the dog know you."

"Are you crazy? I don't want that virus. Besides, I can't. I left the city yesterday. I'm in Illinois with my parents. Drove fourteen hours. Me and Shorty. You've got to get out of there, Romy."

"Right now, I need to worry about that guy and his dog. Its name is Mick? It sounds like it could kill me."

"*Mack.* No, no. Mack is sweet. He's probably scared."

"Okay, I'm going to see if there's a key and try to get inside."

"Listen!" Suzie warned. "My family in Japan have dealt with all this stuff before. You've got to wear something over your mouth. You have any masks?"

"Masks? Of course not."

"Then use a scarf. Or a T-shirt. Cloth napkin. Anything. Put it over your mouth and nose. And sunglasses! It gets into your eyes!"

* * *

ROMY HAD Bill's key in one hand, a plate of sliced ham in the other. She'd gone to the nearby deli for the ham, and it was there she'd seen a sight so unusual that she didn't know how to process it—several people were wearing masks. Some of the masks were white, some black, some patterned, some paper, some cloth.

She'd looked around the store to see if they sold any but they didn't. She also noticed that people were starting to try to keep a distance between each other, though that was extremely difficult to do inside the tight confines of the deli.

Back at her neighbor's door, her vague plan was to open it a few inches, enough to let the dog smell the ham. If ham didn't calm him down, she had no intention of entering.

She put the key inside the bottom lock and twisted but it didn't work. She tried the top lock and heard a click. At that, the dog on the other side of the door, not barking but clanking his nails on the floor, began sniffing. She cracked the door open about an inch and pushed the plate of ham, which she'd placed on the floor, towards the crack, keeping her grip tight on the knob.

The dog's sniffing increased, then there were several eager whines. "Hey there, hey there, how you doing, you hungry, huh? You hungry?" she pattered, in what she hoped was a friendly *I-love-dogs* voice.

She saw a black snout, and instantly the snout had the door open several inches. The snout was stronger than her hold on the knob. The dog appeared to be starving and she didn't have the heart to slam the door shut on him. She stood and pushed the plate through the door gap with her foot. She really wished that she'd had a dog growing up so she wouldn't be so afraid, and irrationally began to blame her parents for this entire predicament.

Romy could hear the dog (Max?) lapping at the ham. Covering the lower portion of her face was a red paisley bandana she'd had balled up deep inside a drawer but she couldn't get it to stay up, so she'd found a bag clip and clipped it to her nose. To complete the ridiculous costume, she had on a pair of sunglasses, making it difficult to see.

Since the dog seemed tamed, she pushed the door open, still speaking in infantile dog-patter, saying things like, "You a hungry boy? Yes, you a hungry boy."

With the door open fully, she saw the dog wasn't threatening-looking after all—he was medium-sized and silver-gray with white speckling on his back and head. His oversized head indicated pit bull in his DNA.

That gave her pause because she'd heard all the stories about pit bulls but the dog's relaxed stance, wagging tail, and slurping of ham indicated he wouldn't harm her. Plus, Suzie had said the dog was "sweet." What was his name again?

Max? No. *Mack*.

"Hey, Mack, hey…" she said, tentatively reaching for his short muscular body. The plate was empty but the dog was still lapping hopefully at it, scraping it along the floor. She picked the plate up and the dog's snout went with it.

"I'll get you more food," she said. "Where is your daddy, huh?" Then, louder: "Sir? Um, Bill? It's your neighbor, Romy. I came to check on you! You didn't sound well. Hello?"

The apartment was laid out similarly to hers, so she put the plate on a nearby end table and headed for the hallway, mouth open so she could breathe with her nose clipped. It scared her that the environs were so silent, with none of the man's moaning, none of his coughing. She was not prepared to come across a dead body.

Gingerly, she walked with one hand out defensively, as if the man might suddenly appear. If he did, she didn't want him too close to her.

At a door, she craned her neck beyond the frame and saw the man lying on the bathroom floor. He was only wearing red and black checkered boxers. He lay on his side, one arm sprawled out above his head on the tile.

"Oh my God," she gasped. "Are you okay? I'm your neighbor. Are you alright?"

The man moaned. She saw him trembling and realized he was slick with sweat.

"Fuck!" she hissed, fumbling in her hoodie pocket for her phone. Her hand was shaking so badly, she couldn't type her passcode. Sensing the dog behind her, she turned to look at him, and his big brown eyes were staring up. Something about his expression made her realize she needed to keep calm and do what must be done. The dog couldn't do it.

Her fingers steadied enough that she unlocked the phone and dialed 911. To hell with what Suzie said about him being worse off in a hospital. Nothing seemed worse off than him lying on the bathroom floor, unable to move.

"Hello, yes, I'm here with my neighbor. Something's happened to him. He's lying on his bathroom floor. I don't know if he's sick or what." The way she said *sick* was code for the virus, and she trusted the dispatcher would understand this. She gave her address, and the female dispatcher said an ambulance was on the way. She hung up and tightened the clip on her nose.

"It's okay!" she said to the man, speaking loudly because she didn't know if he could hear her or was lost in delirium. "An ambulance is coming. You'll be okay, Bill."

He moved very slowly, then doubled over with racking coughs. Romy covered her face with her arm and quickly backed out of the bathroom, pushing past the dog.

"Listen, it's okay," she called out towards the bathroom. "An ambulance is coming. You'll see a doctor."

Not hearing anything, she worked up enough nerve to poke her head around the doorway. Now the man's face was staring upwards towards the door, and it was a frightening sight. His face was red and bloated, his eyes glassy.

"I'm dying," he moaned.

"No. You aren't. It only feels like you are. Trust me."

"Mack," he got out before devolving into a coughing fit. Romy reached for her bandana's bottom and pulled it tight around her chin. Then the man stopped, breathless, and went silent again.

"He's okay," she enunciated through the bandana. "I've fed him."

The man was quiet and motionless; she was scared that he'd died. But then he moved a bit. How long would it take an ambulance to arrive?

She realized that she'd heard the far-off scream of an ambulance but it had faded. Then she'd heard another one but it too had faded. It slowly dawned on her that she was hearing a long line of wails, one after the other, each of them growing louder, then fading as they sped away.

The implication of what she was hearing penetrated her mind in a surreally horrific yet undeniable way— ambulances were responding to calls all over the neighborhood. All at the same time. Ambulance after ambulance, a stream of crisscrossing sirens. More ambulances than she knew the city had.

The man could die. Right here on the floor. Romy could be the last person he saw, her voice the last one he ever heard.

It came back to her—that night. Hunched down in the forest, behind a wide tree. How Heath had loped off to the outdoor changing station in his bathing trunks. Misty, in her white bikini, had looked behind her, then stepped off the platform and went behind the rim of the pool.

Romy had never before remembered that Misty had looked behind her, over her shoulder, towards the woods where Romy crouched, and how her heart had slammed thickly against her chest as she wondered if Misty could see her.

There had been a look on Misty's face, as if she was waiting, expecting something…

A week ago, Romy had watched a movie from her early teen years. She was amazed how much she remembered about the movie—not of its plot, which was fuzzy —but tiny details. Like how the lead actress had goofily jogged up a hill with exaggerated arm swinging. How the lead actor, upon hearing news of imminent world destruction, had made a slack-jawed huffing sound. So much of that formative chunk of her life was burned into her brain tissue as if with a cauterizing pen.

So how was it she could remember nothing, absolutely nothing, of how she got home that night?

"Maaaack," the man moaned. The dog was at Romy's right side. When the man called, the dog thumped past her. He sniffed at the man's body, then whined and hunkered down next to him in the narrow bathroom.

Romy moved towards the man. It wasn't what she should be doing. She should go downstairs and wait for the ambulance, make sure the EMTs could get inside. But who knew when they might get here; her neighbor could be dead by the time they arrived. She couldn't let him die alone.

Kneeling down by the dog, she took the man's hand. It was so sweaty it slipped around inside of her fingers.

"You'll be okay," she said. "Don't worry."

"Are you a pack animal?" he said softly, with difficulty. "Or a lone wolf?"

"I—I don't know. A lone wolf, I guess."

"Good. Then you might survive this. I wish I'd been —" He fell into coughing, and Romy twisted away, covering her face with her arm. "I pushed her and she lost the baby," he said, anguished, breathless. "I pushed her. I said it was an accident but... I was drunk and angry."

Romy immediately knew he wasn't hallucinating. He was making a confession.

A deathbed confession.

No, no. She didn't want to hear it. He was going to survive, and how was she going to look at him again knowing what he'd just said? She feared he was about to say worse.

"She lost the baby and never forgave me." He looked at her with those big, glassy eyes. They were pained and imploring. The most pained look she'd ever seen on a human being. Though he wasn't really looking at her, more through her, immersed in his own tormented world.

"She would forgive you," Romy said. "I know she would. You have to hang on. An ambulance is coming."

She wished the man would stop talking. He was delusional and feverish, and saddling Romy with a memory she didn't want in her brain. The man sputtered, and Romy jacked her head away from the blast of a coughing fit. She waited until it died out.

"You're not the only one," she found herself saying, staring dully at trails of phlegm she could barely see through her sunglasses flung on the white tiled wall. "I was a kid but not a little kid. Old enough to know better."

The man was silent. She heard Mack's thick nails tapping on the tile as he adjusted his stocky body. Then the man rasped and, for a moment, Romy didn't understand him. But the words slowly formed in her ears.

"Tell me…" he said. "Tell me what you did."

Chapter Seven

For five days, Romy was unbearably on edge. That was the amount of time she'd read, on average, before you'd see symptoms.

For those five days, she did everything she'd read might stave off a full-blown case of it. Drank lots of water and Gatorade and took almost hourly doses of Vitamin C and E, and multivitamins, and aspirin. She had everything delivered and instructed the delivery person to leave the bags right outside of her door, and before he'd leave, she'd shove a five-dollar bill through the door crack.

If she got the slightest twinge in her temples, she panicked, for she'd read headaches were a symptom. The few times she coughed, she almost exploded with anxiety. But gradually, she came to believe that no symptoms were forthcoming.

That day, she'd stayed with Bill until the door had buzzed. Then she'd run downstairs and escorted two EMTs upstairs. The EMTs, male and female, had looked absolutely exhausted, on the verge of collapse. Romy had been shocked that they weren't wearing masks.

She'd decided she better bring Mack to her apartment, so she'd done that, and he'd whined and barked until she gave him more ham.

Then she went back to the hallway and the EMTs were carrying her neighbor downstairs on a gurney. He didn't appear to be moving. They'd thrown a rough brown blanket over his nearly naked body.

For the next few days, she'd called nearby hospitals, asking about anyone named Bill from her building's address but it was clear that the city's hospitals were in the thick of a crisis that was quickly overwhelming them, and her calls garnered no information.

She thought about going into his apartment and looking through his things—trying to find contacts for friends or relatives. But she didn't want to tempt fate by going back into a place where the virus might still be hanging around. Not even to figure out what kind of food Mack ate. So, she'd slipped a note under his door, telling him she was holding Mack until he was better and leaving her cell phone number.

When she walked Mack, she was careful to wear her bandana, which she'd figured out how to secure on her face, and kept as far away from other people as possible. She'd never had a dog before and was intimidated by the amount of care he might need, but fortunately, Mack was easy. She took him on a short walk four times a day, and otherwise, he was content to lounge around her apartment, gobbling down any food she gave him.

It was deep in the night that he'd realize he wasn't home and that his owner wasn't with him. Then he'd start to whine, a sad, pathetic sound, like a clarinet.

Romy would get up and pet him, soothing him with dog-patter (*Your daddy's fine, I'm just watching you until your daddy gets home, he didn't abandon you*) until he settled down, which usually took about fifteen or twenty minutes.

During the time she waited to see if the virus would bloom and attack her insides, Romy spoke over her computer with her parents. Her mother encouraged her to come to Hawaii.

"I can't, Mom," she said. "I've got my neighbor's dog. He's too big to put under the seat."

"Put him in the cargo, honey."

"Mom! He's freaked out enough. Besides, no one should be on a plane right now. The virus is airborne and will circulate around the plane and infect everyone."

"Oh, nonsense," her mom scoffed. "Do you have rose hips? Put that in hot water with lemon."

Her father, in khaki shorts and a Hawaiian shirt that rivaled Joseph's coat of many colors, strolled onto the lanai.

"She can't go outside, Steffie," he railed. "She can't go *anywhere* outside. It's everywhere. Stay inside, sweet pea. Keep the doors locked."

"Doors locked, Dad? It's a virus, not a cat burglar."

"Don't scare her, Joe. Romy, take some echinacea. It kills the virus, it really does. I read about it in *Naturopath*."

"Nothing kills the virus, Steffie!" her father insisted.

"They tried to kill it with nuclear warheads, back in '45. What do you think Hiroshima was really about?"

Her parents had always been this way. Complete opposites. Despite this, they loved each other. Romy suspected it turned them on being so different from each other.

After Misty drowned, she could have gone to live with her parents, get far away from the scene of the crime. But she couldn't bring herself to leave her grandmother who, she could see, was starting to rely on her more and more. Getting things down from cabinets. Opening tough jars. Running the heavy vacuum. Raking leaves in fall. Shoveling snow in winter. And most importantly, being companionship for her.

Plus, Romy's parents had always been stressful to live with. She loved them but while their diametrically opposed opinions may have been invigorating for them, it was maddening for Romy, who always felt she should take one side or the other. And her outgoing mother had never liked that her daughter was so insular and was always exhorting her to go out for more extracurricular activities. Romy hadn't wanted that pressure again, so she'd stayed in Glass Town.

"I'll be fine," she told her parents over the computer.

"Honey," said her mom. "Why don't you go to Nana's house? It's sitting there empty. You can bring that dog, can't you?"

"I'm not even sure I can get a car now, Mom. Like I said, don't worry about me."

"Echinacea," her mother stressed. "I'm going to send you a case of it."

Chapter Eight

She was working on a book cover when her phone rang. She was relieved for the interruption, as her current client had asked for his cover's title font to be purple, and Romy had run through every purple on the spectrum but the man kept insisting the font was blue.

One of the more hair-pulling aspects of cover design was that people frequently saw colors differently—this was perfectly normal but trying to align the color the client saw with the color Romy saw could be extremely taxing.

She didn't recognize the incoming call but hoped it might be her neighbor, back from the hospital.

"Hey, Romy, it's Heath."

She let out a long exhale as if she'd been holding her breath. "Hey… Heath. Hi."

"How are you? Getting through this madness?"

"I guess. I mean, I work from home anyway. What about you?"

"I take my bike to the shop."

They were silent. Things were so weird on so many levels that it was hard to know what to say to him.

"I was calling to see if you need a mask or two. I have a bunch of N95s. They're supposed to be the best for this kind of thing. I have them for my restoration work. I called a hospital to see if they wanted them but they said they can't take masks from just anyone."

She was about to tell him she was fine but realized a proper mask would allow her to go back into Bill's apartment and look around for information about anyone she should call. Maybe there was a friend or family member who could take Mack from her.

"I could use one or two. But how will you get here?"

"I can bike."

"Oh, okay." She paused. "I want to be honest that I'm almost positive I was exposed to it. I think my neighbor has it. I was the last person to see him before he went to the hospital. I don't even know if he's alive. I have his dog here with me."

"Romy. That's... oh my God... are you *okay*?" He sounded deeply distressed, more so than her parents had, and this gave her an unexpected warm feeling in her heart.

"Yeah, I feel fine. So far. But..." She swallowed hard and looked at Mack, who was stretched out dead to the world on her rug. "I'll admit I'm kind of scared. Anyway, I'd ask you to leave the mask outside my door."

"Sure. Um, okay." He paused. "This whole thing is so crazy. I—I might be moving back to my old apartment. My roommate isn't being careful. I'm basically not coming out of my room except to use the bathroom and running to the fridge for food. My ex—Tara—keeps calling. Trying to get me to go stay with her."

"Oh," Romy said, an inexplicable sadness spilling into her chest. "If you feel unsafe, that would make sense."

"Maybe." He was quiet. Then, "The thing is... that's the last place I should be. She—she looks so much like her. Like Misty. I'm afraid I'll start the whole thing up again. But I wouldn't mind getting out of this apartment. I looked into Airbnb's but it's impossible right now. Everyone's leaving."

"What about your parents?"

"They moved to Florida a couple years ago. To be honest, I'd rather stay with Tara than them. My father and I have never gotten along, and he's never let me forget dropping out of Georgetown Law. And Mom's as bad." He paused, then nearly whispered, "But how will I ever move on with Misty's face—Tara's face—right in front of me?"

An unwelcome vision arose in Romy's mind. A rundown but charming teal blue ranch house with white shutters. Three bedrooms. Two bathrooms. A window-enclosed porch overlooking a wooded, steep, hilly terrain, more like a small mountain. An acre of land, no close neighbors, and those that were there were blotted out by rows of pine and hemlock.

Her grandmother's house on Sapling Lane. It belonged to Romy. Her grandmother had left it to her in her will. Romy's parents were fine with this, knowing that the house meant more to her than it did to them.

She'd only had the house a year, and hadn't been able to bring herself to clean it out or decide what to do with it. Last year, she'd worked enough to pay off the property tax bill while it sat unused, everything as it was when her grandmother was alive, other than the things her mother had flown in from Hawaii to collect. Nana (or more specifically, her ashes) now had a prime spot on the lanai, overlooking Maalaea Bay.

"I was thinking of going to Glass Town," she heard herself say. "I have a house there."

"You *do*?"

"Yeah, my grandmother's place. She left it to me."

They were silent again. The anticipatory rise and fall of his breath communicated all she needed to know. He was hoping Romy would ask him to come to the house with her, to save him from the Misty lookalike, save him from the cycle of chasing the memories of a dead love.

"Want to come with me?"

Chapter Nine

A week later, the pair drove to the country with Mack, his fat head dangling ecstatically out of the window, his jowls whipped into a smile by the wind.

Heath had a beat-up old Chevy 4X4, which was a good thing because people were now fleeing the city in earnest, and Romy imagined it would be impossible to snag a rental.

It wasn't a comfortable drive, the truck had no back-seat and they didn't dare put Mack in the outside flatbed, so he sat on the door side, Romy squished between his hard muscled body and right up against Heath's thigh, something she couldn't stop thinking about the entire ride.

She kept a grip on Mack's thick leather collar, worried he might excitedly try to make a run for it, despite the fact there was no way he could get through the half-rolled-up window with that fat head. His tail, which Romy was glad was not cropped, was thick as an armadillo tail and kept up a steady *thwack-thwack* against her arm.

Like two million other New Yorkers that March, they made their escape from the crowded city, where anyone walking down the street could inadvertently blow the virus into your face.

And because a lot of people who had the virus didn't show any symptoms, anyone could hold the key to your doom—your mailman, your deli counter guy, your neighbor, your best friend, your lover, your child. Best to get out into the open spaces. So went the thinking at the time, anyway.

Before she left, Romy slipped another note under Bill's door, explaining that she'd decided to leave town but was only four hours away, and could come back whenever he returned. She promised to take good care of Mack.

Despite being in possession of an N95 mask, she couldn't bring herself to open Bill's door. The virus was still so new, so little known about it, that Romy sometimes felt it might lunge out from behind a telephone pole and tackle her to the ground.

She tried not to think about all she and her neighbor had said to each other in those last minutes before his door buzzed and she'd rushed downstairs to let the EMTs inside.

Bill was the only person she'd ever told what happened that night.

Now she was painfully ashamed at what she had told him. But, at the time, she'd felt it would ease his conscience if she unburdened hers. In truth, it had felt good to unlock it from her mind and share it with some-one, someone who had his own burden.

* * *

"MACK, CALM DOWN, BOY!"

The dog was straining on his leash as if a giant pork chop was being brandished in front of his nose. He'd apparently never seen a big yard before and the weed-infested but splendidly blooming lawn with its huge lilac bushes and crops of perfumed lily of the valley was dog nip for him.

Inside, the house smelled the way Romy remem-bered—a powerfully nostalgic brew of dampness, dust, and that indefinable odor that signaled Nana.

"Sorry," she said to Heath. "It looks so... unkempt. I haven't been here in a long time."

After graduating high school and moving to Manhattan to attend art school, she'd visited her grand-mother at least twice a year but stayed at a hotel or bed-and-breakfast, telling Nana she needed reliable and fast Wifi, which her grandmother didn't have, and which was true.

But the reality was she couldn't bear to be in her old bedroom, in that same old bed, staring at those same walls, with those same woods behind her.

She'd thought she would have years left to learn how to sleep in her old bedroom again, how not to lie there and relive that night over and over. But her grand-mother had died a year ago, victim of a massive stroke.

At least she'd died in her own home, watching one of her favorite cop shows.

"It looks great," Heath said, eye-smiling at her from over his white conical mask. The pair had agreed to wear them while they were inside the truck and now they were uncertain what to do.

He tapped one finger against his mask. "If we're going to be living together, there's no real point in them. Unless you think…"

"I agree. But I'm pretty sure my neighbor had it."

"That was two weeks ago, right?" he said. "I locked myself in my room for two weeks."

She nodded. They stared at each other, tentatively.

"Okay," she said. "Let's do this."

They simultaneously removed their masks, then grinned at each other, as if delighted they didn't instantly drop dead. Mack *wroah*-ed his approval, and they laughed. She unhooked the dog's leash from his collar and he began eagerly sniffing every corner.

Romy showed Heath the house, though there wasn't much to show. It was a thousand square feet, tops. Her bedroom looked exactly as it had when she was a teen, including its pop idol posters on the walls. Very embarrassingly including The Jonas Brothers.

"I have no idea how that got there," she said as Heath grinned at her.

She opened the door to the spare bedroom, the one her grandmother had kept a piano in but never played on. Romy would take her grandmother's bedroom. It was the biggest room, and while it would be creepy sleeping in her grandmother's bed, she wasn't going to go back into her old bedroom. She wasn't ready for that.

Especially not with Heath Asher—bizarrely and surreally—here in the house with her. Until long, lean Heath Asher stood in the living room, his overgrown mop of wavy, dirty blond hair almost grazing the popcorn ceiling, she'd never realized how low the ceilings of the home were. It had been built sometime in the 1950s. Were people shorter back then?

"How is this room?" she asked, hand on the doorknob. "It's kind of small..."

The entire house looked minuscule to her now. Cringingly rundown. There was black mold crawling up the cracks of the pink tile in the bathrooms. At least the paint job in the spare room had held up, the springy light green paint wasn't peeling anywhere that she could see but the room, like the rest of the house, had that musty, neglected odor.

He looked down at her, seeming to sense her discomfort. "It's great, Romy. You should see my Williamsburg apartment. It's a slum. My room is basically a large closet. This is a palace, believe me." He turned, spreading one arm. "Man, look at that view!"

He gazed out of the three large windows onto a hot pink azalea bush, as if overlooking the Seine. Nature had continued to flourish without Romy's attention—had probably thrived on the lack of it. After all, the area got plenty of sun and rain.

They put down their things and decided they'd better head into town to grocery shop and buy cleaning supplies and whatever else they would need. The plan was to stay here for a few weeks but both had the uneasy and unspoken feeling it would be longer. The world seemed to be on the precipice of something gigantic.

"Do you think he'll be okay here alone?" Romy asked, looking at Mack, who was already snoozing on the living room carpet.

"Sure. I had dogs growing up. They can stay home alone. Does he chew up stuff?"

"Not that I've noticed."

"Then let's give it a shot. But we should buy him bones and chew toys."

THE GROCERY STORE was another indication that strange days were ahead, even out here in this rural area that still had most of the wide-open spaces it had when it was primarily tobacco land.

The store was crowded and Romy sensed the same human panic she'd sensed in the city, even more so. New Yorkers are accustomed to all manner of craziness, not so much suburbanites.

Many shelves were wiped bare and she was unable to find things she wanted, including cleaning supplies. There was no bleach. No disinfectant wipes. No hand sanitizer. She saw people taking multiple jugs of laundry detergent, multiple packages of soap. She managed to grab two packages of toilet paper before a small mob descended on the remaining ones.

Heath, who was pushing the cart, looked stunned.

"Damn," he said under his breath. "Toilet paper hoarders. Does the virus make people shit more?"

Romy would have laughed except she was too busy frantically eyeing the shelves, wondering what would disappear next. "Let's go over to frozen foods," she said. "That stuff will last forever."

In the frozen foods aisle, Heath turned. "I'll grab some stuff. You guard the toilet paper."

She nodded, knowing this was no joke, and watched him leave, then protectively pulled the toilet paper packages closer to her side of the cart.

"Romy? Romy Renskler? Is that you?"

She turned towards the male voice. The man in front of her looked familiar, extremely familiar... then it hit her.

"Mr. Sands."

He reached out to grasp her hand but yanked it back before his skin could touch hers. "Wait, we're not supposed to touch, are we?"

"I... I guess not."

"Well, Romy! I thought we'd agreed when you graduated you would call me Avery."

Her high school art teacher. Her mentor. The reason she'd majored in design at The New School. The reason she'd even gone to The New School. The reason she had a career she loved.

Mr. Sands.

He looked a bit older but essentially the same—at least from what she could tell with his black cloth mask stretched over his mouth and nose. Trim, lean, about five foot ten. Eyeglasses and deep-set, intelligent, warm brown eyes. The midnight black hair that had formerly been longish, especially for a high school teacher, was shorn close to his scalp and stippled with silver. He still looked good.

Plenty of the high school girls had had a crush on Mr. Sands. "Mr. Manz" they called him. For a lot of the girls, including Romy, he was the only handsome adult male they knew who was not their father.

Romy had not had a crush on "Mr. Manz." She'd respected him in a way she didn't respect any adult except her grandmother, and that included her parents, but her heart was only capable of one deep crush at a time and that spot had been taken by Heath Asher. When Heath left town after Misty died, her heart had decided crushes were not for her.

Mr. Sands—Avery Sands—was also married with two young daughters, or at least the daughters used to be young. Romy supposed they'd be teens now. She and Mr. Sands had kept in touch occasionally by email but like almost everyone from her past, their communications had dwindled to nothing.

"I recognized your bangs, Romy," he said.

Romy touched her thick, pin-straight bangs. She'd always wanted a side part but not with this hair.

"So you're home?" he asked. "I thought you were living in Brooklyn."

"We're here temporarily. We kind of..."

"We? Oh!" His intense brown eyes, ones she had looked into for hours and hours as he talked to her about her art and about being an artist, roamed past her towards the frozen foods. Heath had returned and was plopping bags of vegetables and TV dinners into the cart.

"Heath," Mr. Sands said. "Nice to see you."

Romy was impressed with Avery's name recall—and that he managed to recognize Heath, who was also wearing a mask. Seeming to sense her thoughts, Avery glanced at her and said, "I hardly ever forget a student."

"Oh, um…" Heath snapped his fingers in a gesture of having forgotten the teacher's name.

"Avery Sands. I was the art teacher at Glass Town High. You never took my classes."

"No, umm…"

The words fell between them, both men looked down. Romy knew what was going through each man's mind. Misty had taken Avery's classes, or at least one.

Romy knew this because Misty had sat in front of her for one semester. Intermediate Drawing. Romy had spent oodles of time marveling at the back of Misty's glossy raven hair, wondering how anyone managed to get hair that fabulous.

Occasionally, Misty would turn and speak to Romy, and Romy then marveled at her perfect face, which, because of its perfection, was actually uncomfortable to look at.

The artist side of Romy wanted to draw Misty but when everyone was paired up for the inevitable "draw your partner" assignment, Misty had grabbed one of her friends. Romy had ended up paired with one of the only males in the class, a reticent, bespectacled freshman who looked and acted so bored, practically hostile, that drawing him was a challenge. (He'd then complained how bored and hostile she'd made him look.)

"We came to get a break from the city," Romy said. "We both live in Brooklyn. My grandmother's house was empty, so…"

"Getting bad there, is it?" Avery asked, concern etched around his eyes.

"Yeah." The vision of her neighbor's body on the bathroom tile came to her, his coughing fits.

"What a crazy thing all this is!" Avery said. "Who would have thought we'd live to see this?" He looked around, incredulous. "I came to pick up a few things. I didn't know it would be a mob scene. Let's hope people are overreacting."

"Let's hope," Romy said. "I guess we better keep shopping before everything is gone."

"Romy, Romy," he said, contemplatively taking in her face, or at least the upper half. "So nice to see you. You too, Heath."

* * *

BACK AT HER grandmother's house—*her* house—Romy fed Mack. Then she put away the groceries while Heath took Mack for a walk.

It was a disquieting combination of unreal and natural to be here in this country house with Heath, grocery shopping, walking the dog, making dinner. She recognized that, deep down, a part of her had always anticipated—or *hoped* was a more accurate word—that something like this would happen. Not a pandemic. But being with Heath, doing couple-y things.

At the same time, it was terrible to keep seeing him, keep being reminded of what she'd done. Yet, no one had forced her to invite him here. She could have left him in Brooklyn. But after seeing the condition the virus had left her neighbor in, it became so real to her that she couldn't stand the idea of Heath's roommate potentially bringing it home to him.

She'd already killed Heath's true love and his baby— she couldn't kill him as well.

Chapter Ten

"That was a blast from the past, eh?" Heath said.

They'd cleared the dinner plates and were sitting on the windowed porch overlooking the woods, the ones Romy had used to sneak down to the country club pool. After that night, it made her supremely uncomfortable to look at them, yet here she was, glass of wine in hand, admiring them as if they were nothing but a serene and bucolic tableau.

"You mean Mr. Sands?"

"Yeah. Misty was taking his summer class when I met her. Well, I'd known who she was, had seen her around... but I mean, when we..." He trailed off, tipping a bottle of ale up to his mouth.

Romy was silent and averted her eyes from the woods, pretending to be inspecting scuffs on the porch's wood-planked floor.

"She didn't like school much, you know," he continued. "Neither did I. But she liked art class. Wait, were you in it with her?"

"Yeah, I think so," she said, intensifying her floor inspection. "Not the summer class but my freshman year. I should try to shine this floor up. Do some work while we're here."

"Sure, I could help." He paused. "Sorry, Romy, does it bother you when I mention her?"

"No, no, not at all. I wasn't sure…"

"It's that you're the only person I still talk to who knew her. My parents hardly paid attention to her. We didn't date for long. I don't keep in touch with anyone from school."

"No, it's fine." She straightened back up, sipping at her wine. "I hadn't thought about how we might run into people from high school while we're here."

"Neither had I. I left right after it happened. To D.C. My parents thought I might want to stay, put off school for a semester or a year. But I couldn't be here. I barely came home for the holidays." He laughed a little. "I tell you, nothing but something as lunatic as a killer virus would have made me come back. That and I'd heard Misty's parents moved. They never spoke to me again after it happened, and I can't blame them." He looked at her. "But I'm actually enjoying it here. Thanks to you."

He held up his bottle in a *cheers* gesture. Mack snorted awake from his nap, looking at them expectedly.

"I'll take him this time," said Romy.

* * *

SHE COULDN'T SLEEP and was scared to look at the time because it would confirm how long she'd been unable to sleep, and the anxiety of this would make it even more impossible to sleep.

What had made her think she could stay in this house? Sleep in her grandmother's old bed? Maybe she should move to the couch. But what would Heath think if he saw that? He'd wonder why she didn't sleep in her old bedroom.

She got up and wandered down the dark hallway. Mack, who was snoozing on a ratty, orphaned old couch pillow she'd retrieved from the basement for him, stirred, and seeing it was her and not an intruder, put his big nose back on his chunky paws.

"Wanna go for a walk, Mack?" she stage-whispered, not wanting to wake Heath.

Romy put on a jacket—it was at least ten degrees colder than in the city—and went outside with Mack. The air smelled so fresh. The stars were so twinkly and bright, the sky so velvet dark. It was so quiet. None of the keening wall of sirens she'd heard in the city.

But she worried for everyone there.

As she worked from home, she'd never made close friends other than Suzie, who was also away but she still loved her city and its people. The guy at the deli counter who always said, "Coffee?" with a big smile. The woman she always saw sitting on her stoop with a small, blind white dog. Her postman, whose name was Charlie. They would chat while he put everyone's mail into the metal boxes. He needed to go into dozens of buildings a day. Was the surface of the mail itself crawling with the virus?

Would they all end up like her neighbor? And... Bill. She looked down at Mack, who was intensely sniffing at what was probably a gopher hole.

Would Bill make it out of the hospital? And what if he didn't—had she adopted a dog?

Suddenly, Mack's nose sprang up from the gopher hole and he stood rigidly staring off past the dark mass of trees lining the side of the house. He must have heard a critter. The country must be a sensory jubilee for a city dog like Mack.

"Come on, Mack," she said, pulling on his leash. Her plan was to walk around the edge of the property. Ironically, she felt safer in the city, with its hordes of people and bright lights, than she did out here in the quiet, dark country.

She needed time to readjust to its stillness and darkness. There were only a few streetlights on her street, one of which happened to be in front of the house but walk in one direction or the other and you walked straight into a black abyss.

She took Mack about fifty feet, then he stopped again, muscles tensing, snout directed towards the woods. This time, he emitted an unmistakable low growl. She watched, somewhat amused—no doubt he was growling at what was probably a deer frozen in terror somewhere beyond the tree line. But she noticed her body flushed with tingles of fear.

Mack began barking, loudly and aggressively. Worried he would wake up Heath, she wanted to shush him but fear paralyzed her vocal cords. She pulled on his leash, intending to go back inside, but he started to yank in the opposite direction.

He was strong and dragged her at least twenty feet, barking more loudly—a dark-timbred, surly and threatening bark, not the one she'd heard when she'd stood outside Bill's door. It wasn't a bark that said, *I'm hungry.* It was a bark that said, *I'll hurt you.*

"Mack, Mack, come on!" She dug her heels into the ground and, realizing she needed to seize control or he was going to seize it from her, commanded, sharply, "Mack!" in a voice that told him she was done fooling around. *She* was the boss here.

He stopped, sniffed several more times, then looked up at her as if nothing had happened. Whatever was out in the woods had either darted off or Mack had grown bored with it.

Chapter Eleven

*I*nside, she locked the door, turned, and let out a startled burst of sound, a squeal. In the middle of the living room was a tall, filled-out shadow that her brain took too long to process as Heath. She pressed her palm against her spasming heart.

"Oh my God, you scared me." She laughed nervously. "Sorry about the barking. Mack saw a deer or something in the woods."

He said nothing, and the skin on her neck went prickly. Something was wrong with him. He stood silently, and for a moment, she thought the man in the middle of the living room in shorts and a T-shirt wasn't Heath but a stranger who looked like him and had broken in.

Then her blood curdled. It was Heath, definitely Heath but his expression was blank and robotic, as if he was secretly a monster—someone she didn't know at all, someone about to kill her.

Had she completely misjudged him all this time?

Was he actually a dangerous person? Mack began low-growling, and she took a couple of steps behind the dog, ready to let his leash go if needed, hoping he might attack.

"It was my fault," Heath said in an eerily flat tone. "It was because of me."

Romy's heart was battering against her chest. What was wrong with him?

Then, it dawned on her. With utmost certainty.

He was sleepwalking.

She pulled on Mack's leash. "Mack, sit!" she hissed.

She vaguely remembered hearing or reading that you shouldn't wake a sleepwalker. Why, she didn't know. But what to do?

He was standing, with that zombie face, his eyes open but unseeing. It was the oddest look she'd ever seen on a human being—someone awake but not awake.

"Sit," she hissed again at the dog, and Mack, seeming to comprehend that she was not playing around, sat. She let go of his leash and walked slowly towards Heath.

"Heath?"

"She did it for me," he said.

"Okay," Romy said cautiously, not wanting to startle him. She took his hand and began leading him out of the living room.

Thankfully, he walked with her. She walked him down the hallway, slightly in front of him as the hallway was too narrow to stand side-by-side with him. "Let's go this way," she said, gently but firmly, as if speaking to a child. "Back to bed."

This was the strangest experience. He was following her, yet uncomprehending. However, once she realized what was happening, she no longer felt fear but concern and pity. A motherly feeling washed through her. She wanted to get him back to bed, to safety.

In the spare room, she led him to the bed, and to her immense relief, he crawled back in by himself, then closed his eyes. She pulled the blanket up around his chest.

"Good night, Heath," she said, resisting the strong impulse to kiss him on the forehead. "Stay there," she said, purringly, closing the door behind her.

She wondered if she should figure out a way to lock him in. What if he sleepwalked straight outside?

Chapter Twelve

"Hello, sleepyhead," she said, then cringed. Why had she used such a term of endearment? But he grinned lopsidedly at her and shuffled to the cabinet, took down a mug. She already had the coffee brewing.

"Hello, yourself," he said, pouring a cup. He was in khaki pants and a black T-shirt. Sunshine splashed on his bare arms and she tried not to stare at their muscular luster.

"How did you sleep?" she asked, testing the waters.

He ran one hand through his hair, which was sprouting curls all along the underside. She remembered how she'd spent all summer keeping track of those curls as they grew longer from the start of the season to the end, until they almost reached his shoulders.

"Pretty good. Had some whacked-out dreams though. Being chased all night." He slouched casually into a kitchen chair, sipping his coffee.

"Mack didn't wake you? I took him for a walk and he heard an animal in the woods and started barking."

"Erm. No. Don't remember that."

"Want eggs?"

"Sure," he said, happily, spreading his long legs out.

She took eggs and milk from the fridge, placed them on the counter, and scoured the cupboards for spices. Whatever was in there was years-old but she supposed was still usable.

"I'm not sure how to tell you this." She started cracking eggs into a bowl. "But you sleepwalked into the living room last night."

She turned to catch his face as his hand stopped with his mug halfway to his mouth. "I did?"

"Yeah." She placed the eggshells inside of a small food bin her grandmother had always kept on the counter. "I brought you back to bed. I wasn't sure what else to do."

He raked one hand through his hair again, staring at the table. Its plastic covering was sunshine yellow with a tiny-flower pattern. Her grandmother had probably had it for thirty years, and it showed, dotted with tiny holes and stains.

Why hadn't she considered how shabby and elderly the house looked before she invited Heath here? But she supposed shabby accommodations were better than catching a virus.

"Oh, man," he said, dully. "I'm sorry. I have a history of that but haven't done it in at least eight months."

"Yeah, it was kind of strange." She shrugged, laughing a little. "It really took me by surprise."

"Damn, Romy." He stared at her apologetically. "If I'd thought I still did that, I would have warned you. No wonder I had so many weird dreams last night. It's this pandemic, I guess. And coming here. Where everything happened."

He distractedly sipped more coffee, then leaned into his mug.

"That's actually why I began seeing Loretta—that's my therapist. I used to sleepwalk all the time when I was with Tara but it settled down after I began talking to Loretta. She said it can be triggered by stress." He squinted at her. "Did I say anything?"

"Something about it being your fault. Whatever it was, you didn't say. Just, like, 'it's my fault.'"

"Hmm, yeah. Tara always said I would talk a lot of nonsense." He shook his head. "Well, for what it's worth, I'm told I'm a compliant sleepwalker. She never had trouble getting me back to bed."

"Nope," Romy smiled. "You followed me like a little lamb."

Ugh, why was she always using such corny expressions around him? Sleepyhead? Little lamb? She needed to control whatever this idiocy was that seemed to take over in his presence. He was only a guy. Nothing that special!

Mack trotted into the room and stood by her at the counter, clearly wondering if anything she was making was for him. "You had your breakfast, boy," she told him.

"Come on, Mack-a-roo," Heath said. "Let's go for a quick walk and let Romy cook in peace."

* * *

AFTER BREAKFAST, they sat on the windowed porch, staring out at the woods. She was getting better about looking at them now. Not like she had a choice; she couldn't avoid looking at one entire side of the yard.

Heath's phone dinged and he looked at it. "I signed up for Patch alerts for the town," he said. "I need to figure out if I can do any work while I'm here. Even a few weeks with no money is going to set me back." He stared at his phone for a bit, reading. "There's a town council meeting tonight. How to deal with the pandemic. Also, looks like New York City is under lockdown."

"Lockdown?"

"Yeah, no one can leave their home."

"Oh my God."

Romy was horrified. Seems like they could be in the country longer than they'd anticipated. They'd gotten out in the nick of time. But she couldn't stop thinking about everyone still there.

And what about Bill? It was seriously worrying her that he hadn't gotten in touch yet. Had he died? What obligation did she have to try to track down people who knew him? What if he had family who was wondering where Mack was? And how could she even get Mack to them in this mess?

As if sensing her thoughts, Mack looked up from

where he sprawled on the wood-beamed floor, gave a couple of whistling whines, and laid his snout on his paws, which were almost as big as Romy's hands.

* * *

THE TOWN COUNCIL meeting was in the red brick town hall on Main Street. Despite growing up here, Romy had never had occasion to be in the town hall. It was a thing reserved for adults.

Heath parked the truck and as they walked through the parking lot, they put on their masks. About a quarter of the people heading into the squat brick building also had them on.

Heath cast a glance her way and she could read the look in his eyes—trepidation. He had a dramatic past here—easily one of the most dramatic. While most of the town felt terrible for him, thanks to news articles about him rushing to the pool and frantically bringing Misty to the surface and giving her CPR, some people, Romy knew, remained unconvinced that he couldn't have saved her if he'd *really* wanted to. He was a life-guard, wasn't he?

Now here they were headed into a town hall meeting that could contain those who still saw him as "the boy who didn't save Misty Glass." Impulsively, she reached out and touched his arm. His conical white mask prevented her from seeing his full expression but his eyes crinkled a little.

Inside, the metal folding chairs were all placed several feet apart. *Social distancing* was becoming a familiar term. There were about fifty people there. Several community leaders took their turns at a lectern. The gist of their speeches was they were keeping on top of announcements from the Centers for Disease Control and Prevention and tracking case numbers.

Thus far, there had not been one positive case reported in Glass Town, though the capital, a twenty-minute drive away, had reported several cases, which meant Glass Town had to remain vigilant.

Businesses could make their own decisions about whether masks were required inside but they were encouraged. A local doctor outlined typical symptoms of the virus: high fever, cough, chills, headaches. He also warned, ominously, that one could be a positive carrier and have no symptoms whatsoever. A representative for a local nursing home announced the home was in lock-down, no visitors were allowed. At all.

At the end of the meeting, Romy and Heath stood at a bulletin board. Heath put up several business cards, and took down the number of someone offering workspace.

"Romy!"

Surprised at the sound of her name, Romy turned to see Gillian Frenetti, her best childhood friend. Romy hadn't seen her since high school graduation. Gillian, like Avery, had hardly changed. She'd gained maybe ten pounds but otherwise had the same amber-brown shag-cut, the same pleasant and slightly exotic features, almond-shaped brown eyes, well-defined lips.

How Gillian recognized Romy with a mask on was a mystery. Must be her bangs again.

"Hey, Gilly. How are you?"

Seeing Heath, Gillian's look of intrigue was horribly blatant on her unmasked face. "What's going on?" she asked. "You leave the city?"

"Yeah, we both did."

"Jessica, was it?" Heath said. Romy sensed he was pretending not to remember her name.

"Gillian." She scowled a little, then looked back at Romy. Her expression screamed, *Are you two sleeping together?!* Worried she might be so crass as to actually inquire about this, Romy volunteered, "We both live in Brooklyn and thought we should get out for a bit until this thing passes over."

"It's nuts, right?" Gillian stepped back from them. "Should I get a mask? I have no idea. I can't find them!" She seemed oddly excited about the whole thing, as if the pandemic was a lunar eclipse or category-five hurricane, a freakish and awe-inspiring display of nature's power.

Through the parking lot, the trio made small talk until Gillian veered off to her car. While on the surface the entire mini-reunion was banal, and they kept their discussion to the repercussions of the pandemic, underneath rippled a dark undertow.

Gillian had been friends with Misty. In general, high school students who were two grades apart didn't hang out together but the two girls lived next door to each other. Misty had also babysat Gillian and her younger brother. So when Misty died, Gillian had been extremely distraught. She had also, more than once, made it clear to Romy that she thought Heath wasn't as innocent as he appeared.

A big reason that Romy had spent her freshman summer hanging out by herself at the country club pool was that Gillian lived across town and both were too young to drive. They would bicycle to see each other but each settled into a routine of hanging out at watering holes closest to their homes. Then Romy, after developing a fixation on Heath, lost interest in biking miles to see her friend.

After that night, Romy had folded in on herself, become a near-recluse, and didn't participate in the staples of high school life—football and basketball games, dances, parties, proms. She'd stayed home and perfected her drawing, took college-level design courses, and learned design software programs. High school life was an unfortunate but necessary irritant.

In this small town, no one seemed ambitious for anything other than to procure secure employment, get married, have kids, buy a house. Like millions of artists before her, Romy couldn't wait to "get out"—out to somewhere that allowed, encouraged, and even rewarded artistic expression.

Heath started the truck and it wasn't until the first traffic light that he said anything.

"So, Gillian Frenetti," he said. "You're friends with her?"

"Sort of. We were good friends until I became a sophomore. Then I… began concentrating on other things."

As they were at a stoplight, he turned to stare

straight at her. "She's a big reason the cops kept questioning me."

"Um, what? So you do know her."

"Of course. Just pretended I didn't. She lived next door to Misty. The older brother of one of my friends was a cop, and he told me she went to them more than once, telling them she'd heard Misty and me arguing right before she drowned. If it hadn't been for the surveillance camera, who knows what would have happened to me."

"Sorry," Romy said, unsure of what to say. Gillian had expressed the same sentiments to her, and Romy remembered how ashamed it had made her, knowing the truth, knowing Heath had nothing to do with Misty's death. Another reason Romy had pulled away from Gillian—pulled away from everyone.

The truck started again, and Heath went on, "I mean, Misty and I were teens. I'm sure we had an argument or two. But nothing so loud her next-door neighbor would have heard it. She was making stuff up about me. Trying to get me blamed for what happened."

"I wonder why."

"I think I know why. I think she had a crush on Misty. Lots of people did. Girls, boys. Old people, children. Animals even. I'm not kidding. One time, she rescued a baby squirrel. Fed it with a syringe for a few days. Then it wouldn't go away. Lived on her terrace and would come up through her window. Like she was Snow White or something."

He chuckled—his face soft with a fondness for the memory.

Romy stared out the window at rolling farmland, every fiber of her wanting to scream out what her teenage self had done. She'd killed Snow White! Her chest felt near to exploding with the confession. She'd been fourteen when it happened, and she hadn't done it on purpose. It was quite possible there would be no legal repercussions.

But everyone in the town, everyone who knew Misty, even those who didn't, would hate her. She'd have to leave town, sell her grandmother's house. No sense in owning a house you could never come to ever again. Maybe people would throw stones at it—or her. Or both.

And Heath.

He would *despise* her.

He'd been nice to her. The only boy in high school who had been nice to her, who saw her, acknowledged her, was interested in her as a human being.

She'd repaid this kindness by killing his girlfriend and unborn child. Because she was petulant, immature, jealous. *Delusional.* Delusional that a teen boy on the cusp of adulthood would want a relationship with a *child*.

A part of her wanted so badly to confess, to see the poison in his eyes, hear the rage in his voice. Another part of her, equally as strong, couldn't bear the idea of it.

She was too much of a coward.

Chapter Thirteen

*B*ad woman.

       The voice was inside of her skull, a small, almost whiny voice, a dreamlike voice, with one foot in reality and one outside of it.

Horrible woman!

Romy reluctantly swam to consciousness, eyes still closed. Her first thought was that Heath was watching something on his computer loudly enough that the noise traveled through the walls.

She opened her eyes and blinked at the darkness. The glow of the moon and the lone streetlamp slanted dimly through her bedroom window, giving enough light that she could see the silhouette of the large oak dresser across the room, even make out its knobs.

"Bad lady!"

This time, Romy's heart went berserk, hammering against her ribs, and she quickly turned towards the voice coming from the window, which was open a few inches. She saw a round, white face at the pane of glass.

She tried to scream but the scream was like a rock that had been shoved solidly down her throat. She pushed it out again, and this time the scream erupted from her mouth but it was a paltry scream.

Then the face at the window was gone.

As soon as the window was dark again, Romy began trembling as adrenaline flooded her veins. She tore up from the bed and had her door open, and stumbled shakily down the dark hall.

In the living room, Mack lifted his head and went on alert, jumping up and moving along with her. She threw open the wood door, looked through the screen door out into the dark yard, and saw nothing, heard only the loud buzzing of cicadas.

She closed the door, locked it, and went to the kitchen looking for a flashlight. She found one inside of the third drawer she tried but it was old, the light weak. Mack kept up an anxious prancing next to her. Looking at the circular hand clock above the sink, she saw it was almost three a.m.

She thought about waking up Heath but already her mind was turning against her, telling her what she'd seen and heard was part of a nightmare.

Something so odd—a bone-white little girl with bright white hair standing in her window—simply could not be real.

SHE DIDN'T WAKE up until Heath had knocked several times on her door, calling, "You okay in there, Romy?"

"Yeahhh," she rasped. "I'm getting up."

It was almost eleven a.m. Cold scrambled eggs were on the old electric stove, lukewarm coffee in the pot. She poured herself a cup and microwaved it, still bleary-eyed.

The thing she had seen, the words she had heard, had kept her up until the sun began to rise, pale light sifting into the room. She'd finally fallen into a fitful sleep around seven a.m.

"Sorry," Heath said. "I was getting worried. You're always up earlier than me."

"It's fine," she groaned, putting eggs into the microwave, too. "I had this... it had to have been a crazy dream. But it seemed so real. It kept me awake most of the night."

"What was it?"

"This... she looked like a little girl but kind of a ghost girl. She was white as paper and had blonde hair, and she stood outside of my bedroom window." She didn't tell him what the little girl had said.

Heath was staring intensely at her, a look in his eyes she couldn't quite decipher. "That can be the way my dreams are when I'm sleepwalking," he said. "So real."

"I screamed, but..." She grasped at her throat. "It kind of died in the air. You didn't hear me?"

He shook his head.

"I opened the door to see if I could see her but there was nothing outside. Could it be a neighborhood kid, I wonder?" she asked, speaking more to herself.

The microwave dinged and she got out her eggs but the smell of them gave her faint nausea. She had no appetite and her coffee was already returning to cold.

"Freaky, Romy," Heath said. "I suppose it could have been a kid. What time did it happen?"

"Around three o'clock."

"Hmm. How old did she look?"

"Hard to say. I only saw her for a few seconds. I'd thought young, maybe ten. She didn't look quite... human though."

"Are you serious?" He gaped at her.

"Very serious. It was the *strangest* thing I've ever seen. I almost let Mack out to chase after her but was worried he wouldn't return."

Also, if Mack ended up biting a neighborhood teen or child, there could be severe repercussions.

Heath dabbed at his lips with a cloth napkin, then got up and brought his plate to the sink. He turned to her, putting his hands on her shoulders. It was the first time he'd ever touched her and despite her preoccupation with the thing she'd seen in the window, warm excitement pulsed through her extremities.

"That must have been really scary, Romy. Why didn't you wake me up?"

She stared at his chest, unable to make eye contact. Too much feeling was coursing through her and she didn't want him to see it in her eyes. "She was gone. Then... I wasn't even sure if she was real."

He moved his face in such a way that it was impossible not to look directly at him, it would have been obvious that she was avoiding eye contact for reasons that she was sure he would surmise—that his hands on her arms, that his face and body so close to hers, was making her terribly uncomfortable because of her powerful attraction to him.

His sleeping down the hall was beguiling and she often fell asleep fantasizing about walking down the hallway, opening his bedroom door, and…

She forced herself to look into his strangely arresting eyes, with that blue the color of china, irises that seemed larger than average, and barest intermingling hints of gold, gray, and green. Eyes that pulled you in and pushed you away at the same time.

"It was probably a kid having fun," he said. "But don't be shy about waking me up, okay? I thank you, I really do, for everything you've done for me. I'm here if you need me, alright?"

"Okay," she said, weakly, as he let go of her and began washing the dishes. His back to her was a simultaneous relief and small anguish.

A kid having fun.

But one who'd called her *horrible woman*, had called her *bad lady*?

Chapter Fourteen

*O*ver the next week, Romy and Heath developed a routine. He'd found a space to restore furniture and already had a couple of jobs. Romy designed covers in her grandmother's room. They both had careers perfect for an infectious virus—they could work with no one else present.

In the morning, they had breakfast on the windowed porch, talking about anything that popped into their heads. Their conversation flowed easily, as if they'd known each other forever, which they practically had.

In the late morning, they'd split up to work. Around five p.m., Heath, who was in the town's center, would bring home groceries, and they'd use their combined limited cooking skills to make dinner.

If it was warm enough, they'd eat on the porch, then have some drinks. Romy found a portable CD player in her old bedroom and they'd play her childhood CDs— Jane's Addiction, Madonna, and yes, The Jonas Brothers —and dance around.

Before dinner, they usually went running. Both were athletic and liked the challenge of forcing themselves up the hilly rural terrain.

They'd run past a field of horses, a chicken farm, and a tunnel-like house built into the treetops. Mack would run with them, though Romy was careful to keep him on his leash as she still didn't know if, given the chance to roam free, he would return.

Sometimes, running up these hills, she felt a strong sense of déjà vu, something that started her running faster, and faster, running away from something, until she could almost outrun Heath and Mack had his long, pink tongue flapping out.

"Hold up, Miss Talent!" Heath would pant. "Damn!"

But she couldn't stop until she reached the summit of the hill and all the way up it chased her, hounded her —the urge to get away.

Since it was a Saturday night, Romy and Heath had more wine than usual, as if they worked regular work-days. Then they sat on the porch doing what they usually did—staring into the woods.

At dusk, a family of deer picked its way across the lawn. Romy marveled at the two delicate, speckled baby fawns. Mack didn't even bark at them.

She'd forgotten how much the country called to her. How loud the songbirds warbled at daybreak. How velvet dark was the sky, with millions upon millions of stars, so bright she could see their constellations again—the Big and Little Dipper, Orion, Hercules. There were the burning reds and mauves of the sunset, the vast and clear powder-blue sky.

But she knew the downsides of country life. Termites and fat black ants got into everything. There were brown spiders that could send you to the hospital. Wasps. Hornets.

Romy had probably grown too squeamish to live in the country. Her grandmother had thought nothing of trapping mice and squirrels in the walls and birds in the chimney, of chasing belligerent raccoons from the outdoor garbage cans, and scraping dead possums from the road.

The house was a lot of work, too. There was a water well somewhere out in the yard, and Romy didn't have the faintest clue what to do with it. Ditto the "leach field" for draining the septic tank. There were gutters that her grandmother had cleaned—how did she know when to clean them?

Winter was harsh, with snow to shovel, and hilly, icy roads to navigate. There were storms that tossed trees down on power lines and outages were common, sometimes lasting for days, even for a week or more. The smart ones had a generator.

Come to think about it, Romy wondered how the hell she'd ever lived here for so long. In the city, she'd learned how to deal with disturbed humans—avoid eye contact and get away from them as soon as possible. Disturbed nature was another thing entirely.

As if reading her thoughts, Heath asked, "Ever think about moving out of the city?"

Romy sighed and shrugged. "I don't know. I'd always wanted to live around artists. That's why I went to New York. But it turned out it was harder to meet people than I thought. Those Meet-Ups are excruciating. I haven't made many friends." She didn't want to say she'd only made one, Suzie.

"I haven't either." He poured her more wine, a fizzy rosé.

"When did you and Tara break up?" she asked.

The wine had gone to her head. All this time they'd spent together and she hadn't asked anything about Tara. She'd rather not think about the woman he'd been engaged to and, judging from their online photos, had seemed happy with.

"December. Right before Christmas, so I felt like a real bastard. We lived together in Brooklyn, and I found the first room I could. Hence my bad roommate situation. But she's actually from around here. Milton, an hour away. That's how we met. I was home visiting, and she was visiting a friend from college. Met at a bar, turned out we both lived in the city. A few months later, we were living together." He stretched out his long, jeans-clad legs. "She still calls me. I told her I'm fine, I'm out of the city. Haven't heard from her for a few days now."

"Maybe you two can work it out." She didn't sound convincing even to herself.

"Nah. It was a mistake."

They both had their arms slung down and simultaneously made hand gestures, causing their tumblers to collide and splash wine onto the wood-planked floor.

"Oh!" Romy laughed as she popped up from her chair.

"Damn, sorry."

Romy went to the kitchen and returned with a hand towel. She sank to her knees and began sopping up the liquid, then Heath was there on his knees too, his hand over her hand, swishing the towel around. She was drunk, he was drunk. The sexual tension was palpable.

And then—it was so fast she would never know who moved in first—they were kissing.

Oh my God, they were kissing. On their knees, on the floor. His lips and tongue were everything she'd ever imagined they might be but so much better. The man knew how to kiss. She hoped she did, too.

"Oh wow, Romy, wow," he breathed, pulling away slowly. "I'm sorry." He stood up and put his hand out for her.

"Why are you sorry?"

"I mean... I'm taking advantage of your hospitality."

"Oh, get over it," she said, wrapping her arms around him, pressing her chest against his. "Take advantage of me."

She was too full of unbridled lust to think clearly. She tilted her mouth up to his, like a baby bird wanting sustenance, and he obliged. Everything was in order again. The world had righted itself. They were kissing.

Chapter Fifteen

ad laaaadyyyy…
   Baaaaaad laaadddyyyy…

The sound cut unwelcomely into her snug cocoon, her bubble of sleepy rapture. Heath's arms were wrapped around her, his beautiful, silky-smooth naked body pressed smack up against hers. They were tightly coiled together on the twin mattress in his room, the spare room.

She barely remembered leading him there, unable to bring herself to have sex in her grandmother's room, on her grandmother's bed. She'd have to get a new mattress at the very least before that happened.

The sex had been wildly good. The kind of sex that could make you a little crazy, make you do bad things to keep getting it. And he seemed to think so too, the way he'd breathed, "You're Miss Talent in more ways than one, aren't you?" She liked the slightly possessed look in his eyes as he had his way with her.

It was hard to deny the fundamental corporeality of

sex between men and women—the man entered; the woman was entered. This always left Romy feeling a little outside of herself, a little less of herself, a bit more of someone else. With Heath Asher, a man she'd dreamed about since she was essentially a child—the enmeshing felt far more pronounced.

Leave this place!

She snapped to reality, her eyes popping open. She instinctively looked towards the window.

The white face was there, the bright white-blonde hair, and this time, there were also glowing blue eyes. A young girl was staring at her with pure hatred in those otherworldly eyes. And that voice... odd and drawling, deranged.

Heath... Heath! She called out in her mind but nothing came out of her mouth. She had gone rigid and mute with fear.

Then she screamed but it was a pathetic thing, more like a squeak. Heath grunted beside her, and she turned to him, her breathing quick and raspy.

"Heath, Heath!" She pushed on him. "Get up! Get up!"

He made a groaning noise.

"Move! Move!"

She scrambled over his dead-weight body, and Mack, who'd heard the commotion, was in the doorway, snuffling and whining. He let out a few *what's happening?* barks.

This finally roused Heath.

"Whah is it?" he slurred.

"She's back!" Romy yelled. "The little girl!"

Romy careened down the dark hallway and went to the kitchen, yanked open a drawer looking for the flashlight but instead grabbed a seven-inch chef's knife. Then she was zooming through the living room and trying to unlock the door with a shaky hand but she kept doing something wrong and it wouldn't unlock.

"Romy!" Heath called.

She turned and saw him pulling up his jeans. "What are you doing?" she cried. "This isn't the city! You don't need to be dressed!"

Mack was prancing anxiously and barked a few more times. She was going to let him out. Let him out to chase down that little bitch.

She finally got the door open and was poised to unlock the screen door when Heath was pushing in front of her. "I'm not going outside naked if there's a kid out there," he said. "You stay here. And keep that dog! We don't need him biting a kid!"

She had never heard Heath speak so dominantly before, so she pulled Mack back by the collar and watched Heath descend into the night. Remembering the front light, she flicked it on, which made it impossible for her to see anything beyond the screen.

Why was a little girl running around the town in the middle of the night? Why did she look so odd and ghostly? Why had she targeted Romy's house?

Had she really said, *Bad lady*?

Had she really said, *Leave this place*?

* * *

SHE WASN'T sure how much time passed, maybe ten minutes, when Heath loped up the steps and opened the door. The look on his face said he hadn't seen the little girl.

"Not there," he said. "Don't see anyone."

He locked the door, looked at her knife.

"Were you going to stab a kid, Romy?"

"I don't know what she was!" Romy cried, her voice high-pitched with hysteria. "She didn't look like any girl I've ever seen!"

"You called her a little girl."

"She's like—a little girl but not one! Okay?!"

Mack was pacing and whining. She went to the fridge and took out a can of his food, instantly placating him.

"Heath," she said, firmly. "I can't explain it. This girl, this *thing*, whatever she is… is pale as a ghost. She almost glows. She has these big, weird blue eyes. And… she's whispering. Or speaking quietly. And saying these bizarre things."

"What things?"

Romy began slowly shaking her head, her nose tingling, staring at the floor. How could she tell him what the little girl was saying?

"She says… ah… oh, I don't know. Forget it!"

She stomped off and curled up on her grandmother's bed, the knife still gripped tightly in her hand. A minute later, Heath crawled into the bed. Admittedly, this was a test. She wanted to see if he would console her, would take her side against this crazy thing happening, this ghostly pale little monster.

He gently pried the knife from her hand, placed it on the bedside table, then played with strands of hair around her face.

"Listen," he said, soothingly. "When I sleepwalk, I'm having a dream that is so real to my brain that my body believes it's happening." He was quiet for several moments, then wrapped his arms around her, squeezing her tight. "This whole thing is stressful," he said, his mouth right up to her ear. "Us being out here. The pandemic."

"I'm not sleepwalking," she said, her throat thick, threatening tears of frustration.

Chapter Sixteen

*T*he next morning, she got up before Heath and went to shower. As she lathered up her hair, she couldn't stop thinking about the little girl in the window. Mostly what she was saying.

Bad lady. Horrible woman.

She had never told anyone about Misty. Except for Bill.

And the ghostly little girl in the window certainly wasn't Bill, the rather large, middle-aged, gray-haired neighbor who was probably dead or on a ventilator in the hospital.

So how was it this little girl could be saying the things she was saying, as if she knew what Romy had done?

What if Heath heard her saying these things? Wouldn't he want to know why a strange little girl was not only running around in the middle of the night but had fixated on Romy and was calling her bad? Wouldn't he begin to ask questions? *Why are you bad, Romy?*

In the kitchen, Heath shuffled in about ten a.m., bleary-eyed. It hadn't been a restful night for either one of them.

"Morning," he said with a lopsided grin, his hair mussed, those deep blue eyes, the ones she thought she would be perfectly content to look into for eternity, blinking at her.

If only the little girl hadn't shown up, what a morning this would be. She'd finally had sex with Heath Asher. It had been great sex. The best she'd ever had, by a wide margin. If the little girl hadn't shown up, how happy she would be right now.

Or would she?

Deep down, a dark, shadowy lesion was expanding —the memory of what she'd done that night. What Heath would think if he knew. She'd crossed a line she should not have—had made him inadvertently enter into a physical relationship with the killer of his great love and his unborn child.

"Morning," she responded, drearily.

He sat down next to her, and they drank their coffees in silence that stretched on until it became awkward. He finally broke it with, "I want to tell you something" and reached one long finger out, tapping it a few times on her hand. "You're not, like, quarantine bae."

This actually caused her to smile. "Quarantine bae? Is that a thing?"

"I read about it. So." He tapped again. "You're not. I'm going to confess something."

Oh no. She didn't want any more confessions. Bill's confession was enough! She glanced warily at him.

"This is embarrassing but… I had a crush on you back in the day."

She jerked her head towards him, eyes wide, unable to believe what she'd heard.

"But you were, what? Thirteen? Fourteen? A kid. I wasn't," he said.

"Are you serious…?" she breathed.

"Definitely. But there was nothing I could do about it."

"I—I thought I looked like a little mouse."

"You kind of did. But a cute mouse."

"Heath, I had the *biggest* crush on you. It was terrible. I sat there all summer staring at you."

"You think I didn't know that? Your stare was like a laser. Even behind those sunglasses."

She laughed, but inside, was absolutely woozy with embarrassment.

"If I'd been younger… or you older…" He trailed off.

"Yeah," she nodded.

"So… when Misty made it clear she liked me, I took that as a way of forgetting about you. Because I was starting to think things about you that were very inappropriate."

He took a sip of his coffee and stared out through the window above the sink. "Which isn't to say I didn't like Misty. I did. I was eighteen, she was gorgeous. I'm not a saint." His gaze came back to her. "Once I got to know her better, saw how good and kind she was, then… I did fall in love. Very much in love. We only dated, what? Month and a half? At that age, it felt like years. When you're young, it's like dog years. That summer felt like it went on for a decade."

"Why are you telling me all this?" she whispered.

He pried her hands off her coffee mug and held them. "Because I want you to know this isn't about getting laid because we're stuck out here together. Not for me anyway."

"It's not for me either," she said.

He kissed her hand, then released it. "Good. So we're set."

This would have been the most euphoric moment of her life so far, except that it wasn't. It was too full of trepidation. Too full of guilt.

Could... could she tell him? Would he believe that she hadn't meant for it to happen? Would he forgive her?

"Heath..." she said, shocked by the strong tremble in her voice. "Um..." Her bottom lip was shaking, she felt ready to dissolve into tears. "What... what if... there's something... I should tell..."

Once again, he reached for her hand, kissed it. Then he said something that stopped her breath, stopped her heart. He looked deep into her eyes and said, "I know what you did."

"Oh, God!" she wailed, her other hand flying to cover her mouth.

At her cry, Mack barked and jogged into the kitchen, thinking she needed help. She pulled her hand from Heath's and reached out to soothe Mack, rubbing his skin-like fur.

"How—how did you know?" she gasped, one hand

petting Mack, the other at her mouth, trying to stop herself from crying. But she couldn't cry, she couldn't cry. She was frozen.

"Well," he said, softly. "It was pretty obvious. Young girl like you at the pool all summer, staring at me. You should have been with friends. I mean, I was flattered. Like I said, I was more interested in you than I should have been."

"But how did you *know*? I never told anyone."

He shrugged. "Who else would have done it? There's no one else who would have bothered."

The word "bothered" sent a peculiar chill along her spine, but she figured he must be in as much shock as she was, this buried secret finally spoken between them.

"Why didn't you *tell* me you knew?" she asked, her voice thin and pleading.

"I'm telling you now."

"But why not sooner? Oh my God! I've had so much guilt!" She was still shaking, and she wrapped her arms around her shoulders. She was cold, so cold.

"Aw," he said, rubbing her bare leg. "You don't have to feel guilty about it, Romy. I know you didn't mean any harm. I appreciate what you did."

She stared at him for a few moments, bashed into silence. Then she shrieked, "What?!"

"You only did it to help me out. You're taking this much worse than I thought you would. It's not that big of a deal, you know?"

"Shit, what…?" She shook her head, and a strange feeling washed through her. "Heath… what exactly is it you think I did?"

106

"What do you mean? You've been buying up my books, right?"

"Oh my God! Oh!"

"What the heck did you think I was talking about?" he chuckled.

Mack clattered his nails on the floor, wagging his tail. He let out a few more barks.

"Mack has to go," he said and stood up. "Come on, boy."

Mack shook his stocky body back and forth in delirious anticipation as Heath grabbed his leash off the kitchen island.

"Jesus, Heath," Romy said, the relief so extreme it was frightening. Then she began laughing, almost hysterically. "How—how did you know that?"

"For one, my rank tanked right after we came here," he said, snapping the leash on Mack's collar. "But my publisher has always known that one person was putting in a lot of weekly orders. They didn't know who it was. We kind of joked about it, my savior, that kind of thing. I figured it was a fan who was reselling the books at cons." He looked down at her. "But as soon as we came here, my publisher reported the sales had stopped. We thought it was because of the pandemic. But I started thinking about it and… it's you, isn't it?"

She nodded, her heart rate beginning its slow descent back to normal. "You got me," she said.

He was halfway through the living room with Mack when he stopped and turned, looking contemplative. "But how did you know I was Helen?"

The words poured so smoothly out of Romy's

mouth that she was impressed with herself. Perhaps she'd anticipated this question coming to her sooner or later. "I was curious what you were up to, so I dug around and found your URL registration."

"Huh." He was almost out the door with Mack when he turned again. "I thought I'd done that anonymously."

Romy only shrugged and opened the refrigerator, desperate to hide her face. She should tell him the truth —that she's Golden-Eye. That she'd seen his name on his PayPal account.

But she was so vastly relieved at having narrowly escaped being pinpointed as Misty's killer that she didn't have the emotional fortitude for any other confessions.

Chapter Seventeen

"I'm glad you got in touch," Gillian said.

The pair sat outside at a farm and winery on the far south side of town, staring into a boundless field of grapes, the sky streaked with a dazzling pink and mauve sunset.

On the rustic table before them was the winery's specialty, a tray of glass samplers of their special wines, not only red and white but apricot, raspberry, peach, and even beet.

By now, people were gathering, if they had to gather, in outdoor areas, and keeping at least six feet apart from each other. Romy and Gillian were playing it safe and had double that amount of space between them, which forced them to talk a little loudly.

"I want to apologize for basically disappearing on you when we were kids," Romy said, the tangy taste of beet wine on her tongue. "Once we got to high school, things got a bit tough for me."

"Yeah," Gillian said. "With your parents leaving?"

"Not so much that, I'm the one who wanted to stay with my grandmother. It's that… I didn't fit in. I wasn't into sports or parties. I wanted to get into a really good school and get out of here. No offense to Glass Town but it's not exactly an artist mecca."

"I get it," Gillian said, sipping her peach sampler. "Woo! This is sweet."

"I felt I should apologize."

"Thanks, I appreciate it."

They stared out over the glaringly beautiful sky. At a time like this, with the clean-smelling air, the soothing quiet, the technicolor horizon, Romy was tempted to move back. But how could she? The town was forever tainted.

Sometimes, the familiar homes, streets, and shops gave her the sensation of being off-kilter, living in a fun house.

"Sooooooo…." Gillian drawled, the tone of her voice letting Romy know exactly what subject lay directly ahead. "Heath Asher, huh?"

Romy shrugged and switched to the raspberry wine sampler. She'd figured the topic would come up but her need to see Gillian outweighed her desire to avoid talking about him.

"Okayyyyy…." Gillian drawled again. "He's a hot-looking guy. But…"

"I know you think he had something to do with Misty Glass's drowning. I can definitively tell you he did not."

"And how would you know that?"

"You saw the same camera footage I saw, Gilly. It

was on the news. It's probably still on YouTube somewhere."

"All I know," Gillian said, turning towards her, the words eagerly tumbling out as if she'd spoken them before without much effect. "Is that I heard them arguing a few days before it happened. I was in my bedroom, and they were in her driveway. He stormed out of the house, and she followed him. I distinctly heard him say, 'I want nothing to do with you anymore.'" She raised her brows triumphantly. "Later, I saw her in her yard and went over to ask if she was alright. She told me he could be jealous and sometimes she was scared of him. 'There are two Heaths,' she said. 'One is very sweet but the other one…' I told her she should break up with him but she said she couldn't. That it was impossible at that point. I didn't know what she meant but when it came out she was pregnant, I did."

Romy couldn't believe what she was hearing. *Scared* of Heath? He'd always come across as so pleasant and laid-back as a teen. And now? Same.

"I told the cops," Gillian continued. "But his friend's brother was the lead detective and it seemed like they'd made up their minds. Plus, I was fourteen. No one took me seriously. Even my own parents didn't care what I had to say. I biked to the station by myself. Twice!"

"They had an argument. They were teens."

"A few days later, she drowns? Misty couldn't swim. Everyone knew that."

Romy shifted uncomfortably and with her sampler

tried to hide whatever expression must be on her face. *Everyone knew that.* No, everyone *didn't* know that.

"Cops said the hook came off the tarp when she jumped on it... but really? How convenient for him. Who put it on at night? Him, I bet."

Romy finished off the sampler and started another. She desperately needed the edges of her mind dulled. "Look," she said. "I might as well tell you that he and I are involved."

Gillian ruefully shook her head. "I figured."

"So, I don't want to hear all this. I know for a fact he didn't do anything to the tarp. End of story."

"I don't know how you could know this, but fine," she said, obstinately.

They gazed out at the sky as dusk shuttered down. Heath was still out doing a furniture restoring job and Romy had told him she was taking Mack for a run into the hills. In reality, she'd called a car lift to meet Gillian. Mack lay at her feet, contentedly snuffling at the grass.

"Did you know she was pregnant?" Gillian asked, unwilling to let the topic fade out.

"Yes. It was in the news. I presume they did an autopsy."

"I'm only saying," she stubbornly continued. "I think they got into an argument about it, and he didn't want it. Then—"

"Alright! What do you want me to do about it?" Romy finished off the apricot sampler, then said, "Sorry." She couldn't alienate Gillian. Not now, when she needed her. "I know you were close to her. But he loved her. He really did. He wanted their baby."

"Okay, let's change the subject," Gillian relented.

They moved onto Gillian's son, Jacob, who had started preschool, though it had closed down due to the pandemic. Gillian was married to Reggie, her high school boyfriend. Romy was hoping that since Gillian had never moved out of town, and her son was in the school system, that she would be a good source of information.

"I have to ask you something," she said. "Can you tell me if there's a little girl in town, about ten years old, who has blonde hair and bright blue eyes? Like eerily bright blue eyes?"

Gillian looked uncomprehending for a few moments. Then she said, "Little girl with blonde hair? They're all over town. We were settled by Dutch and Germans, you know. Whitest damn town ever."

"But a little girl who looks kind of creepy? Kind of…" It hit her how unhinged she sounded. "Is there a little blonde girl around town who is kind of a trouble-maker? Maybe she has emotional problems? Anything like that?"

"Huh? I have no idea." Gillian sounded almost insulted, as if Romy was insinuating the troublemaking child was representative of the town's offspring.

"Or whose parents aren't responsible? Maybe they'd allow her to run around at night?"

Gillian was laughing and helping herself to another sampler. "Doesn't sound like any kid I know but she could exist. Why?"

Romy sighed. "Because twice a little blonde girl has come into my yard in the middle of the night. She gets right up at my window and says the strangest things."

"Really?" Gillian was gaping.

"Yes, and she looks ten, maybe eleven. But she's the creepiest, oddest little girl."

"Ummmm." Gillian shook her head, staring into her wine. Something about the tone of the *ummmmm* made Romy almost certain that Gillian didn't quite believe her. "That's really weird. I don't have a clue what kid could be doing that. I mean, I used to sneak out at that age. Didn't we all? But I wouldn't get in anyone's window and draw attention to myself. Do you talk to her?"

"No, she runs off. So quickly, I can't find her. Let me know if you hear of anyone like that, okay?" Romy pressed. "Please?"

"Little blonde girl. Creepy. Troublemaker. Got it." Gillian chuckled and finished off her sampler.

Chapter Eighteen

*R*omy stopped into the grocery store before heading back to her grandmother's house—which she still had trouble thinking about as her own house—to pick up things for dinner. She texted Heath her plans.

It was gratifying how naturally they'd slipped into a domestic routine, and how comfortable it all felt. Yet, there was an almost continual back and forth in her mind of whether she should tell him about that night.

Only it would be more than telling *him*. She should then go to the police, which would finally free him from any lingering suspicions from the stubborn ones such as Gillian. But she knew she faced losing everything—not only the man she was growing to love in an adult way, but also her identity.

Once she confessed, she would never again be the artist, the talented young woman who went to The New School on a partial scholarship, who moved to New York City and became a designer.

From then on, she'd only be the one who killed Misty Glass, town princess, descendent of town's forefathers, saver of squirrels. And for good measure, she'd be a baby killer, too.

She had no doubt her budding relationship with Heath would be terminated. She'd spent her entire adult life, from high school and into college, and then post-college, feeling awkward and hopeless around the young men who'd shown a romantic interest in her. Yes, she'd dated. Yes, she'd had sex. But a part of her had always been biding her time, waiting for what she finally had— Heath Asher. And he'd turned out to be as wonderful as she'd dared to hope.

All of this stuff about Misty being scared of him in high school. Romy had spent so much time watching the couple as they interacted at the pool. She'd never seen any sign of it.

In fact, Misty had appeared the initiator in their exchanges, constantly looking up at his lifeguard station for attention, even to the point where Romy had wondered how Misty was allowed to sit there distracting him from the important job of keeping people from drowning.

There are two Heaths.

Romy had seen only one of them. Sure, they'd been living in the same house for only a few weeks. But they'd spent almost all of that alone together. Wouldn't she have seen a flicker of the "other" Heath by now?

IN THE PRODUCE AISLE, she was trying to decide between two large, lumpy purple organic tomatoes when she heard, "If it isn't Romy Renskler."

She instantly knew the voice. "Mister—" She shook her head and smiled. "Avery."

His warm dark-brown eyes, no eyeglasses this time, crinkled over his mask. "Thank you. None of that Mr. Sands stuff. Makes me feel ancient."

He was pushing a cart with a few staples in it.

"I see you got lucky," Romy said, indicating his package of toilet paper.

He slung his thumb over his shoulder. "They got a delivery. You should hurry before the toilet paper vultures descend."

"I'm good," she said, laughing. "Stocked up last time."

"Smart." He winked and tapped his temple. "I always knew you were smart. Hey, we should get together and catch up—outdoors, of course. I want to hear how it's going with you these days."

"Going as it's going for everyone, I guess," she said. "Though I'm lucky I can work from home."

"Lucky for me I took early retirement last year," he said. "Couldn't have timed it better."

"I know you always said you and Mrs. Sands wanted to travel the world. Now you can do that. Though probably not this year."

His face darkened and he looked unsettled, rolling a plump, unripe mango around in his hands.

"Alicia lives in Saybrook with the girls," he said.

"Suppose she'll do the world traveling with her new man."

"Oh. I—I'm sorry to hear." She internally kicked herself for not checking his ring finger—which was bare —before she'd brought up his wife. This was difficult news to take in. The couple had always seemed so perfect for each other, so in love.

"It happens." He deposited the mango into his cart. "People get older, grow apart. A marriage starts to lose its spark. Well, it didn't for me, but it did for her." He hung his head, staring into his cart. "Sorry. What am I unloading this on you for? Inappropriate."

"No, no. It's fine. I'm sorry to hear."

"And you? You and Heath?" he ventured, eyes twinkling.

Romy felt herself beginning to blush, and she was thankful for the face covering. "Yeah." She nodded, "It's new but..."

He reached out and touched her hand. "You be careful, will you?" Then he pulled his hand back, as if he'd touched something hot. "Sorry, we're not supposed to touch, are we?"

"It's fine, but... be careful? You mean the virus?"

"Well, that and..." He hesitated, and looked around for a moment, as if a shopper might be eavesdropping. "I never told you this, but Misty... she was quite talented. Could draw very well, very realistically. Didn't have the magic that you have but I thought she might do something with it. We had a few advisory sessions, where she might like to study if she pursued art. But one day she told me she had to stop coming to see me. That her boyfriend had forbidden it. I thought she meant that football player, what was his name..."

"Patrick," Romy said, her stomach sinking.

"Right, right. Patrick Dugan. Remember, I rarely forget a student. But they'd broken up by then. She meant her new boyfriend. Heath Asher."

Romy swallowed hard. The garish fluorescent lighting of the store was giving her the pinging of a headache.

"That—that makes no sense. Heath loves art. In fact, he writes novels."

"Oh, I'm not sure it had anything to do with the *art...*" he demurred, his voice dipping conspiratorially. "I got the feeling he was overly possessive of her. Jealous, you could say. Which was concerning, given I was her teacher, twenty years older, and happily married. At the time." He grinned—she could tell by the crinkling eyes. "But high school boys aren't very mature. I'm sure he's matured by now," he finished, generously.

Romy wanted to get away. Away from all of this. Two people in the course of an hour telling her Heath Asher used to be a jealous maniac. The man she'd been in love with since she was old enough to have any concept of what romantic love was.

Couldn't they tell that *Romy* was the bad person, not Heath?

Seeing what must have been distress on her face, even though he could only see half of it, Avery adopted an easygoing, apologetic tone.

"Don't mind me. This was over a decade ago, and my memory is probably all haywire. If Heath is good to *you*, that's all that matters. Still…" His voice became solemn. "Tragedy about Misty, wasn't it? Utter and complete tragedy."

Chapter Nineteen

That night, Romy and Heath lay in each other's arms, squished together in the spare bedroom's twin bed.

"What if we bought a new mattress?" he murmured. "There must be pick-up somewhere."

"It's not the mattress. It's the entire room. It's my grandmother's. She's only been dead a year and I can still smell her in there."

"We could do a deep cleaning. Use laundry detergent. Romy, two of us in this bed is…"

"I know, I know."

She kissed him on the lips, snuggling contentedly into the crook of his arm. Happiness saturated her, the kind she'd only ever read about and had suspected wasn't real.

Lying on his chest, listening to the beat of his heart, was so beautiful that her eyes welled with tears of joy. She absolutely loathed the idea of disrupting this moment. But she had no choice.

"I have to ask you something," she said, plucking at a few of his sparse chest hairs.

"Shoot," he said, drowsily.

"It's about Misty."

She felt him shift, and she began soothingly stroking his bicep. "I saw Mr. Sands—Avery—in the grocery store today. We got to talking about her a little. He mentioned she was a talented artist. He said that... well, he might have been mistaken..."

"Said what?"

"That he thought he remembered you forbidding her to go to advisory sessions with him."

"Forbidding? Who said this?" He sounded bewildered.

"Mr. Sands. Avery."

He sighed heavily and adjusted his arm so it was no longer around hers but up by his head. "I definitely don't remember that. Forbid her to go somewhere? He told you this?"

Now Romy began to feel she had betrayed Avery's confidence. He'd confided in her as a way of warning her, putting her on guard, and she'd run to Heath and squealed.

"Forget it. I'm sure he was mistaken."

"Why would he tell you something like that? Does he have designs on you or something?"

He didn't say it angrily, rather more like he was genuinely curious. But the words made her uneasy—proof that Heath did indeed have a jealous streak.

"*Designs*. You sound like a forties movie," she teased,

trying to lighten the mood. "Of course not. He's always been one-hundred percent professional with me."

"Okay then," he grumbled. "I don't know what he's talking about. Why would I forbid her from going anywhere? That makes no sense."

But Heath didn't move his arm back to her, it stayed on the pillow. Romy felt so bad about her accusation that she couldn't bring herself to ask the next question—whether he'd argued with Misty a few days before her drowning.

What did it matter anyway? Romy knew perfectly well what had happened that night. *She* had unhooked the tarp. *She* had set up Misty to drown. Not Heath, who'd sprinted from the changing station, plunged into the pool, and wailed like a wounded animal when he couldn't revive her.

Hours later, she awoke out of a dream about making love to him. The dream got her so aroused that she began caressing him with the explicit intent of getting him in the mood.

After a minute or so, he began to respond, and soon, he was on top of her, driving into her with thrusts so deep and burning that she was on a spectacular and unstoppable train to orgasm.

That's when she saw the little girl in the window, a lascivious look on her face, a lurid smile on her lips.

Romy's loud cry was of ecstasy and terror, sickeningly mingled.

* * *

HEATH AND MACK traipsed back to the house, Mack straining at his leash to get inside and go to bed. Heath shook his head at her, then continued to the kitchen, gave Mack a dish of water, and poured himself a glass.

"I'm telling you, she was there," Romy insisted. "In the damn window again. And she saw us fucking!"

"Then we need to pull the drapes."

"I want to know if she's out there. How the hell is she running off so fast? Mack didn't bark or anything?"

"Nope." Mack finished off his water, then Heath picked up the water dish. If they didn't pick up the dish, Mack usually knocked it over sometime in the night.

"I don't get it," she said, despairingly. "How can she disappear so quick? Could she be a feral child who lives in the woods and nobody knows about her?"

"For sure, Romy, she lives out there with the wolves. Are there wolves around here? With the fisher cats."

When she scowled at him, he came over and laid his hands on her shoulders, a gesture that warned he was about to get paternal. "I know you don't want to consider this possibility..."

"Yeah, yeah, I know. It's all in my head."

"I'm not judging you. I have similar issues with my sleepwalking. Loretta says these things are usually linked to repressed memories."

"Repressed memories," Romy snorted, plucking his hands from her shoulders. "This woman sounds like a bad Lifetime movie."

"Well, she's helped me a lot. I used to sleepwalk all the time. In the past year, I only did it that one time, here. Would you at least consider talking to her?"

Mack let out a long, whining yawn, circled a few times, and plopped on the old stuffed couch pillow.

She couldn't get the little girl's smile out of her mind's eye. It was so creepy, so knowing. Wouldn't a young girl, seeing a couple having sex, have looked baffled, curious, or even disgusted? Even if the girl had —ick—walked in on her parents in the past, that look still hadn't fit the face of a young girl unfamiliar with sex.

Could this really be all in Romy's head? Why would her mind invent an impishly scary-looking little blonde girl of all things? And why, oh why, would she conjure her up at the most inopportune time imaginable?

"I'll think about it," she told him.

Chapter Twenty

Hey, Golden!

I hope you're doing well with this crazy pandemic thing! I wanted to give you a head start on my new book. It will be the last in the series. It hasn't sold very well. But I do have a few fans out there and I can't disappoint them by not wrapping things up.

It's called *Missy's Child*. That's right, Missy and Prince Holden are married, so of course, they must produce an heir to the throne! I haven't settled on a name yet, but it will be a baby boy. I'd like the cover to have Missy holding him when he's about two, which is when the story will pick up.

For inspiration, attached please find a photo of

the most adorable towheaded little boy you've ever seen! He's my nephew.

Let me know if you have any questions.

Best,
Helen

*R*omy held her breath, an ominous foreshadowing in her gut, and opened the attachment.

The photo was a bit faded. The boy was, indeed, towheaded and adorable enough to be a child model. But he was no "nephew." It was obviously a picture of Heath as a toddler, with those same sublime china-blue eyes with the barest flickers of golden-green embroidered in over-large irises.

In the photo, Heath was platinum blond and pale as soap. His hair had, like most blond children, darkened over time. Thanks to long, lifeguarding summers in the glaring sunshine, his skin was almost permanently tanned, not this alabaster color.

Toddler Heath and the little girl in the window could easily pass for siblings. Even fraternal twins.

The implication of this made Romy clench her teeth, hold her breath—the little girl looked like she could be Heath's daughter.

* * *

"HELLO, Romy, I'm Loretta Hale. It's so nice to meet you. Heath said you'd like to talk. I need to inform you that to comply with patient confidentiality and HIPAA law, we can't discuss Heath's therapy at all."

On Romy's laptop was a woman of about sixty, with long reddish hair and large, half-dollar-shaped eyes. She was wearing a bright, multicolored dress in a zigzag pattern, and gave off a hippy vibe.

"That's fine," Romy said.

"What would you like to speak about today?"

"Okay. So." Romy began spilling out, rat-a-tat-tat style. "You probably know that Heath and I came here because of the pandemic. I have a house. Shortly after we moved in, I was woken up by this... whispering or low talking. I saw this... it was a little girl. Staring into my window."

Romy was gesticulating so animatedly she knew she must look sort of crazed but couldn't help it. "She was very blonde and really pale. She ran off and I couldn't find her. When I saw her a second time, her eyes were strangely blue, almost glowing. But again, I couldn't find her in the yard. The third time, Heath and I were... um... doing what adults do... and there she was again! In the window! Heath went out with the dog but neither could find her."

The woman was studiously blank-faced as if she heard such tales on the regular. Finally, she said in a very smooth, reassuring voice, "Does Heath see her?"

"No. She always runs off."

"Have you called the police?"

"No. She's gone so fast. What would be the point of

calling them?" She didn't mention she had a fear that the police would bring up bad memories for Heath. Or maybe, recognizing him, they'd start poking around in the death of Misty again.

"Can you describe the girl to me, was she transparent... or...?"

"Transparent? No. But very pale."

"What was she wearing?"

"It's hard to say. I only see her for a few seconds, and her face comes up to the windowsill. She seems about ten or eleven years old."

Romy felt her nose tingling harshly as if she was about to cry, so she pretended to be jotting notes on a nearby notepad.

"What I want to know is, could this be in my head?" she asked, trying to sound clinically detached and not hysterical.

"It's certainly a possibility," Loretta answered, without hesitation. "You said she's speaking to you? What does she say?"

"Ahhh... she says..." Romy's voice went very quiet. "*Bad lady.* And... um... *Leave this place.*"

"By 'bad lady'—she means you?"

Romy nodded.

"Does the little girl remind you of anyone?"

Romy paused for a long time, staring off at the opposite wall and its framed pictures of her grandmother, mother, and herself when she was younger. She'd told Heath he had to leave the house during her session, and he'd given her no arguments, loping off into the backyard, where they'd started a garden. But she turned and checked to make sure the door was closed.

"Yeah, she does." She kept her voice low. "She reminds me of... *Heath*. When he was a little boy."

Loretta was silent for several moments, then got to the crux of the matter. "Romy, did anything happen to you when you were little? Something involving Heath?"

Romy was absently kneading the muscle of her thigh, over and over, with the knuckles of her fist. "Is this confidential?"

"Of course."

Romy nodded tightly and sighed out, "Something happened. Yes."

"So... you did something you feel responsible for? When you and Heath were little?"

"Something like that," she mumbled.

She had to stop looking so damn guilty. Heath must have told Loretta about Misty. If Romy continued to ooze guilt, continued to hint around about a bad thing she'd done that involved Heath—how long would it take for Loretta to piece together that Romy had something to do with Misty's death?

But Loretta's expression was the very picture of kindly nonjudgment. "Would you like to share what happened?" she pressed.

"No. I don't." Then, startled, she gasped, "You won't tell Heath this, right?"

"Absolutely not." Loretta paused, then smiled benignly. "It sounds as if this little girl is a manifestation of your conscience. I think when you resolve this issue, she'll go away."

"But how do I resolve it?" Romy asked hoarsely.

"What about sharing what happened with Heath? He's been your friend for a long time. The two of you are basically living together now."

"I—I can't."

"Romy… if you made a mistake, or a misjudgment, that had consequences that, at the time, you didn't understand, you need to forgive yourself. You wouldn't be worried about this if you weren't a good person, and good people make mistakes." She paused ominously. "However, if the consequence was the death of somebody, you would need to go to the police as there is no statute of limitations on death."

The counselor smiled benignly again, and Romy couldn't tell if the woman did think she'd killed somebody or was only saying that because it was in her repertoire of counselor-type things she was required to say.

"Romy, we aren't going to talk about Heath," she continued, "but since I know you know about his sleepwalking, I'll make a small exception. It sounds like the two of you have deep issues from your past that you're grappling with. Do you think now is a healthy time to start a relationship?"

"Maybe not. It just happened. We're sort of stuck together."

"I understand."

As the woman nodded, her big, round eyes pulsing with maternal concern, Romy had the oddest flash of intuition that the woman was in love with Heath.

Something about the way she said his name, drawing it out slightly, *Heeeathhh*, as if she enjoyed rolling his name around her mouth. Something about the way she'd asked if they should be starting a relationship—the way the question had gone up at the end with a slight inflection of disapproval. More than disapproval, a smidgen of irritation.

"What I suggest," Loretta went on, "is try talking to this little girl. Tell her she's a figment of your imagination, of your subconscious." Her voice was so tranquil, it was hypnotic. "Tell her that you forgive her. Because you're really telling yourself."

Chapter Twenty-One

"How did it go?"

Heath's hands were grubby and a smear of dirt was on his cheek. Romy had found a pair of gardening gloves on the porch but they were her grandmother's size, not a man's size, so Heath had happily been digging into the dirt with bare hands, like a kid in a sandbox. She'd started to notice dirt under his nails.

Heath had gone garden-mad and was planting every vegetable he could think of. This despite them not knowing if they would be here in the time it took for the seedlings to become harvestable.

"It was okay," she said, reluctantly, hoping he wouldn't ask any more questions. There was no way she could tell him about her "subconscious" taking the form of a creepy little blonde girl who looked like she could be his child, the child who'd died because of Romy's adolescent temper tantrum.

"Glad to hear it." He washed and dried his hands,

kissed her, and went to take a shower. Twenty minutes later, they were on the porch with drinks and a tray Romy had assembled of sliced cheeses, olives, and bread.

Things weren't looking good in the city. Cases were soaring. What news she could bring herself to consume was filled with gruesome tales of hospitalizations, deaths, and so many bodies that they were being stacked in meat trucks and buried in a potter's field on Hart Island.

She realized that she, like everyone else in the city, had been wandering around without a clue that something invisible and deadly was lurking in the air, expelled from people's noses and mouths. How she'd most likely come face-to-face with it in Bill's bathroom.

She tossed a pitted olive to Mack, who deftly caught it with his mouth and sat looking expectantly for another. Thinking of Bill, she was starting to feel less like she'd done him a grand favor by caring for his pet than that she'd stolen a dog from a dead man.

She should do more to track down his friends or family. But how? Suzie didn't know his last name, and as his apartment was a rental, Romy had been unable to locate a record of a Bill or William linked to her building's address.

"Heath," she said, looking over at him. He had his eyes closed and was wearing a contented smile. The pair had spent the evening before changing the glass panes to their accompanying screens, and now a breeze tinkled the elaborately tiered sea-glass and seashell wind chimes hanging in one corner.

Caroling songbirds clustered in the trees on one side of the porch, filling the air with their musical warbles, and a tuft-tailed squirrel squatted on a nearby pine branch, cackling and nattering at them.

A much more pleasant ambiance than the one she imagined she'd be subjected to in the city. But how long could they realistically stay here? All of her belongings were still in her apartment. And obviously being back at the scene of the horrendous thing she'd done as a teen was beginning to drive her mad. Presumably, if Romy left town, the little girl would be left behind.

"Hmm?" Heath said.

"I need to ask you something."

He didn't open his eyes but sighed as if he knew his serenity was about to be cut short.

"I want to be honest that I met up with Gillian the other day."

He still didn't open his eyes but his silence was charged as if he was listening hard.

"I didn't tell you because I know you don't like her, and you have a good reason."

"Yes, Romy?" He sounded a bit exasperated. "And?"

"And… like you told me…" She took a sip of hard seltzer, trying to bolster herself. "She mentioned that she'd heard you and Misty arguing a few days before… what happened. She was very adamant about it, and even said Misty confirmed it to her."

She couldn't bring herself to repeat Gillian's version of what Misty had said about being scared of him.

He opened his eyes and put down his bottle of ale as

if preparing himself for something. Possibly to get up and leave. Then he leaned forward contemplatively, staring out into the woods, vigorously circling his thumbs.

"What are you saying?" he asked, not looking at her. "Are you like Gillian? You think I killed Misty?"

"Of course not."

"Then what?" he asked evenly. "I knew I shouldn't have come back to this town. I thought it would be okay because I was with you. That *you*, at least, knew the real me."

"I do know the real you."

Why was she interrogating him? She knew what had happened. Yet she couldn't stop thinking about not only Gillian but also Avery having their doubts about him. She couldn't completely ignore that, could she? At the very least, she should have a better idea about whom she was currently living with.

"Then why do you keep asking me about not only the worst time in my life but a time I hardly remember?" he said. "I was *eighteen*."

He raked his hand through his half-wet hair, then retrieved the beer bottle and tipped it up to his mouth. He put it down and after a minute or so of wire-tense silence, he said, "We didn't argue much that I recall. If you must know, we spent most of our time having sex. I mean, we were kids. Horny kids."

"Okay," she said, quietly.

"But… " He rocked against his legs, gripping the beer bottle tightly. "There was one day, I was at her place. Her parents worked, so they were never around."

He kept his focus fixed on the woods, even when Mack approached his knees, thinking he might be a likely candidate for tossing an olive. When none was forthcoming, the dog grunted and trotted into the kitchen. "I don't know... it was like she was trying to provoke me."

"*Provoke* you?"

"Yeah. As I said, we'd just had sex. She'd always seemed very, um, *happy* with it. But that day, she didn't. She told me she wanted to go back to her ex-boyfriend, that football player, Patrick something... because he was better in bed." Looking down, he shook his head and laughed a little. "Now, as an adult, I'd react differently. But back then... she was only the second girl I'd ever had sex with. It really set me off. I put on my clothes and wanted to get out of there. She followed me down the stairs, saying things like, 'He's better than you, and he's bigger than you.'"

Romy's mouth was hanging open. She couldn't imagine the genial Misty saying such things. Nor did Romy like the way he'd used the word *provoke*. It was the kind of word a man used when he was making excuses for his own behavior.

He went on, "In the driveway, I said I never wanted to see her again, or something similar. That has to be the argument busybody Gillian overheard. She always had her head half out the window, spying on us."

"I thought you said Gillian was making up the argument."

"Well... I didn't want to admit this one, okay? It's rather embarrassing?" He glanced sidelong at her, a spark of challenge in his eyes, then went back to his tense staredown of the forest.

"But you two stayed together?" she asked.

"Yeah, the next day, it was a different Misty. She came to my place, telling me she didn't mean any of it, that... that we were so good together, she was scared. Scared I'd leave her. She'd wanted to hurt me before I'd hurt her."

Kneading his hands, he continued staring off into the woods as the atmosphere began to imperceptibly darken, a scattering of dusk fireflies starting to glow. "So, I reassured her that I'd never hurt her. A few days later, she told me she was pregnant." He paused. "Then she was dead."

Romy was gutted to see that his lower lip was trembling, as if he was barely holding back tears.

"Why couldn't I save her? Why wasn't I faster?"

Romy leaned over and grabbed his forearm. "It's not your fault," she blurted.

"I knew she didn't swim well. We'd stay on the tarp. I thought she'd be safe." He pulled his arm away, lost in his memories. "Her leg went halfway through a rip once. We knew about it, we'd stay away from it. But with what she told me that night, our minds were elsewhere. When the whole thing came off on that side, she went under and panicked. If only I'd gone on it first, like usual, I would have stopped her... but I lost my phone that day. I heard it ring from the changing station, where I'd left it."

He looked at her, his eyes glistening. "Romy, it was my job to put the tarp on at the end of the day, me and my boss. Too many critters had died in the pool, so it went on every night. I hooked that corner. Did I not fasten it tightly enough?" He shook his head. "It clipped and that was it. And I always pulled on it to make sure. Always. But we shouldn't have been on it. How stupid I was!"

He tossed his neck back for a moment, then hung his head between his shoulders, as if in agony. Romy had grown mute, her fingers squished up against her mouth.

She'd never known that he was the one who'd fastened that corner of the tarp, as Gillian had theorized. All these years, he'd been living with the guilt of thinking he was directly responsible for the tarp coming off.

He *had* fastened it tightly—she remembered how hard she'd had to tug to get the latch off the bolt. She needed to tell him.

Without even feeling herself move, she pulled herself onto his lap and buried her face in his neck. "I'm sorry I brought it up. You *have* to know it wasn't your fault."

She couldn't say it. Couldn't say it. It wouldn't come out of her throat. It wouldn't. He didn't respond but relaxed into her, and she felt she'd comforted him.

She was crawling with shame, interrogating him about his jealousy—when it was *her* jealousy that had killed Misty.

Chapter Twenty-Two

*F*or the next three nights, the little girl failed to make an appearance, though Romy kept the window cracked open a few inches, letting in the pleasantly balmy night air.

It was nearing May, and positive virus cases had climbed so high in the city that most of it was shut down. Even here in the country, things had changed. Restaurants could only have thirty percent capacity. Gyms and schools were closed. There were no live events. Most people were working from home.

And positive cases had been identified in Glass Town —approximately two hundred of them. It seemed there was no mass of populated land on the planet that would be immune.

She'd also finally agreed that she and Heath could sleep in her grandmother's bedroom. She'd ordered a mattress online and two masked men had delivered it, leaving it outside.

She'd spent two days taking down all of the framed

photos on her grandmother's wall, wrapping and storing them, and giving the room a deep clean with the bleach-infused spray she'd finally snagged at the grocery store. It was the last one on the shelf, and she felt almost as if she'd found a nugget of pure gold.

The room still felt like her grandmother—Romy could swear she still smelled her, as if her molecules were embedded in the walls—but she figured nothing was ever going to change that. Now her plan was to paint the room, and she was in the midst of checking out colors online, leaning towards a cheery yellow to offset the doom of the world outside.

She had to admit having a queen-size bed was heavenly. Not only for all the things she and Heath could comfortably do to each other on a larger bed—and they did quite a lot—but how they could stretch and laze and have their own space, as well as curl into each other and cuddle.

But Romy made sure to draw the musty drapes when they got physical. Real or not, a freaky-eyed little girl leering at them when they had sex was a real mood killer.

Romy slept on the window side and did everything in her power to summon the girl in her mind in order to do what Loretta had suggested and confront the girl.

Tell the girl—tell *herself*—that she was forgiven for what she'd done.

Despite Loretta's contention that the little girl was nothing but a mirage, a visual symptom of Romy's guilty conscience, the idea still terrified her. But it was the only thing that gave her any hope the situation would go away.

It felt like every hour, she startled awake and stared out the window, heart pounding, silently urging the specter to appear. But for three nights, the rectangle of moonlit space remained empty and she dared to hope the issue had corrected itself.

But on the fourth night, she awoke out of a fitful sleep, thinking she'd heard something outside. She stared at the window, clawing the sheets, bracing herself for seeing that otherworldly, alienesque little face and radiating blue eyes.

Instead, she saw a head of blonde hair pass by the window. Pass quickly by and not look inside. Romy's breathing quickened and she forced herself to quietly get up and move out of the room, closing the door behind her so as to not wake Heath.

As she approached the darkened living room, she saw Mack standing rigidly at attention, staring towards the door. He too had sensed the little girl. What did this mean? Wouldn't he only be standing alert if the girl was real?

Romy grabbed the flashlight from where she kept it ready, new batteries installed, on the kitchen island, and walked to the door. "Down, Mack," she hissed.

She turned the lock and it made a metallic click, then she grasped the doorknob and turned it as soundlessly as she could. Keeping the front light off, she opened the wooden door and saw nothing through the screen. Still, she sensed a presence in the dark.

"Hello," she called softly, the adrenaline of fear

lighting up every part of her body. She thought if the little girl's ghostly face appeared in front of her, she would probably drop dead of fright.

"Are you there?" she asked in a husky whisper. "I know you're me. I—know why you're here."

Mack stood next to her and let out a long, low growl. "Mack, go lie down!" she commanded, pushing him back with her palm. He shuffled off.

Romy still saw nothing outside, only heard the shrill racket of cicadas and crickets livening the still night. A breeze rustled through the screen door.

"Little girl?" Romy asked, tone rising, a feeling of ridiculousness beginning to poke through the fear. "It's okay. I—I forgive you."

She opened the screen door several inches and peered outside into the dark. She thought she saw something small and white on the lawn near the lilac bush.

It could be a stone or… a foot.

"Little girl? I for—"

Mack slammed by her and was out the door.

"Mack!" she yelled, stumbling onto the door. "Goddamn it!"

Turning on her flashlight, she was pushing out the screen door when she heard a scream. A female's scream. She froze. Mack was somewhere in the dark. Growling.

"Help!" Romy heard. "Get this fucking dog off me! Help!"

Romy rushed forward, sweeping the flashlight's beam from side to side. The little girl wasn't a little girl. Romy could tell by the voice. And she was painfully real.

"Mack!" Romy hollered, trying to track the sound of his growls.

On the opposite side of the lilac bush, the flashlight's beam picked up Mack on top of... a blonde woman. A teen? Definitely not a little girl.

"Mack!" Romy ordered harshly, giving her voice as much authority as she could manage. "Down!"

She got up to the pair and dragged him back by his thick collar. She could definitely see that the woman on the ground was an adult. Romy feared she might see blood and what that could mean for Mack but it was too dark to tell how much damage he might have inflicted, and the woman was wearing long, dark sleeves.

"Romy!" It was Heath's voice. "Romy!"

"I'm over here!" she called.

The woman was crawling along the lawn. Her clothing was all black, so Romy could only see her blonde hair in a ponytail and her pale hands.

"Who are you?" she screeched at the stranger. "What are you doing here? What do you want?"

"Are you kidding," Romy heard and turned around. Heath was standing nearby, naked, his manhood dangling. He was stock-still and appeared shocked.

"Heath..." she gasped. "Don't... ah... you better..."

"Don't worry, honey," came the woman's voice from the ground. "I've seen it all before."

* * *

INSIDE THE HOUSE, the woman sat pressing one hand on her arm, which Mack had bit. Romy found an old tube of antibiotic ointment in the bathroom, handed it to the woman, and watched as she rubbed the ointment on the red mark on her forearm. No doubt the tube had expired but Romy wasn't about to volunteer this information.

It was now abundantly clear that the intruder, despite being blonde and not brunette, was none other than Tara, Heath's former fiancée. Romy recognized her from all the time she'd spent staring at her on his social media profile.

Heath disappeared with Mack, then came back out in shorts and his most-worn T-shirt, a faded ocean-blue that brought out his eyes. Mack remained in the bedroom. "What the hell are you doing, Tara?" he demanded.

"That dog," she said, glaring at him. "You're lucky I don't press charges."

"You're sneaking around the yard. *You're* lucky he didn't kill you!"

She sulked, keeping her hand pressed on her arm. From what Romy could tell, Tara's long-sleeved shirt had saved her from a deeper bite. But given Mack's steel-trap jaw, Romy suspected he'd merely decided to toy with her.

"What are you doing?" Heath repeated. "How did you even find me?"

"The find-your-phone app," Tara offered. "I've been worried about you."

He pointed at her. "I *told* you I was fine. I *told* you to stop calling me."

Tara turned her ice-blue eyes on Romy. She definitely had a strong resemblance to Misty but the core of Misty—luscious and luminous—wasn't there. Tara looked rough, like someone you wouldn't want to get on the wrong side of. Seemingly not finding anything worth continuing to examine, she brought her attention back to Heath.

"It's not right how you disappear after three years together," she said.

"Disappear? I've been talking to you. I told you where I was."

"You said Glass Town but you didn't say you'd moved in with another woman." She didn't bother to look at Romy as she said this. "I don't think Loretta would approve. You went from me, the Misty clone, to a girl from your childhood." She brought her turquoise gaze back to Romy and flailed her good arm at her. "Did you know Misty?"

Romy was taken aback to realize that not only had Tara managed to track down Heath's whereabouts but had uncovered the owner of the house he was in.

"I knew her a little."

"It's not healthy, Heath," Tara said, shaking her head.

Heath cackled as if to say, *Can you believe this shit?* "You're a fine one to talk healthy. Stalking and spying on me." He looked at Romy. "This solves the mystery, I'd say. Look at her, she's blonde. Why are you blonde, Tara?"

"Because I thought if you saw me on social media looking less like Misty, you'd give us another chance, that's all," she said, sounding sad and pathetic, not the fighter she'd appeared a minute ago.

Tara looked so genuinely distraught that Romy felt bad for her. She must have loved Heath as much as Romy did—probably more, given how long they'd lived together. And she clearly *still* loved him. It wasn't Tara's fault he'd chosen her because she looked like Misty, then dumped her for the same reason.

"Unbelievable." He sighed, throwing his hand through his mussed hair. "You've been coming down from Brooklyn to spy on me?"

"No," she pouted. "From Milton. I moved back home because my dad got sick. I'm helping him out."

At the word "sick," Romy and Heath each instantly retreated into the living room's far corners.

"Not the virus," Tara stressed. "He has appendicitis, okay? We've been quarantining."

"Well, I'm sorry about your dad," said Heath. "But this is… How long have you been spying in the window? You've been scaring Romy to death."

"This is the first time," she insisted, peevishly. She looked down at her arm. "Do you have any Band-Aids?"

"I'm sorry, I couldn't find any," Romy said, straining to be polite, worried that Tara might report Mack for biting her. Police may not care that she was trespassing. Mack obviously had a lot of pit bull in him and that was going to work against him. Some places even banned bully breeds and she didn't know if Glass Town was one of them.

"Is this her?" Heath asked Romy. "The little girl you've been seeing?"

Romy peered at Tara more closely. The pale-blonde hair, alabaster skin, and vibrant blue eyes matched—but there was no way. The little girl was so odd-looking and she definitely appeared much younger. Not at all a woman in her twenties.

"I don't think so," Romy said, though her voice lacked confidence.

"Little girl?" Tara looked flummoxed. "I only wanted to confirm that you're living with a woman, Heath. You should have told me that."

"Why? We're not together. Haven't been since December."

"I'm only saying, it's not right to ask me to marry you, give me a ring, then run off."

"I didn't run off!" Heath said, impatiently. He'd clearly had this discussion or variations on it before. "We talked and talked and you didn't want to hear it. I said I'm sorry a million times. I don't know what else to say."

Tara turned to Romy—her eyes steely. "He'll do the same to you. He seems all sweet and cute, but he'll cut you to the bone. He's in love with a dead girl. His cloud password is Misty Glass. He's had that password for everything since high school. Who can compete with a dead girl? She makes no demands, has no opinions, and never gets old!"

Romy had to admit Tara was making some valid points.

"Thanks for revealing my password to the world, Tara. Do I need to call you a car or anything? Because you need to go."

Tara stood, seemingly trying to hike up her dignity.

"No. I parked across the street in that ballpark. I don't know why I'm here. I guess dealing with my dad, losing my job, losing you, this pandemic, I've gone a bit nuts."

"I can show you out," Romy offered, not thrilled about having to move closer to a maskless woman she'd never met before.

"I'll do it," said Heath, seeming to read her thoughts. "Next time you decide to drop by unannounced," he told her, "at least wear a mask."

"Goodbye, Heath," Tara said, sucking in her breath. Then, to Romy, "You're lucky that dog didn't break the skin."

Heath opened the door for her and she disappeared into the night. He closed the door, locked it, and stood staring at it.

"Heath?" Romy prodded.

He turned, exhaustion all over his face. "I can't deal with this drama," he sighed, walking down the hallway. He opened the bedroom door and Mack came trotting out as if nothing had happened.

THE NEXT MORNING, Heath was tense and quiet and didn't want any breakfast. After coffee, Romy retired to her room to work, including on his book cover. She spent a couple of hours looking for a photo of a little blond boy who resembled him when he was a toddler.

There weren't many children—even child models—who were as beautiful as toddler Heath was, so it wasn't an easy task. But she found a few that might work.

She wondered how she was ever going to confess to being Golden-Eye. It was bad enough he'd figured out she'd been buying his books—he must already consider her a world-class liar.

She'd put the finishing touches on another client's cover when he knocked on the door and she quickly shut her laptop. Thank God he was a knocker. She didn't need him knowing she designed book covers, that might get him introspecting in a way she didn't want yet.

She turned and smiled at him as he popped his head in but the look on his face conveyed he was about to say something that was going to change everything, and not for the better.

"Listen," he said, nervously massaging his jaw. "I should head back to the city for a bit. I've got tools there I need for these jobs. My belt sander and polisher are too expensive to be going out buying new ones. And I've got outstanding jobs I abandoned when I came here. I should get to them."

She was silent for a few moments, then said, "Why do I get the feeling you're going for more reason than that?"

He slouched against the doorway, the late morning sun stage-lighting those spellbinding eyes. Sometimes she wondered if he didn't have those if she'd be so enchanted with his looks.

"I'm sorry Tara showed up," he said.

"It's not your fault. I'm only glad Mack didn't tear her arm off."

He emitted a burst of edgy laughter, then turned serious again. "It's got me thinking. Everything she said.

How I went from her straight to you. Loretta thinks I'm codependent. She says I need alone time."

"Loretta wants you to herself," Romy heard herself snap and immediately regretted it.

"Wow, what?" He shook his head, sadly, as if disappointed that Romy couldn't see the genius of Loretta. "She's been so helpful. I used to sleepwalk all the time until we started hypnosis."

Hypnosis? This was the first Romy had heard about hypnosis but she couldn't deal with the strangeness of this declaration right when it appeared he was taking off and she didn't know when or if she'd ever see him again.

"I feel," he continued, "with you having suspicions about me, and Tara stalking me, I need a little break from women."

"I don't suspect you of *anything*," she insisted. "I only had some questions." But even as she said it, she realized it wasn't completely true.

He looked awkward and fidgety—like he wanted to get away from her. The more he looked like that, shifting restlessly against the doorway, the more she wanted him to go away. It's better to be alone than to be with someone who doesn't want to be with you. "Well, I don't think it's safe to go back to the city but if you want to go, you should go," she said.

"I'll be careful. Going to get my tools, work, and sleep in my room. Avoid my roommate." He smiled weakly. "Virus can't come through walls."

"According to my dad it can," Romy said, rolling her eyes, and they shared a laugh that made her heart ache.

She already missed him.

* * *

HEATH WANTED to get ahead of traffic—if there was even much traffic these days—so an hour later, he had his things packed and the two of them stood in front of his beat-up old jalopy.

"You'll be okay without a car?" he asked.

"Yeah, my grandmother's Volvo still runs, so I might try that even though it's uninsured. Or I'll rent a car."

"You'll be alright with that little girl running around?" The way he said it made it clear that he, like Loretta, thought the girl was in her mind.

"I've got Mack."

He put his hands on her arms and unexpectedly hugged her. The delicious feel and smell of him made her want to cry. The idea of not seeing him all the time cracked her heart but she also wanted him to leave quickly so she could indulge in a private weeping session.

"Are we breaking up?" she was mortified to hear herself asking. "I mean if we're even together?"

He held her face in his hands and said, "I have some thinking to do. I need to figure out a way to move on from Misty once and for all. I don't think the way to do that is being in a relationship, which is what I used to think."

"What would help you move on?" she asked, hoarsely.

He looked down for a few moments, then past her into the yard, and finally locked her with those peculiarly arresting eyes. "What haunts me is the idea that I didn't run fast enough on purpose. That I didn't do all I could on purpose." He paused, his bottom lip trembling ever-so-slightly. "That's what haunts me. Because I don't quite remember it all."

Romy thought about his wails. The bone-chilling cries of the worst grief imaginable—grief she couldn't imagine experiencing. She could never forget them. He wouldn't have made those sounds if he'd wanted Misty to die, would he?

Unless…

"Romy?" he asked.

"Ah," she said, forcing herself out of the disturbing thoughts threatening to engulf her. "No, um…" She felt herself pulling away from him, couldn't tolerate the feel of his hands on her.

"Romy," he said, "can you tell me you don't wonder the same? I had a ticket to Georgetown. Prelaw." Then, in a monotone, he gave voice to the very idea that she was trying so hard to shove away. "I knew there was a camera."

There it was. Those cries of grief, the ones she could still clearly hear if she put her mind to it…

Could it have been an act?

Had Romy inadvertently started something that Heath decided to finish? The opportunity had presented itself, and he'd simply let it play out. There's no more perfect murder than a death that isn't planned, just not prevented.

Once he saw Misty was in serious trouble, all he had to do was get to her a little later than he should have. All he had to do was pretend to be blowing air into her lungs, pretend for the camera.

How utterly, ingeniously perfect. A murderer who appears for all the world (or at least the town) like a pitiable victim.

"No, Heath—" Her throat was screwing shut, chills were assailing her body. She shook her head, unable to speak.

He kissed her on the cheek, and she felt herself wince. Then he tossed his two bags into the passenger side, came back around, and climbed into the driver's seat.

"Wait," she said. "Wait here."

Spontaneously, she ran to the house and grabbed her apartment keys, which were hanging on the pegs by the door. She jogged back and held them up through the driver's window. "Stay at my place if you need to get away from your roommate."

He tried to wave her off but she forced the keys into his hand. "Please? It will make me feel better. The little key is my mail key if you can grab the mail."

She'd filled out an online change of address form, and mail was beginning to trickle into Sapling Lane but her city mailbox must be stuffed to the point of being useless. "If you see the guy who lives next door, his name is Bill. Tell him I have Mack. Have him call me."

"Okay," he said, staring ahead out the windshield. "Thanks. I'll at least go over and get your mail for you."

"And you might want to change your password unless you want Tara following you back to the city."

He looked down at her, smiled a little. "Already did.

154

By the way, Misty's only my password because I'm really bad at coming up with new ones." Then he gunned the engine.

Watching the truck carry him away down the hill was a heavy blend of sadness and relief.

That night, she slept on a blanket next to Mack's dog-smelly pillow. "Are you a lone wolf or a pack animal, Mack?" she murmured into his neck as he nonchalantly licked his paw.

Chapter Twenty-Three

"*R*omy, Romy… so good to see you. And your whole face this time."

Avery Sands sat across from her at a local restaurant that had a large outdoor seating area warmed with heat lamps. He was almost fifty but had kept in shape and had only grown deeper and more comfortably into his brooding good looks. Though there was a new dash of dolor in his dark brown eyes, no doubt emanating from his divorce.

They ordered a bottle of Vinho Verde to share and looked over the heavily seafood-oriented menu.

"Cheers," he said, clinking her glass. "To better things than a pandemic. Though it's put us back in touch, so there's a little silver lining."

"I'm sorry we lost touch. Things got crazy with work."

His eyes gleamed with genuine pride. Besides her grandmother, he was the only person who'd ever looked at her that way, and now that her grandmother was gone, this made him the sole purveyor of pride in her artwork.

Sure, her parents were gratified she made a living but they didn't really get it, and could still be tetchy that she hadn't gone into the type of business they understood, one where the product came in a jar.

"I'm really so proud of you," he said, echoing her thoughts. "You know I can honestly say that you are still, to this day, the most talented student I ever had."

"Thanks," she said, unable to control her smile, and feeling her cheeks starting to warm. She knew he meant it.

They spent the next hour or so talking about her design business and the trends in covers, topography, and images. By the end of dinner, they'd each had a couple of glasses of wine, and Avery started to open up about his marriage.

"I was under the impression things were fine but men can be obtuse, which is a kinder word than stupid." He grinned sheepishly as she shrugged with a *You said it, I didn't* look. "I know there were things I should have improved on. Spending more quality time with the girls. Helping more around the house. Listening better. Talking less. All the things that men—or at least me—can be bad at."

"It came out of nowhere?"

"Yes and no. I'd definitely noticed she was spending more time with one of our neighbors. He's a stay-at-home dad and our kids were friends with his kids. I was commuting from Saybrook to my last year at the school, so the neighbor—Morris—kind of picked up the slack.

In more ways than one, as I discovered. And discovered in an up-close-and-personal manner I wish with all my heart I could cauterize out of my memory."

"Ouch. I'm really sorry."

"Morris. Who has an affair with a guy named Morris?" The server appeared and cleared their plates, and Avery asked for another bottle of wine.

"I really shouldn't," Romy demurred. "I took my grandmother's car here."

"Take a car service. On me. Then come back tomorrow for your car, also on me."

"Oh, I don't…"

"Come onnnn," he pressed. "I haven't seen you in ages. Though I suppose Heath is waiting up for you."

"Um." She stared disconsolately into her near-empty wine glass. "We broke up. If we were even together. Whatever. He needs space."

"Space!" Avery cried. He mockingly shook his fist. "Why I oughta… how dare he." He grew serious. "Maybe it's for the best, Romy. I felt bad about what I said in the grocery store but… I got the feeling from what Misty said that he wasn't the best boyfriend. In fact, given what happened…"

She shook her head as the waitress appeared, uncorked the new bottle of wine, and began pouring. "I can't hear it," she said. "I know what some people in town think. But he didn't do anything to hurt Misty. He may have his faults, we all do. That just isn't one of them."

"Sorry," he said. "I know how painful it is to hear unpleasant things about the people you love. *Believe* me, I know. Somehow all my friends knew about Alicia before I did. I actually cut off a few good ones because they *dared* to tell me she wasn't all I thought."

An hour later, they were in front of the restaurant. Romy wasn't smashed but decided she shouldn't drive back to the house. Besides the four-and-a-half glasses of wine she'd consumed, the town's streets could be pitch-black with sharp, unexpected bends, and deer that suicidally leaped out from the roadside. Best to be crystal-headed when driving these roads.

They were supposed to be standing six feet apart but given the two bottles of wine they'd downed, their perception was off and they drifted closer.

Romy had to admit he was a handsome man. Different from the way Heath was handsome. Darker, shorter, more compact and masculine, with heavy brows and deep-set eyes. She wasn't into older men, but if she *was* going to be into them, he'd be at the top of the list. But that would be far too awkward. He'd known her since she was a kid.

"Avery, I forgot to ask you, do you know of any little girls in town who are very pale and blonde and have kind of eerie blue eyes?"

"Um." He looked like he was trying not to look too perplexed. "Well, my girls are teens now, so I don't know many little ones anymore. What age are you talking?"

"Ten, eleven?"

"Can't think of anyone in particular, not with—did you say—'eerie' blue eyes?"

"Sorry, it's a dumb question. I wish I could describe

her better. She almost looks like she crawled out of a grave."

He almost did a spit-take. "I'm sorry, what?" As they were only a couple of feet from each other now—virus notwithstanding—he put his hand on her wrist. "What's going on, Romy?"

She sighed, casting around to see if anyone was nearby. Luckily, people were keeping their distance these days. "It's crazy but I think... Did you know Misty was pregnant when she died?"

"I believe I read that, yeah."

"I think—I think her unborn child is..."

He stared intensely at her.

"Well... I feel like..."

He gripped her wrist tighter, only a few inches from her. "What is it?"

Once she crossed this line, she knew there was no coming back from it. But she could think of no other person in the world she could tell. Besides, she was drunk; inhibitions were lowered to the point that what she was about to say didn't sound that bizarre.

"I think Misty's child is haunting me."

SHE AND AVERY took the car service to a nearby bar that was serving outside at big picnic tables. The weather was warming but still chilly at night. The bar, like most of the local restaurants, had set up towering, red-glowing heat lamps outside.

"I know this sounds insane," she said after the masked server took their order.

They'd said virtually nothing on the short car ride over, an unspoken agreement between them that they would save the ghost talk for their destination. During the ride, she'd begun to regret her rash impulse to tell him the spirit theory she'd recently started to entertain in earnest.

"What's making you think this?" Avery asked, doing an admirable job of sounding like he didn't think she'd lost her mind.

"There's this little girl who's been peeking in my windows. She looks at the age Misty and Heath's child would be if she'd lived. Heath showed me a picture of himself when he was a toddler. The girl has the same coloring. After she comes to the window, I try to find her but she completely disappears."

The server delivered their orders and they halted their conversation until she left. "Do you believe in ghosts?" Romy asked him.

Avery took a thoughtful sip from his pint of beer. His expression of sincere contemplation gave her the rising hope that comes with finding someone who won't judge you for your most outlandish musings.

"I've never seen one," he said. "But that doesn't mean they don't exist. 'There's more in heaven and Earth than is dreamt of in your philosophy, Horatio,' to quote a man you may have heard of." He smiled, then he gazed curiously at her. "Are you saying ghosts age in real time, like living beings do?"

"Well..." She tipsily pondered this knot in the thesis.

"Maybe this one did."

"But why would she haunt *you*?"

Romy burst out with sputtering, nervous laughter. "I don't know other than she's not happy I'm with—or *was* with—her father."

"Have you told Heath about this?" he asked. "You say the ghost figure is a girl, does he know if his baby was a girl?"

She squirmed, staring down into her wine glass, her stomach filling with acid, and wishing she hadn't ordered more booze.

"He thinks she's a kid from the neighborhood," she sighed. "Or maybe I'm sleepwalking. He sleepwalks, so he thinks everyone does." She sucked in a deep, ragged breath, trying to tamp down her queasiness. "I couldn't possibly ask him about the baby's gender. I don't even know if he knows that. He never spoke to Misty's parents after that night."

They were silent, and when Romy spotted the waitress at a nearby table, she hailed her and asked for a glass of water. Avery's unblinking gaze was brimming with concern.

"Perhaps the girl will go away now that you and Heath aren't together." The way he said it was not as if he was humoring her but wanted this for her. "If that is what's disturbing her spirit, that disturbance is gone."

Romy nodded, thankful for his noble attempt to speak to her seriously about a ghost-child.

But given that she knew the *real* reason the little girl might be haunting her, she didn't feel optimistic that the girl was placated.

Chapter Twenty-Four

The next day, Romy was tweaking the title colors for *Missy's Child*. She'd finally found a child model who resembled Heath as a toddler—but who didn't look like he was hamming it up for a cereal commercial—when Heath called.

She let the phone ring until it was about to go to voicemail before picking up with a distracted-sounding "Ahh, hello?" as if she was too busy to have checked the caller ID.

"Hi, Romy," he said, softly. "It's Heath."

"Ohh… heyyy," she said, attempting to sound as if she'd half-forgotten who he was. "What's the city like?"

"It's… well, pretty much everything is shut down. The streets are weirdly empty. Easy to get parking. There's a chicken game thing going on with people coming down the sidewalk. Who will first move out of the way? Everyone claps at seven for the frontline workers."

"That's nice. Wonder if they'd like a raise, too."

"Good point." He paused. "I miss you."

Her soul melted and all pretense of nonchalance evaporated. "I miss you too. A lot."

"I miss our garden."

The way he said *our* garden made her giddy but it didn't make her giddy that *she* was the one doing all the work on *their* garden, especially as he'd planted a ton of vegetables that needed constant watering, weeding, and trimming. "It misses you too," she said. "Some of the tomato plants are drooping. They're sad."

He made a low chuckle. There was a tiny but deep crinkle that formed vertically between his brows when he gave that soft, low chuckle and she pictured it, thinking how much she liked it when it made an appearance.

"Why are you in the city if you miss us so much?" she asked. "Get your tools and come back. Make sure to bring my favorite tool, the really hard one."

Much as she'd developed some trepidation about Heath, her loneliness and hearing his tender, sexy voice was too much for her. Perhaps because she'd met him at the onset of puberty, his voice resonated in a key that plugged directly into her heart—and between her legs. She wanted to reach through the phone, grab him, and pull him back to her.

Another muffled chuckle came down the phone but he said, "I can't yet. I'm starting deep intensive work with Loretta to get to the bottom of my sleepwalking."

"Deep intensive work? Let me guess, this takes place in her apartment."

"What? No."

"Sorry." Romy was letting her jealousy get the better of her. Heath's sleepwalking was a genuine concern. If Loretta could help him with it, more power to her. But Romy refused to dismiss the libidinous drawl she'd heard in Loretta's voice when she'd said his name, couldn't shake off that unprofessional gleam she'd definitely spotted in Loretta's large, egg-shaped eyes.

Why Romy was jealous of Loretta and not Tara, she didn't know. Perhaps it was that Tara seemed to be a person Heath was running *from*, while Loretta had something he was running *towards*.

"We do the sessions online," he continued. "I don't go to her apartment. Pandemic, hello?"

"Alright, I'm just a little miffed because it's clear you leaving was her idea."

"She only suggested it. I'm the one who decided."

"Fine, she's a saint," Romy relented, staring out the window into the emerald expanse of sun-splashed, overgrown front lawn. She'd have to figure out the ancient, oily lawnmower in the shed, and would probably hack off a few toes in the mowing process. "Tell me more."

"I had another incident a few nights ago. Scared the crap out of my roommate, who apparently almost hit me with a spatula." He paused. "Loretta is convinced that my sleepwalking has something to do with a memory I've repressed about... *that night*." He said this in almost a whisper. "I haven't wanted to dig around about that night. But recalling that memory might be the only way to stop my sleepwalking. Eventually, I'm going to hurt myself or someone else."

"Okay," Romy said, not liking where this was going.

"I know I often say things when I sleepwalk but Tara could never make out the words. But you did, right?"

"Umm, I think so."

"Something like, 'It's my fault'?"

Chewing her bottom lip, she watched a fat bumblebee levitating over the lilac bush right outside her window, preparing to land on a violet cluster.

It was my fault... She did it for me.

My fault.

Oh God, if she told him that, he'd become even more convinced he was responsible for Misty's death.

She did it for me.

Had he really said that? What *had* Misty done for him? Surely, not getting pregnant. From what Romy overheard of their conversation, it had sounded like the pregnancy hadn't been planned.

"Hmmm..." she stalled. Mack wandered into the room, did a lap, and not finding anything interesting, trotted back out. "I think it was, 'It's not my fault.'"

"It's *not* my fault? That's what I said? I thought it was the opposite."

"Heath, you were freaking me out. I'm not sure what you said. Is Loretta licensed to be doing hypnotherapy? That stuff plants false memories, you know."

"She's only ever wanted the best for me," he insisted.

"Why don't you go to my apartment so if you sleep-walk again your roommate won't kill you with a kitchen utensil? Do you open doors when you sleepwalk?"

"Haven't that I know of." His voice went deep and gentle, the way it did when they were snuggling in bed together after making love. "Thanks, Romy. I'm doing this for us too, you know. The sooner I get past this, the sooner I can come back to water your garden, if you know what I mean."

She laughed. "It's definitely getting dry over here."

"And the little girl?"

"Haven't seen her. Maybe she got bored."

"Romy?"

"Yes, Heath?"

"I'm doing this for us. I really am."

She smiled to herself, her heart swelling. At the same time, it was ready to break, for how could she ever plan a real future with him? How long could she keep from telling him the truth?

Each day, she became more despairingly convinced she had to stop betraying him. She couldn't take the push and pull of wanting to share a life with him and yet carrying the weight of this worst of worst secrets.

She'd read of people who'd gotten away with murder but decades later walked into a police station and spilled their guts. Those people didn't seem so misguided to her. Guilt gnawed and gnawed and gnawed like a hungry rat until anything—a prison cell, loss of your family, loss of the love of your life—was preferable to one more minute of it.

"That's sweet you want to do it for us," she said. "But Heath. Do it for you."

Chapter Twenty-Five

He doesn't love you. He loves me.

Misty was in Nana's living room. She looked ridiculously gorgeous, a goddess. It wasn't all pleasant to see that kind of beauty, like staring straight into the sun. But she wasn't dead. It had all been a mix-up.

Romy asked her where she'd been all of this time, asked in her own head, didn't hear the words or feel her mouth moving.

"I was traveling," Misty said.

Romy knew she was supposed to be happy that it had all been a mix-up and Misty was alive. But she could only feel dejected and anxious that Misty would reclaim Heath for herself.

Then they weren't in her grandmother's living room. They were down at the country club pool. The top of Misty's white bikini barely covered her ripe, woman's breasts, and she wandered around the pool area, a legato of sensuous movement.

Romy sensed that Heath was at his usual place on top of the lifeguard station but she couldn't see him.

She had the small, dispiriting hope that he might reject Misty, that he would realize it was Romy he truly loved. After all, what did he and Misty have in common except sex? How could he choose Misty over her when Misty had said those horrible things to him, things Romy would never say?

But it was no use. Misty was Misty. She was also pregnant with Heath's child. The time had come for them to be a family. Overwhelming sadness spilled into Romy's chest, knowing she was about to lose Heath again.

Tap, tap, tap.

Misty was knocking on something. Did she have something in her hands?

Tap, tap, tap.

Misty looked over her shoulder, expectantly, as if she was waiting for something. Something out in the woods. Or someone.

Tap, tap, tap.

The noise finally pierced the barrier between sleep and wake, and Romy realized it was coming from the window. Her eyes bolted open and her heart rate skyrocketed.

The white face in the window. The alienesque, slightly inhuman white face. Those ghostly blue eyes. And something Romy hadn't seen before—a little white hand.

The girl was knocking at the glass windowpane.

Romy kept it closed now, as only a screen between her and the girl had been too frightening.

The words came slightly warbly through the glass pane.

Baaaad lady!

Romy could hear her own raspy, panicked breathing, feel her heart slamming so hard in her chest she thought she might pass out. Her jaw trembled as if she was in a freezer.

Then she heard Mack. In the room with her, barking lowly at the window. *Wruh! Wruh!* Deep, guttural growling. He dashed quickly and lunged up at the window. *Wruhh! Wrrrrruh!* His claws *scratch-scratch-scratched* on the sill as if trying to dig his way out.

The little girl was gone.

Chapter Twenty-Six

"This should tell you whether we're dealing with a ghost or not."

Avery held up a round, black plastic ball, about the size of a lemon, with a lens in the middle. "Got it when these little shits—excuse me, misguided youth—began breaking into my garage. The cameras came in a pair, you can have this one. Where does she usually appear?"

"Right out here." Romy opened the door and they went outside. She gestured at the windows on the outside front wall. "The last couple of times, she was right there, in that window."

She pointed to the main window in her grandmother's room. The house was set back far from the street and Sapling Lane was so sparsely populated that the little girl—if she was real—didn't seem to have an ounce of concern that a car might drive by in the middle of the night and spot her.

Avery officiously walked up and down the length of

the small house, then peered up at the doorway. He squinted, pointing.

"I'm thinking right there would be the best place. There's that bush"—he pointed back to the neon-pink azalea bush between Romy's grandmother's room and the spare room—"so it won't get anything on the other side of that. But it should catch her coming and going. It's motion sensitive."

The next fifteen minutes were spent watching him climb up a ladder, secure the camera with backside tape on the wall area between the door and the roof, and repeatedly test whether it was working by walking in and out of its line of vision, then staring into his phone.

He showed Romy his cell screen and what he'd recorded: himself. She downloaded the app, logged in with his account and password, and watched the same video.

"Amazing," she said. "But will it see anything at night?"

"Sure, it's got night vision. I could set it to use a small floodlight when it detects motion but whatever she is—kid, ghost—we don't want to scare her off, do we?"

The way he said "ghost" in all seriousness, not making her feel like a lunatic—she appreciated it so much she had the sudden urge to lean over and kiss him, then fiercely hoped that stray thought hadn't announced itself on her face.

"Do you think it would catch a ghost though? On film?"

He rubbed his chin in thought. "I don't know." Then he smiled impishly. "Guess we're going to find out."

The twitching of his body and the slight uptick of tension in the air let her know he was about to leave. And she didn't want him to.

"Mister—" She shook her head. "Avery. I was thinking of shrimp scampi tonight, a salad with iceberg I've got to pick from the garden before it's eaten by slugs, and a Pinot Grigio. If you'd like to—"

"You had me at shrimp scampi."

* * *

"THIS IS HEAVENLY," Avery said, staring out at the woods.

"Aren't you near woods?"

"Nope. I'm on a cul-de-sac that's gotten crowded over the years. Used to be woods behind us but now there's a scraggly line of elms and behind them a bunch of cookie-cutter tract homes."

"Shame."

"How'd you escape that fate?"

She raised her arm to the woods, as if saluting them. "Those are state woods. And the incline is very steep. Don't think they could ever build there."

Avery somberly turned his dark, slightly hooded eyes on her. "Those are the woods you used to cut through?"

She nodded. "The country club pool is down at the bottom. It's very isolated. But in summer, I could hear noises coming up the hill."

He took another sip of wine, then reached for the bottle and finished it off in their glasses. The table was spread with their empty dishes, both of them having thoroughly cleaned their plates and gone back for seconds.

"Pandemic is turning us all into alcoholics," he said, squinting one eye shut, pretending to scour for drops in the empty bottle.

"I've got another bottle if you're desperate," she laughed.

"Better not." He made a motion of his hands on a car wheel, driving. "Delicious dinner, by the way."

"Thank you. And thanks for helping."

Mack stood by expectantly, waiting for scraps. Romy refused to hand any over, worried it would start a habit she'd never be able to break. But she couldn't take his wishful face anymore so she walked him into the kitchen and closed the door.

"I miss that whole dinner routine," Avery said as she sat back down at the table. "My wife usually did the cooking, I'd clean up. Even when the girls got older, we insisted to them that we sit down to dinner as a family. No exceptions. No cell phones." He grinned at her. "Sometimes that was a real struggle."

The alcohol was definitely responsible for what came out of Romy's mouth next. "I can't believe she left you." Mortified, she covered her mouth with her hand. "Sorry. That was rude."

He laughed awkwardly. "But true. Listen, I wasn't the perfect husband. Maybe I should have been doing more cooking than cleaning all those years."

"I'd rather have someone clean."

They fell into a silence that was easy but charged in

an oddly pleasant way. She'd known him for so long but he was always her mentor, her teacher. Never just a man. A man with a wife, kids, troubles. She liked knowing this side of him, knowing he wasn't a godlike mentor but a regular old, frail human being.

"Tell me about you, Romy," he said. "I was sorry to hear about Ella. I remember her well. She was so encouraging of your talent."

"Thank you, I appreciated your card."

"And your life now? How are your parents? They're still in Hawaii?"

"Yep. My dad thinks the virus will wipe out humanity within the next three months and my mom insists everyone only needs a kale smoothie with turmeric. A few weeks ago, it was all about echinacea, but she's since done more" —she hooked her fingers into air quotation marks—"*research*."

He laughed. "At least they have each other. It's tough going through this alone. I haven't even seen my daughters in several weeks. It's a terrible time to be separated."

"It is tough. I have Mack though. I had Heath for a bit, but then…"

"For what it's worth, if he left you, he's a complete numbskull."

Finishing the last dregs of her wine, she looked pointedly at him and asked what only the alcohol buzz gave her the determination to ask. "Would you be honest with me about something?"

"If I can, of course."

"Will you tell me exactly what Misty said about him

to you? I mean, *exactly*. Don't sugarcoat it or think I can't handle it."

"Yikes." He massaged his sloping forehead, his brooding countenance becoming even more brooding. "That was a while ago."

"What you remember. Best as you can."

He took a deep breath, lost in thought. Then he started nodding almost imperceptibly, staring off a few feet in front of him, as if he was back there in the past, back with Misty.

"I was advising her about art as a career," he said. "I'm not trained to be a social worker. But as a teacher, you have to be prepared for the kids to open up to you." He paused, sipped more wine, and started to look uncomfortable. "I was teaching a summer advanced placement class, which Misty was taking for college credit. One day, she didn't seem like herself. She was normally very bubbly. A little too bubbly to be an artist, if you ask me. But you don't need to be a tortured Van Gogh type to be a graphic designer, which is the direction I thought she might go."

He cleared his throat.

"She seemed very down, so I asked her to stay behind after class. I asked her if anything was troubling her. She said her boyfriend—at first, I thought she meant that football player but then she used his name, Heath—didn't want her coming to class anymore. That he was jealous and possessive of her time and attention."

Romy couldn't respond, her throat had thickened

with trepidation about where Avery's story was going, what she was about to learn.

"I gave her the usual spiel—that wasn't what love should be. That he sounded insecure and could even prove to be dangerous."

At the word "dangerous," Romy found her voice and instinctively almost jumped in to defend Heath but stopped herself. She'd asked Avery to tell her exactly what had happened, and she needed to listen, even if she didn't want to hear it.

"It's hard though," he continued. "All the movies, books, music—it tells kids love is like that. Wailing and gnashing of teeth. Romeo and Juliet. Then I come along and try to say love should be staid and boring." He smiled regretfully. "And maybe right there is why Alicia left me."

There was the hopelessness of the situation in his eyes—one stuffy teacher against a much more thrilling world of messages that encouraged the most primitive, impulsive behavior. Romy couldn't imagine having spent two decades inside of a high school with all its attendant juvenile drama. She could barely stand it as a teen, let alone an adult.

"Now, because this was summer," he continued, "I couldn't tell her to go to the guidance counselor. I did say it was important that she speak to her parents, and she promised she would. But Romy, you never know what a kid's relationship with their parents is. She kept coming to class. Then another day, she found me in my office. I was grading projects. She…"

He stopped, furrowing his sloping forehead. "She had a large bruise on her wrist. She showed it to me, told me that she and her boyfriend had been in an argument. That he'd accused her of wanting to go back to her old boyfriend, the football player." He swallowed hard, shook his head. "Accused her of thinking that the old boyfriend was better in bed, something like that. I cut off that part of her narrative quickly. What a sixteen-year-old does in her private time like that, I can't get into, you understand."

He closed his eyes, dragging up the memory, then opened them again. "I wanted to help her but we have protocols. I told her I would need to call the police. Report him if he'd hurt her."

He took a sip of wine, then put down his glass, clasping his hands around the stem. "Then she changed her story. Told me that she'd tripped while they were arguing, and that was why she had a bruise. Not that he'd touched her, and she'd deny he'd touched her. I said, 'Misty, you've got to tell your parents. If you don't, I'm calling them myself.'"

"What—what did she say?" Romy whispered.

"That her parents were in Martha's Vineyard, somewhere like that. It was a Friday. At home, I told Alicia that I was concerned for my student. I figured I'd call her parents on Monday, let them know they should talk to their daughter. But it was the next night..." He sucked in a big breath and let it out slowly. "You know what happened."

There was a long stretch of silence, during which Romy heard her heart pumping thickly in her ears.

During which she could see Misty—her confusion, her anguish, her bruised wrist. All the while knowing she was pregnant and scared to tell anyone, including her boyfriend.

Scared of Heath.

It seemed impossible, yet there it was. Avery was confirming everything Gillian had said. Even Heath had admitted he and Misty had argued over her ex-boyfriend—only in Heath's version, Misty was the instigator, not him. And he certainly hadn't mentioned grabbing her wrist.

"So you believe he had something to do with her death," Romy said, the hard lump in her throat making her voice sound strangled.

"I saw the surveillance tape on the news like everyone else," Avery responded. "He pulled her out and gave her CPR." He appeared genuinely conflicted. "I thought about going to the police, telling them about her bruise. But what would that look like? Trying to pin the blame on the kid when he may have just gone through the most horrific experience. No one—the administration, the town, the parents I have to deal with on a daily basis—would have appreciated an insinuation like that."

"Did you ever tell her parents about your last conversation with her?"

Looking ashamed, he said, "No. I didn't want to risk heaping more trauma on a kid who'd already been traumatized. Maybe it was the wrong decision, but at the time, the news was filled with that video of him trying to save her. It seemed perfectly real to me." He turned and stared out over the woods, then looked back at her, his dark eyes slightly haunted. "I'm sorry to tell you these things, Romy, because I can see you care deeply for him."

"Yeah," she said, quietly. "I did." It took her a moment to realize she'd used the past tense.

He continued, "You asked if I think he had something to do with her death. Put it this way. I don't think he did." Pause. "And I don't think he didn't."

* * *

THAT NIGHT, she couldn't stop thinking about the implications of Avery's story.

There's two Heaths, Misty had said.

He seems all sweet and cute, but he'll cut you to the bone, Tara had said.

Two Heaths. The charming, amiable man who made women fall in love with him without even trying. And this other Heath—one with a nasty, violent jealous streak. One who'd bruised Misty's wrist. One who may have allowed his girlfriend and their unborn child to drown so he could be rid of them and attend Georgetown unencumbered.

Perhaps, as a young girl, Romy had seen a glimmer of the two Heaths—the one who'd acted like her friend, interested in discussing art and books with her. And the one who'd instantly forgotten her as soon as Misty came along with her promises of the flesh.

And yet...

He'd appeared happy down at the pool when Misty

had told him about the pregnancy. Romy remembered him triumphantly throwing up his arms, twirling her around. Getting on his knees and asking her to marry him.

I knew there was a camera.

He knew there was a camera, but at the time he'd asked Misty to marry him, he couldn't possibly have known she was minutes away from drowning... could he?

* * *

ROMY AND HEATH had gotten into a routine of speaking around midnight as both were in bed and ready to drift off to sleep.

But that night, when he called, she couldn't bring herself to pick up the phone. Within a minute, he began texting.

Romy, you there?

You okay?

Where are you?

I'm getting worried.

She finally texted back, *I'm fine, fell asleep early. Will call you tomorrow.*

In return, she got a smiley face and a heart emoji.

By the way, I think I'll take up your offer to stay at your place. My roommate is starting to bring girls home. Crazy. You still cool with that?

She sat staring at the message. Then she finally typed, *Sure, I'm cool.*

A string of kissy faces appeared.

Any little girl sightings?

Nope, she appears to have left the chat.

Glad to hear it. Good night, Romy. <three kissy faces and a half-moon>

Night, Heath.

Chapter Twenty-Seven

*T*wo days later, she was busy working while Mack lazed near the open door of Nana's room, when her phone rang. No name came up, but the 718 area code of Brooklyn did, so she answered.

A male voice asked for her, but the unfamiliar voice was quiet, weak, as if the man was trying to catch his breath.

"This is Romy."

"Romy," the man said, still sounding faint. "It's your neighbor. Bill Jenkins."

"Oh my God, Bill!"

Seeing her agitated reaction, and perhaps understanding his owner's name, Mack swung his head up from the floor and stared at her.

"I'm so glad you called. Are—are you okay?"

"Better," he said. "I was in the hospital all this time and got home a few days ago."

"I have Mack! He's right here!"

Hearing his name, Mack trotted over as if he'd been

called. She rubbed behind his ear as he lolled out his tongue.

"I've spent every day since I got home calling animal shelters but a lot of them are closed for quarantine. The city pound never picks up the phone or answers emails. I'd gotten to the point where I'd assumed he'd been put down."

"Didn't you see my notes under your door?"

"I think what happened is when my sister-in-law came to get Mack and he wasn't here, she thought animal control had taken him. She began cleaning and the notes got thrown out. But there's a guy in your apartment. He saw me and said to call you."

So Heath was definitely at her place. She hadn't heard from him last night and had decided not to initiate contact.

"Well, I'm glad you called," she said, though distress clutched at her heart at the thought of giving up Mack.

Not to mention being in the house alone. Mack had provided her with a sense of protection.

"He's been here in the country at my grandmother's house," she said. "He loves it. I'm sure he'll be so happy to see you."

"That's another reason I'm calling," he said, then took a shaky, ragged breath. "I'm still weak. Mack is an energetic dog and as much as I'd love to see him, I can't take him on long walks, and he'll go nuts in the apartment. Is there any way—"

"Say no more. You want me to keep him longer?" Her heart soared. Mack sat, whined, and looked expectantly at her with his expressive brown eyes.

"If you could. If you can't, I understand. But I've got no way to get him. This thing knocked me out."

"It's no bother. He's got plenty of room here and seems quite happy. I should be back in the city in the next few weeks and can bring him with me then if you're ready."

"I should definitely be ready for the Mack Attack by then." He laughed, wheezingly. There was a long pause, and Romy's mind turned to that afternoon in Bill's cramped bathroom. His racking coughing fits. His burning hand.

Those things they'd said to each other…

Maybe in his fever and illness and long convalescence in the hospital, he'd forgotten it all.

"Romy…" he said, his voice low and guttural. "We said some things to each other."

She was quiet, then finally said, "I guess we did."

"So now we're… bonded."

"I—I suppose so."

"Let's keep in touch. I want to see my boy again. I just can't right now. It wouldn't be fair to him."

"I understand."

"I want to thank you. For everything. Goodbye, Romy."

She hung up, and a feeling of uneasiness rippled through her. Mack—appearing to be bewildered by hearing his owner's name but having no follow-up—let out a whining yawn and wandered out of the room.

Now we're bonded.

She couldn't tell if Bill had been reassuring her that their secrets were safe with each other, or if now he felt he had something he could use against her, and she against him.

She may have lived next to this man for a few years but she didn't know him at all. He could be a friend. He could be a foe.

I pushed her. I said it was an accident, but…

She lost the baby and never forgave me.

Bill was the one person on the planet whom she'd told about that night down at the pool.

And he was living right next door to Heath.

Of course, Bill wouldn't know to *whom* he was living next door. In telling her story, Romy had not used Heath's name. There would be no reason the new neighbors would ever have a discussion about Misty.

But having each of these combustible elements—her secret, Bill's secret, and Heath—all in close proximity for the first time made her supremely uncomfortable.

* * *

When Heath called that early evening, she made the decision to pick up. She'd had a couple of glasses of wine, and was feeling relaxed and reminiscent and her persistent solitariness was making her, well, lonely.

She wondered if she should have stayed in the city this entire time—at least there, she could walk down the street and see people, even if there were fewer people on the street than usual.

Out here, days easily slipped by without her seeing a soul. In fact, the only time she saw anyone was when she masked up and went to the grocery store or pharmacy.

Occasionally, someone would pass her when she was out running with Mack. But she and the person would keep a wide berth and not stop to acknowledge each other.

Gillian had hunkered down into quarantine with her husband and son, and Romy hadn't seen her since their drinks at the winery.

She'd speak to her parents every few days over the computer and had chatted with Suzie the same way, but for long stretches, it was only her and Mack. She was, indeed, a lone wolf.

Accustomed to lengthy periods of alone time, she hadn't expected to feel so hollowed-out and empty, as if the rest of the world had vanished—yet she knew millions of people must be feeling the same way, and there was odd comfort in that.

Of course, there was the little girl in the window. But even she hadn't made an appearance for several nights, not since she'd *tap tap tapped* on the window.

Maybe the girl had spotted the surveillance camera and that was enough to deter her from her behavior— that is, if she was an actual flesh-made little girl. Though Romy wondered if a girl of ten or eleven would not only spot such a small camera but would understand its significance.

"Hi, Heath," she said into the phone.

"You're harder to get a hold of than Lysol spray," he joked.

"Sorry, I've been swamped with work. Seems like everyone has nothing else to do but write books."

"Huh." He paused. Romy reflexively scrunched her

face, realizing she'd slipped up. "So you... design covers?" he asked.

"I just started."

There was a silence she imagined to be tension-filled, then he said, "Hm. That's what I'm trying to do as well. Write. But it's not coming to me, the whole Misty—ugh, I mean, Missy—storyline. Doesn't interest me anymore."

Sensing he'd thoroughly accepted her explanation and moved on from the topic, she relaxed.

"But I've got to finish up the series or the few fans I do have will hunt me down," he continued. "I'm picturing *Misery*-type scenarios."

"*Missy-ry*," she quipped.

"Ha. Good one."

She sipped her wine, torn between wishing he was here—her body continually yearned for his body—and wanting them to leave each other alone so they could both move on from their pasts.

"How's it going with Loretta?" she asked, a self-flagellating question she wished she had the willpower to resist asking.

"I think we're getting closer to a breakthrough," he said, voice low. "There's something about that night I've blocked out. I know I blocked out a lot of it but there is something *big*. At least we think so."

Romy wandered to the opposite side of the porch and stood staring out into the woods. There was a blazing red fireball of a sun sinking below the rim of treetops.

"Are you sure you want to remember?" she asked. "Sometimes we block things out for our sanity."

"No. I'm not sure at all. But I can't keep sleepwalking. One day, I'll end up in the middle of the street or falling down stairs."

Romy was feeling floaty with the wine, and the more she heard Heath's mellow voice, the more she excused what Avery had said about him. Heath, grabbing Misty so hard that he'd left a bruise on her wrist?

Even if it *had* happened, they were immature, hormonal teenagers whose brains were still developing. She shouldn't be judging him for what he may or may not have done twelve years ago any more than she wanted him to judge *her* for what *she'd* done—not that she'd given him that chance.

"Oh, I saw the next-door neighbor," he added. "I told him to call you."

"Thanks, we spoke. He's still too weak to handle Mack, so I'll keep him here. But I'm glad he's better. I didn't know if he'd died." She paused. "Will you do me a favor?"

"You know I will."

"Will you… not talk to Bill about me? I'd never met him before the night he was sick and I ended up with Mack. I'm a single woman living alone and it's…"

"Of course. I had no intention of talking to him about you. I only gave him your number because you told me to have him call you."

"Thank you."

Mack was looking longingly at her. It was normally the time she took him on a run but she didn't feel like running after two glasses of wine. Maybe a nap and then a run.

"I guess I better go take Mack for his run," she lied. She suddenly wanted to get off the phone.

"Romy... I'm feeling distance from you lately. Is it anything I've done?"

"You're the one who left, not me," she said, more snappishly than she'd intended. He's also the one who'd planted it in her mind that he may have let Misty drown on purpose—*of course* she was going to feel distant. She didn't say that part.

"My jobs are easier to do here," he insisted. "I've got all my tools here. And it's easier to have discussions with Loretta without someone else around."

"You mean without *me* around."

He said nothing, and her gut began to squirm. "Are you talking about me to her, Heath?"

"Well, sure. You and I are in a relationship—sort of. Or might be in one at some point. I'd thought. I don't know!" He paused, then added, testily, "I'm allowed to discuss what I want with her."

"Goodbye, Heath."

"Romy, lis—"

She hung up and turned off her ringer. Then, tipsy or not, she decided to take Mack for a run.

Chapter Twenty-Eight

*T*he woods lit up as if they were a stage that had been flooded with catwalk lights.

She saw everything around her—the white birch trees like thin, still ghosts, the carpet of amber pine needles at her feet. Then the light was gone and the woods were plunged back into darkness.

Heat lightning. Or as they called it in these parts— summer lightning. Silent lightning that would illuminate the entire sky, but no thunder, no rain.

In those brightly lit seconds, when Misty had looked back over her shoulder seeking something in the woods, she'd seen Romy.

And she must have told Heath. *Romy is watching us. That little girl who sits there staring at us all day long.*

Romy was scrambling up the mountain but in her rush to get away she was forgetting to plant her feet side-ways and she kept sliding back, and back, and back into danger.

Someone was chasing her. She could hear herself

panting, as well as panting behind her. A man panting. Her arm was snagged on a tree branch and she stumbled, then flopped to the ground, slipping and sliding down the hill.

The man was on top of her. He was so much bigger and stronger than she was. The heat lightning struck up again, illuminating his face.

It was Heath.

You did it, didn't you? You unhooked the tarp.

His voice was that of a completely different person. His hand was at her neck.

You unhooked the tarp, you stupid little bitch.

You killed my girlfriend. You killed my baby.

The pressure on her neck was so intense, there was no way she could fight it. She was losing the ability to breathe. Couldn't breathe. *Help!* She called out in her mind. *Help!*

There was a crack of thunder and she awoke with a gasp, her heart thudding crazily, clammy sweat oozing from every gland. She had the disorienting sensation of still being in the dream, the dream being her reality.

This had happened.

Thunder rolled away in the distance. She instinctively looked towards the window, saw the little girl. Her fantastically white face and dreadfully lurid expression.

Baaaaad laaaaaady, the girl mouthed.

Then she was gone.

* * *

192

FIVE MINUTES LATER, all the lights were on and Mack was in the room with her, his muscular body and big shark head giving her a sense of safety. Her hands stopped shaking enough that she could open the camera app. She went to the video and rewound.

The moon and lone streetlamp dimly lighted the side of the house, the camera's night vision giving the scene a slightly greenish tint. She watched and watched but no one appeared in the frame. She rewound and watched half an hour's worth of video.

She saw no one approach, saw no one leave.

Could the girl have come so much earlier? Could she still be out there, crouched down by the window, perhaps behind the azalea or hydrangea bush?

Her insides clenched as she accepted what this could mean—that the girl was indeed not real. The girl was a figment of Romy's imagination... or the ghost of Heath's child.

The dream—the nightmare—was less real to her now, yet she couldn't shake the bone-deep conviction that it hadn't been only a dream, it was a memory.

She never did recall getting up the hill back home. Didn't recall opening her window, removing the pillows meant to fool her grandmother, and crawling into bed.

She did remember hearing the wail of an ambulance as it passed her house and headed for the country club pool while she lay in bed trying to reverse it all, undo it with her mind. She was still young enough to think that kind of wizardry could happen.

All day Sunday, she lay in bed, telling her grandmother she was sick, hardly able to speak, only moaning.

When her grandmother would insist that she down soup, she would regurgitate it back up.

What happened had completely transformed her. And it had all happened in a flash, all gone sideways and wrong from how it was supposed to go.

Her life had veered sharply and permanently, and her adolescent mind hadn't the slightest notion how to adjust. Should she confide in someone? What would happen to her? A dark and crushing fear of the unknown kept her paralyzed.

When Monday came, the bruises on her neck had faded. She found her grandmother's powdered foundation in the bathroom cabinet and applied it to the remnants of the bruising, and wore a T-shirt with a high collar.

She had no memory of what caused them and assumed that in her mad scramble up the hill in the dark, she'd smacked straight into a tree branch.

As Romy held her phone, still watching the surveillance video that showed nothing but the moon-drenched, green-tinged dark, she brushed her fingers along her neck, remembering the bruising she'd acquired that night.

Bruising she now felt had been caused not by a tree branch... but by a human hand.

Chapter Twenty-Nine

*R*omy watched as Avery climbed down the ladder and stalked in and out of the line of vision of the camera. He stood staring into his phone, his mouth a tense line.

"Appears to be working," he said, holding his phone out for her.

On screen, she watched him walk back and forth. Then she went to her phone, pulled up the camera's app, and watched the same video.

"Could it have been too dark to catch her?"

She asked because it was a thing she had to ask. But her mind had already drawn the inevitable conclusion that the little girl was a phantom, either of her imagination or of the beyond.

"*You* could see her, right?" Avery stared into his phone again. "I can see the silhouette of that bush." He pointed to the hydrangea. "And that bush." He pointed to the azalea. "I can see the moon."

He walked over to her, showed her the screen, and pointed at the glowing white dot in the black sky.

"So, we should be able to see her."

* * *

"Okay. We're dealing with something unknown," Avery said, pouring her a glass of merlot.

After confirming the camera was working, the pair decided to have a drink on the porch. Avery had helpfully brought a bottle this time.

"Apparently so," she sighed. Confounded, Romy palmed back her bangs, stared at him. "Could she really be a ghost? You *do* believe I'm seeing her, right?"

"Yes, I do. I absolutely do." He paused. "Romy, have you thought about going back to the city? If you can work at home, you might have an easier time than being here."

She crossed her arms, wondering how much to reveal about her conflicted feelings towards Heath. But Avery was the only one she felt she could open up to these days.

"The problem is that Heath is there. I'd told him he could stay if needed. I can't see being in a one-bedroom with him and a pit bull."

"Doesn't he have anywhere else to go?"

She shrugged. "Not really. I mean, he's got his own place but his roommate isn't being careful. And his parents are in Florida. Besides, this is my grandmother's home."

She swept an arm out, taking in the porch's clutter

of old furniture and antiques—some things valuable, including an original Thomas Edison phonograph, handed down from Nana's parents—and other relics of her grandmother's eighty years in one house.

So much history Romy hadn't been able to bring herself to dive into yet, figure out what to keep, sell, or trash.

"Everything she owned is still here. If the girl is real, I want to make sure she doesn't break in." She sipped her wine, then said, more jokingly than she felt, "If she's a ghost, I suppose she could float through the wall. In fact, why *hasn't* she floated through the wall?"

"Maybe she's a ghost who respects property laws," Avery said, and they shared an uneasy laugh.

Romy didn't tell him the main reason she didn't want to be in the same apartment as Heath—by now, there was an undeniable undercurrent of doubt about him that edged into prickly apprehension. The dream of him strangling her was still acute in her mind.

You unhooked the tarp, you stupid little bitch.

For the first time, she'd begun to think deeply on the significant block of time from that night of which she remembered nothing. It wasn't unusual to have large swaths of your childhood forever lost in the unfathomable depths of your brain. But even back then, she'd known a portion of that night had simply been erased from her psyche.

And Heath. He was working with a therapist to dislodge his own sealed-off memory. One that was tormenting him to the point that he sleepwalked as his subconscious perpetually relived it.

What if… she and Heath had entombed the *same* memory?

And that memory was that Heath had tried to kill Romy that night. In a fit of rage. Because he knew what she'd done.

Summer lightning had struck up, causing Misty to turn her head and look into the woods. She did this *before* Heath left for the changing station, not after. At that exact moment, she'd caught sight of Romy and whispered what she'd seen to Heath. When the tarp came unhitched, he must have known who'd fooled with it.

While he didn't remember chasing Romy down and strangling her, the violent act left an imprint on his subconscious that he'd long mistaken for purposefully allowing Misty to drown.

There were questions though. If Romy's dream had really happened, how had Heath gotten from the pool area to where she was in the woods so quickly?

The pool was surrounded by an iron fence. She doubted Heath could slip through the same bent metal bars that she herself used. He would have gone to the open gate and come back around.

Had Romy blacked out, allowing him enough time to find her? How had she gotten away from him?

Avery's phone jangled, pulling her out of her reverie, and he retrieved it from his pocket, held up his finger. "Sorry, I should take this."

"Of course." She nodded at him, and as he strode towards the porch door, she assumed he would step outside for privacy. But instead, he stopped at the wall of windows, keeping his back to her.

"Hi, Alicia. Thanks for getting back *finally*," he said, stressing the last word. "I'm here with Romy Renskler, you remember her? I wanted to see Skylar and Savannah soon. ... Yes, I realize it's a pandemic, I've been extremely careful."

He looked over his shoulder at Romy. "She's safe, she lives here by herself. ... Oh, really, they can see Morris but not their own father? ... I don't care that he's in your pod, Alicia, if that's what you're calling it these days, they're my children." He sighed, exasperated. "I can't discuss this right now. I'll call you later. Please pick up the phone next time."

He hung up and sheepishly looked at Romy. "Sorry," he said.

As soon as he got back to his chair, Romy poured him more wine.

"Nice double entendre about the pod," she said.

"Thanks," he smiled. They were silent, each drinking, then he said, resignedly, "I don't want this single business. The few single guys I know my age, they're busy chasing girls in their twenties. They look like fools."

"You wouldn't though," she said, truthfully.

"Maybe, but I have no interest in that. I've got nothing in common with women that young. Except perhaps you," he laughed.

The air got a little warmer. Romy leaned forward, pretending to be fascinated by something on the edge of the woods. Where was a family of deer when you needed one?

"I'm going to ask you something," he said in a serious tone, forcing her out of her performance. "It's at the risk of alienating you but I won't feel right until I do."

She waited.

"Would you like me to stay here with you?" He held his palms up disarmingly. "As a friend. I sleep on the couch, the floor, here on the porch, whichever. Then you've got me here to help you deal with this, hopefully witness this girl."

"That's so nice of you. It's not alienating me at all." She looked down at the snoozing Mack, and propped her foot on him, kneading the tire-like muscle of his neck. "But I've got Mack. Besides, if she's not real, there's nothing to worry about, is there?"

She didn't want Avery staying overnight because she was fairly certain what would happen. They'd end up sleeping together.

It was everywhere—the pulsing *frisson* of sexual tension that had sprung up between them, likely born out of mutual loneliness and shared history, a link to the past, when things were less complicated.

It was tempting to ask him to stay, and possibly—no, probably—end up with a warm body next to hers. Plus, she was highly curious about what he'd be like in bed. The feminine intuition that conveys if a man is good in bed or not was insistently telling her he'd be very good.

Something about the way he walked, self-assured and masculine. How his hooded brown eyes got a little more sparkly when he looked at her. Yes, it would be fun alright.

But then would come everything afterward, the questions about what they meant to each other. She'd learned in college that "no strings" sex wasn't interesting to her. She didn't need another entanglement.

Besides, the memory of how her body perfectly melded with Heath's was too fresh. Whether or not sleeping with Avery would technically be cheating, it would feel that way.

"I appreciate the offer," she told him. "But Mack and me—" The dog drowsily slit his eyes open at the sound of his name. "We're set."

Chapter Thirty

*S*he was working in the garden, digging out weeds around the tomato plants, when Heath called.

Staring at her screen, she debated picking up but knew if she didn't, he would start texting her panicky messages.

"Hi. I'm in our garden." She smiled at the "our." Even now, she couldn't help herself.

"I only wanted to tell you that Loretta and I had a real breakthrough yesterday. And this is going to sound crazy, Romy. But whatever memory I've buried, well… it might have to do with you."

She went cold. As if the temperature had plummeted. As if there was no sun on her face or arms and it wasn't almost summer.

"Isn't that nuts?" he asked, nonchalantly. "I mean, there's no way you could have anything to do with anything. I'm thinking about stopping with her. You mentioned false memories. Maybe that's happening."

"What did you remember? About me?" She didn't know how she got the words out but she was utterly astonished at how normal she sounded.

"Nothing. Just… a feeling… a strong feeling… that I *saw* you that night. But so far as I recall, after that night, I *didn't* see you. I'd already graduated. I didn't go back to the pool, for obvious reasons. I didn't even go to Misty's funeral. I couldn't handle it. You and I didn't see each other again until the book signing. But Loretta wanted me to ask if you remembered anything from that night. If there might be any truth to this feeling."

Romy sank into the dirt. Didn't remember doing it. Only sank, her legs crossed in front of her.

"Heath."

She stared at the ground, the turned-up dirt, the green weeds poking up around the tomato plants, weeds that looked similar to tomato plants, so she tried to examine their leaves closely before ripping them out of the ground. Friend or foe?

"I need to tell you something," she said in a breathy voice that sounded as if it was coming from outside her.

A beep came through the phone. "Ah, crap," Heath said. "That's a client. He's already left a couple of messages and is getting agitated. Can I call you right back?"

"Sure." It slurred out as *shhurrrrrr*. As if she was drunk, as if her body was shutting down.

He hung up and she sat staring at hundreds of little translucent-gray, multi-legged beetles skittering through the dirt, stampeding around in aimless circles, desperately trying to bury themselves back in the cool, damp ground. Every single one of those bugs had a better life than she did right now.

A butterfly marbled with black, red, and turquoise hues landed on the tomato plant in front of her, whisking its wings. The kind of butterfly she never saw in the city. It opened its varicolored, translucent wings and flew to the edge of the garden, Romy's gaze following its trajectory as it swooped towards the ground. In the dirt, she noticed something white and papery.

A note?

Crawling to it, she spotted its loops and realized it was a mask. A paper one, with one side white, the other side light blue. The mask didn't belong to her or Heath. They'd used their N95s or cloth masks.

She put one gardening glove back on, picked the mask up and examined it, held it to the light but saw nothing that would indicate if the wearer had been male or female. The yard was too far away from any other yards for the mask to have been blown in by the wind.

Someone had dropped it. Someone who'd been in her backyard. They'd either had it in a pocket or looped on their wrist, and it got loose.

Her first thought was Tara. Heath had changed his cloud password. His ex-fiancée could no longer track his movements, and likely thought he was still here. She was sneaking around again, trying to spy on them. And this time she'd heeded Heath's warning to wear a mask.

Romy's second thought was the little girl.

Ghosts don't worry about viruses. Neither do figments of the imagination or manifestations of a guilty conscience. Even a little girl wouldn't bother with a mask.

Unless an adult told her to bother with it.

Romy's phone rang. Heath again. "Sorry about that. Anyway, you have something to tell me?"

"I'm only glad you're close to getting to the bottom of this with Loretta. Sorry I wasn't supportive before."

"Oh." He paused. "No insight on anything, huh?"

"No, Heath. We didn't see each other that night or after that night. Not until the book signing."

"That's what I thought. Hm. Well, it was a crazy thought. Ignore me."

Once they hung up, Romy slowly stood and looked around her acre of property. Her gloved fingers squeezed the mask, crinkling it up into a ball, as her chest swelled with renewal, a feeling of rallying the strength to take on a challenge.

Someone was messing with her.

Chapter Thirty-One

*S*he had to go back to ground zero, the axis around which all the other bodies revolved, the vertex at which all angles converged.

Misty.

The last thing Romy wanted to do was lay eyes on Misty's frozen-in-time, forever-youthful face but she was possessed with the need to dig into what may have happened that she wasn't remembering or was misremembering.

In her old bedroom, she scrounged through her dusty bookshelves, sliding out her high school yearbooks. There were four of them, one for each year she'd attended Glass Town High. She found her freshman book—when Misty was a junior, the last year of her life.

Legs folded in the lotus position on top of her musty-smelling braided area rug, Romy leafed through the book. In the middle were several collages of students doing extracurricular activities and hanging out on school grounds.

These middle pictures tended to be dominated by the popular clique and the students who were on the yearbook committee. It was almost as if those same two dozen people were the only ones who went to the school, which easily contained over five hundred students.

Misty wasn't any of the things that usually guaranteed membership in the popular clique—a cheerleader, a clothes hound, or living in one of the big, new McMansions. But she was a Glass and dating Patrick Dugan, who *was* part of the in-clique, given his status as quarterback. The pair had been voted "Hottest Couple" as well as Junior Prom King and Queen.

Except for when Misty was featured prominently with those superlatives, she only appeared at the edges of crowd photos, always smiling but Romy felt Misty's eyes were melancholic, with an older, resigned look about them.

The unwelcome idea flashed through her mind that, on some level, Misty sensed her time was nearing an end. The thought made a sore lump form in her throat, and then the tears came. She barely made any sound as she cried, but Mack sensed it anyway, and came trotting into the room, then sat next to her, guarding her grief, offering her stalwart comfort.

She found the junior class and Misty's profile photo. For once, Misty wasn't smiling. But she looked stunning, like those supermodels who never appear as beautiful as when their makeup-free, unposed faces are casually snapped with a Polaroid. Fat, pouty lips. Catlike, light blue eyes. Shining black hair that hung perfectly tousled yet appeared coolly unbrushed.

Underneath her photo was the tragically prescient quotation: *Live as if you were to die tomorrow. Learn as if you were to live forever.* —Mahatma Gandhi

Misty's yearbook entry was the usual high school mishmash of shout-outs and cryptic insider gobbledygook.

Mom&DadLoveYou, LauraLeeBFF, I Wanna Be a Cowgirl, SpringbreakFL Quiet down!!! Home games, Gooo Chieftains!!! Patrick, I LOVE YOU, The Glamour Pusses Emma, Naomi, Melinda. Ladies Night! Danny UR best brother ever. Dancing in the moonlight. Beers @ the Hollow. Camping @ Cherry Tree Hill. Grandma, Grandpa, Love you! WildNFree. AR&AJ

At the end was Misty's email address.

A thought began to work through Romy's mind, crawling and then accelerating until it came to clear-headed fruition.

Taking the yearbook with her, she went to Nana's room, Mack trailing, and sat down at her laptop. She logged out of her email and put in Misty's address, which used the same extremely popular email provider that half of the country used.

His cloud password is Misty Glass. He's had that password for everything since high school.

If Heath's password was Misty's name, then...

In the blank bar for a password, Romy typed "heathasher" but the message "incorrect password" appeared in red. She tried "HeathAsher" and got the same result. Then she tried each variation ending with a one and 01. Finally, the account locked up with the message, "Have you forgotten your password?"

On social media, Misty had either never had an account or it had been deactivated. But it was easy to find Patrick, though if he hadn't been friends with Gillian, Romy would never have recognized him.

Patrick Dugan, onetime quarterback, prom king, and general "stud" of the school was now an overweight, mostly bald man. He was only twenty-nine or thirty but easily could pass for being in his forties. Kind of shocking, really.

Romy sent him a friend request and a message asking if he could chat. Since she had numerous people from high school in common with him on her friends' list, she was fairly confident he'd respond.

The next person was easy enough to find as well. Loretta Hale, LPC (Licensed Professional Counselor), had a social media page. Romy aimlessly clicked around on her public photos.

Loretta appeared to be living the typical life of a city dweller who had an active social life, was apparently single, and made a good living. Dinners at various restaurants around town. Birthdays and holidays with friends and family. Vacations at locales both snowy and tropical.

Romy wasn't certain what she was looking for—just a clue into Loretta's psyche. Did she have a significant other? It didn't appear so. Did she have children? Not that Romy could determine. Did she have pets? Yes, there was a small dog, a tan and white chihuahua mix named Butter.

Romy saw nothing that would confirm what she was half-heartedly hoping to find—that Loretta was romantically drawn to much younger men.

But she did see something that gave her pause. A long pause. And she'd almost missed it.

A couple of years ago, Loretta had been at a restaurant with what appeared to be extended family. Next to her was a little blonde girl, about eight or nine. In the picture, Loretta smiled from ear to ear and was leaning into the girl, who had on a big goofy grin. The pair obviously knew each other quite well. The untagged photo was captioned, "So happy to spend quality time with my beautiful niece!"

The girl in the photo was a harmless-looking pixie, not the maniacally grinning girl who haunted Romy's window.

But slather white face paint on her, give her contacts to make her eyes strangely vibrant, and coach her to look and act fiendish—and it wasn't out of the realm of imagination that Loretta's niece could be the little girl in the window.

The things the girl was saying—*bad lady, horrible woman, leave this place*—all pointed to Loretta suspecting that Romy was responsible for Misty's death. And wasn't it rather clairvoyant how Loretta had instantly sensed that Romy's past mistake may have led to a death?

Heath's hypnotherapy sessions. If he talked in his sleep, he could be talking in those as well. And if he'd blotted out the memory of seeing Romy in the woods but the memory surged forth when he was under hypnosis, then Loretta would know what Heath didn't yet know, at least on a conscious level.

Heath's therapist, after hearing from him that he'd moved in with none other than the woman who'd killed Misty, might have decided to start playing games. But why? If Loretta knew or suspected what Romy had done, why not tell her client, tell Heath?

Did she not wish to traumatize him further, as perhaps what Romy had done that night was tied up with Heath trying to commit murder? Or was Loretta's only goal to separate Romy and Heath so she could move in on him herself?

If coaching her niece to pretend to be the ghost of Heath and Misty's unborn child was her way of coercing Romy into confessing to him, then this extremely unorthodox—not to mention unethical—method was also batshit crazy.

But not so batshit crazy if you consider that it almost worked.

* * *

THE NEXT DAY, Romy was working at her laptop when a blurry ring came out of it and a chat box popped up bearing the name Patrick Dugan and his profile photo.

She wasn't ready for this but it had to be done, and who knew when she'd be able to get in touch with him again.

The puffy-faced man on the screen looked even more out-of-shape, ruddy-complexioned, and hairless than he had in his photos. Truly hard to believe that a little over a decade ago, this man was considered one of the hottest young lads Glass Town High had to offer.

Patrick had no idea who Romy was but he knew Gillian. Not only because Gillian had lived next door to Misty when the pair had dated but because neither Patrick nor Gillian had ever moved out of town. They also had children in the same pre-school, which Romy figured out from seeing mutual tagging on their children's photos on Gillian's social media wall.

They said their greetings and had about fifteen minutes of catch-up, during which Romy learned that Patrick owned a local car repair shop and had three young children. Romy decided she better get to the point before she lost all her nerve.

"Patrick, I hate to do this to you, because this might be traumatic for you but I'd like to ask you a little about Misty Glass."

"Ohhhhhhh Mistyyyyyy…" he drawled, exhibiting a rather blank expression. From the response, Romy couldn't tell if he even remembered dating her. "Ahhhhh, what is it you wanna know?"

"She was your girlfriend for a while, right?"

"Mmmmm hmmmmmmm," he drawled, again seeming as if the name Misty Glass was someone he was struggling to recall.

"I guess what I want to know is—if you'd be willing to tell me—why, ah, why you two broke up?" The last part of the sentence rose to a high-pitched crescendo and she made an exaggerated cringe-face, embarrassed for her own nosiness.

"Hmmmmmm...." He rubbed his ruddy cheeks. "That's a strange thing to ask."

"I know. It's... I'm fictionalizing the tragic case of Misty and doing research..." She trailed off, certain her explanation didn't sound convincing.

"Fictulizing?"

"Making a fiction story out of the Misty tragedy. A *novel*."

"Oh!" he said, unexpectedly interested. "That's cool. I don't read much, but I like movies." He grinned at her, and for a moment she saw the echo of hunky, athletic Patrick. "Let's see, Misty and I dated, what? A year? Something like that." He slowly shook his head as he traveled back in his memories. "She sure was beautiful. I thought she looked exactly like Megan Fox."

To make her story stick, Romy picked up a nearby pen and began jotting notes. "You two were the king and queen of the school," she said, the ego stroking a calculated attempt to get him to open up. She was betting on the idea that Patrick wouldn't mind reminiscing about his "glory days."

He chuckled softly, casting his grayish eyes down at his lower half. "Hard to believe. Look at me now."

"You look great," she said, smiling stiffly.

"Misty... yeah, yeah. She was the prettiest girl I'd ever seen. Still is, don't tell my wife. Lucky boy I was." He began making *mm-mm* noises, practically smacking his lips, self-satisfied with his youthful ensnaring of a Megan Fox doppelgänger.

"But something happened?" Romy prodded. "I remember you two broke up. The whole school was shocked." In reality, Romy had only surmised the pair had split when Misty began appearing at the pool without him but he didn't need to know that.

"Yep, yep... well, you know..." His eyes glazed over as he delved further back into his memory. "At the time, I thought we might get married someday. She wasn't Catholic but we'd work it out. Then one day she..." He snapped his fingers. "Told me it was over. Told me while we were sitting in my Jeep, in the school parking lot, right before school ended for the summer. Oh boy. I definitely didn't expect it."

"Did she give you a reason why?"

"Nothing major. Something about wanting to be free. The next thing I knew, she was dating another guy, that lifeguard down at the country club. So I assumed that was the real reason why."

"Did you two talk after? Did she tell you anything about her new boyfriend?"

"Uhhh... no."

Romy heard dramatic wailing in the background, what sounded like a little girl having a temper tantrum. Patrick craned his neck around the computer, apparently looking towards the door. When the sound faded, he returned his attention to her.

"Oh yeah," he said, his sleepy eyes flickering with a retrieved memory. "There was that one day, the last time I saw her. She came to my house. This was the summer. I was outside playing basketball with my brother and there was Misty on her bike. We went upstairs and, uh...." He trailed off awkwardly.

"You had sex?" Romy grinned.

Patrick looked like he'd been slapped.

"No, ma'am," he said. "I'm a good Catholic. None of that until marriage. Misty and I never got conjugal like that."

Romy sat in a state of disbelief. Hadn't Heath said that Misty had taunted him about Patrick being better in bed than he was, being "bigger" than he was?

"So you never... nothing? All that time?"

"No, ma'am." He rocked back and forth, then his face lit up. "Ah, now I remember. Yep. She came over and told me she wanted to get frisky. Wanted to do the deed."

"She did?"

"Yeah, now I think on it, she was a little insistent. Kind of, well, she got down there and..."

A guilty grin spread across his face, and again Romy could see a trace of the former studly quarterback, could envision him as she'd spied him in the hallways—standing a foot above most of the boys, broad-shouldered, floppy-haired, oozing athleticism and testosterone.

She wondered what had gotten him to his current washed-out looks and had the melancholy suspicion alcohol was behind it. Had Misty's death started him drinking? Romy felt a stab of guilt that she shoved away before she could spiral into more guilt than she already had.

"Was this while Misty was with her next boyfriend? The lifeguard?" Romy probed.

She hoped Gillian and Patrick weren't so close that her childhood friend would have mentioned that Heath was back in town—and living with Romy. She doubted it, especially as the pandemic meant schools were closed so they wouldn't be coming into casual contact.

"Not sure, to be honest," he said. "But like I say, J.C. wouldn't have approved. J.C. comes first, even before Misty. Not an easy decision, I admit."

He touched a silver cross pendant hanging down his white shirt, which Romy hadn't noticed until he'd started the Catholic talk.

"So, she left. And that was it. Never saw her again. I heard that when she died, she was pregnant." He smiled mournfully. "I guess the lifeguard gave her what I wouldn't."

Chapter Thirty-Two

*I*n bed that night, Romy lay staring out the window up to the moon, which was full and low-hanging, much brighter, more defined than it looked in the city. She could clearly see the gray craters pockmarking its surface.

Romy kept pondering what Patrick had revealed in their conversation, that he and Misty had never had sex.

Someone was lying—either Patrick, Misty, or Heath.

Heath would have his reasons. Gillian Frenetti had reported to police an argument she'd heard him having with Misty mere days before her death. Romy had questioned Heath about that very argument, and he needed a story.

Why not blame it all on Misty? Make her sound unusually crass and *provoking*. Who wouldn't blame a young guy for getting upset if his girlfriend had told him that he had shortcomings not only in bed but in his pants?

Patrick would have his reasons. He was a "good

Catholic" who wouldn't want to admit to anyone, especially not to someone about to "fictulize" the tragedy of Misty, that he'd had sex before J.C. (and his wife and family) would approve. Nor would he want any hint of suspicion that he, not Heath, was the father of Misty's unborn baby.

And Misty herself. All the things she'd told Heath about his deficiencies and preferring Patrick—if she'd actually ever said them—could have been her trying to make Heath jealous for some reason. Maybe she'd felt ignored. Maybe she liked to see him worked into a frenzy. She'd been sixteen at the time of her death, and sixteen-year-olds weren't exactly known for high levels of relationship maturity.

There was something else that kept needling Romy. In her bones, she felt the argument between Heath and Misty, at least the way Heath had relayed it, didn't sound quite... *real*.

A girl telling a guy her ex-boyfriend was better in bed and had a larger penis was the type of argument that might be in a movie or book, but did women *really* talk like that? Especially a sixteen-year-old?

But this was twelve years ago; she couldn't expect Heath to have perfect recall. And perhaps Misty, being a teen, had read one of those books or watched one of those movies, and parroted the things she'd hoped—for whatever reason—would get under Heath's skin.

Romy tried to sleep but kept snapping her eyes open and staring at the moon. Sleep was a precious commodity these days anyway, as a freaky little girl sticking her face into the window wasn't exactly conducive to dreamland. But she needed to know if the girl appeared so she could rewind the surveillance footage again. Maybe this time, it would catch her.

At least if the girl came by tonight, there would be plenty of moonlight to illuminate her movements. So much moonlight that perhaps Romy might spot Loretta in the background as she orchestrated the performance of the little girl—who was none other than Loretta's niece.

It was only a four-hour drive from the city, less in the middle of the night with no traffic. Did Loretta's niece sleep over occasionally so they could make these trips? How could Loretta guarantee her niece wouldn't mention them to anyone?

The niece theory was fantastical—but not any more fantastical than a ghost or a guilt-induced hallucination.

As Romy stared at the brilliance of the full moon, she wished that it had been a full moon the last time the girl appeared. It's possible the girl had managed to get to the window in a roundabout way that hadn't been caught on camera. After all, the camera at the country club pool had managed not to catch Romy unlatching the tarp.

Romy's gaze roved from the moon to the popcorn ceiling. She stared and stared, her mind beginning to turn and twist and meander down various pathways.

She sat up and found her phone on the bedside table, logged into the home surveillance app. She watched the saved video of the last time she'd seen the little girl in the window—but nothing had appeared on the tape. The moon was a soft glowing dot in the darkness of the sky.

Every twenty-four hours the video would automatically erase itself unless Romy saved it. So she went to tonight's video and rewound it to five minutes ago, then hit play.

Tonight's big, fat, balloon-round moon looked exactly as it had on the night Romy had last seen the little girl. The night she'd *tap tap tapped* on the window.

Either the camera was terrible at picking up far away objects—not only far away but light-years away— or Romy was looking at the *same* video footage from the night the little girl appeared.

Or rather, she was looking at the *same video footage every night*.

Because the video was playing one night in a continual loop.

She got out of bed, put on her slippers, and walked to the door. Mack popped his head up from his pillow and followed her, thinking he was going for a walk.

"Stay, boy," she said, opening both doors, then closing the screen door. He sat right on the other side, panting, confused as to why he wasn't being taken with her.

She walked up and down the length of the house, in the line of vision of the camera. Stopped and gave the middle finger to the lens. Back inside, she rewound the video footage on the app.

She did not appear.

Chapter Thirty-Three

"*I*t's so good to see you, Romy," said Alicia Sands.

The two sat outside Alicia's small but adorable Cape Cod-style beachfront home in Saybrook.

Alicia was at one end of a large, round cast-aluminum patio table, Romy at the other. They weren't six feet apart—more like four—but given that they were outside and both had been quarantining, they took their chances.

Despite being on a raised patio at the back of the house, the Atlantic Ocean was so near they could hear it crashing along the stone jetty protecting the homes on the shoreline.

Romy had contacted Alicia through social media the day before and received a message in the morning. The message only said, "I can't speak about my soon-to-be-ex-husband but if you'd like to come for an outdoor visit, let me know."

There seemed to be a wink-wink-nudge-nudge in the

message—as if Alicia was willing to speak about Avery, but not where there could be a permanent record of her words.

So, Romy took Mack out for his morning walk, then settled him on the porch with water, his pillow bed, and plenty of chew toys, and left to make the hour-long drive to Saybrook.

Romy remembered Alicia as she would stand next to Avery at school art fairs, looking stylish, maternal, and attractive, like one of those wives in a G-rated movie, smiling and proud of her husband's achievements and the students who were clearly drawn to him, his classes that had a waitlist.

Romy had no way of knowing if the surveillance camera not filming—and seeming to be repeating the same footage in a loop—was simply a glitch.

If it wasn't that simple, that meant her former teacher and the adult male she'd been closest to in her youth, much closer to than her own father, truth be told, was up to something. But this wasn't anything she could come right out and ask him. Not to mention she didn't have a clue why he might not want to record the little girl in the window—especially as he'd been the one to set up the camera.

"Avery always said you were one of his most talented students," Alicia said, serving them both iced tea and keeping a distance as she poured.

She looked much as she had a decade ago, though like many women during the pandemic, she'd stopped visiting her hairdresser, so her ash-blonde, shoulder-length hair was streaked with silver. It flattered her delicate features and gave her a bit of an edge.

"You said you can't talk about him but I didn't know... well, I have some questions," Romy began awkwardly.

"Depends what you want to talk about, I'm afraid," Alicia said, sitting and folding her hands primly on the table. "According to the terms of the settlement, there's not much I can say about him."

Romy had no idea how to broach anything—least of all the reasons behind the couple's divorce. But she decided to plow ahead with as much diplomacy as possible.

"I've been speaking to him since I got back to Glass Town..."

Alicia's eyes glinted suspiciously, as if Romy had been sent by him for a nefarious purpose.

"All I mean is... Look, I'm going to be totally honest with you. There's been strange stuff happening at my childhood home. I don't know who is behind it but I'm looking into everyone. That means Avery, too."

"Strange stuff?" Alicia sounded perplexed but intrigued.

"Yes, really strange. This is going to sound like I've lost my marbles, to use one of my grandmother's expressions." She took a sip of iced tea, hoping to calm her gut which was fluttering nervously. "But there's this little girl who's been showing up in my yard, looking into my window. Saying weird things. She looks... bizarre. Very pale, with extremely blue eyes." She didn't volunteer what the girl was saying. "Avery set up a surveillance cam for me, hoping to catch her on video. But the camera seems to either not be working or... maybe he set it up that way on purpose."

Romy had noticed that Alicia's slate-blue eyes had steadily grown wider and wider. It was alarming how wide they grew. Her small pink mouth hung open in an oval shape.

"Romy," she said breathily. "Does this little girl have an accent?"

"An... accent?"

"Yes, an Eastern European accent?"

"I—I don't..." She tried to think back. The girl sounded *different*. But the things she'd been saying had been so quick and elementary it was impossible to detect any kind of accent, let alone pinpoint its origins. "I couldn't say."

Alicia started to slowly shake her head, her expression growing more and more disturbed. She chewed on one side of her lip, then finally said, "I'm not supposed to talk about her."

"Excuse me, *her*? You know this little girl?"

Alicia seemed to be struggling mightily—wanting to talk and yet under direction not to. She turned in her chair, looking up at the second floor of the beach shack. "My girls are home," she said, lowering her voice conspiratorially.

Alicia crossed her arms, and Romy worried she'd decided to stop revealing anything. But then she said, "If it's who I suspect it is, she's no little girl. She's twenty years old."

"What do you mean?" Romy sputtered. "She looks

ten, maybe eleven or twelve, tops." Then she remembered that knowing, leering look the girl had given her when she'd caught Romy and Heath having sex.

Alicia put her finger to her mouth in a *ssh* gesture, took another sip of iced tea, then stood and quietly said, "Come with me."

INSIDE, their masks back on, Romy followed Alicia through a wide living area to a small, dark-wood-paneled side room that contained a desk and computer. Romy could hear hip-hop music pulsing upstairs. Alicia closed the door behind them.

At her monitor, Alicia clicked around, then pulled up a newspaper article. On it was a large photo of a very young girl with a runner's number pinned to her chest. "Is this her?" she asked, angling the monitor towards Romy.

Romy stared at the girl's face. Platinum hair, extremely pale skin, distinctive blue eyes. "Yes," she said, fingers pushed up against her mask in shock. There was no doubt. It was the type of face you didn't see often, if ever. "That's her."

"Her name is Katya," said Alicia. "She has a pituitary gland growth hormone disorder—Highlander Syndrome or dwarfism or both. Either way, she's always going to appear much younger than her actual age. She also has Waardenburg Syndrome, which affects the pigmentation in skin and hair, and gives her eyes that surreal blueness. According to her, and my research, she must be twenty. She used to live next door to my husband and me."

She pointed out the window to a two-story, shingled, cottage-style house.

"I thought, the couple next door thought, *everyone* thought that she was a little girl. They'd adopted her five years ago when she was supposedly seven. But she was about fifteen at the time."

Alicia looked at Romy over her mask. Her eyes went big and haunted. "One day last year, while the girls were still in school, I came home from work early and… my husband was in bed with this supposed child." She pressed her chest. "I'd—I'd never had such a—Romy, I screamed. I screamed so loud. I—" Unable to continue, she sat with her palm flat on her heart, as if trying to push it back into her chest.

"You don't have to…" Romy said.

"No. I must tell you. Thinking about it gets my heart racing. Walking in on your husband with another woman—that's bad enough. But to walk in on him with a *little girl?* That's…" She appeared ready to collapse in her chair.

"Want me to get you a glass of water?"

"No, no. All I can say is, if he wasn't the father of my children, I would have killed him. *Killed* him. Picked up the nearest object and…"

She clenched her hands, balled her fists with remembered rage. Then she started robotically stroking her thighs.

"I ran downstairs and tried to get outside to scream to anyone who would listen to call the police." She seemed on the verge of hyperventilating. "That my hus —my *hus*—was a *child rapist*."

Her whole body was shaking. Romy sank to her knees and stared at her.

"But he caught me at the door. Dragged me back kicking and trying to punch him. He was buck naked. Then the girl—Katya—came in. She had a shirt on and was utterly still but looked... How to explain it?... She looked pleased with herself."

Alicia turned back to the monitor, staring at Katya's picture—a glum, pony-tailed girl in a sleeveless T-shirt and shorts, with the runner number 1755 pinned to her shirt.

"Avery swore to me she wasn't a child, she's an adult. And that if I didn't want to embarrass our children forever, I'd listen to him."

She turned her attention back to Romy. "So, I very reluctantly did. They told me about her hormone disorder. She'd been pretending to be a child so she could be adopted and brought to the U.S. I yelled at him, 'How the hell do you know this is true? Because *she* tells you so?' That's when they began showing me news articles about her. Ones written in her home country, the former Yugoslavia. She grew up in an orphanage and was a champion sprinter by the time she was thirteen. She'd even been at a qualifying event for the Olympics but I don't know what happened there. Far as I can tell, she never got to the Olympics."

Romy stayed on the floor in front of Alicia, wide-eyed. So *that's* how the "little girl" kept darting off so quickly, even outrunning the nose of a dog.

"She managed to get papers saying she was seven... God only knows how. After Avery retired, we moved here full-time. While I was working and he was supposedly enjoying his newfound retirement interests, they developed a bond. A very *close* bond."

"Unbelievable," Romy breathed. "He told me *you* were the one who'd had the affair. That he'd walked in on you with the neighbor. Morris."

She laughed, sharply. "That's my neighbor's name and he's quite happily married. Romy, I don't mean to spoil your view of a man you look up to, but if this is Katya bothering you, I need to tell you the truth."

Unfortunately, this *had* spoiled Romy's view of her Mr. Sands, the man who'd helped her so much in her teen years. The man she'd recently felt she'd grown close to again. But she couldn't stay in denial. She needed to know as much as she could get out of Alicia.

"This girl—I mean, woman—lives with him?"

"He claims not, tells me she moved out west. But I never believed him. That *woman* latched on to him like he was her salvation. She saw a way out of pretending to be a child, and that was to get Avery to take care of her. She told the adoptive couple everything, which confirmed what they'd started to suspect. The wife had found tampons and razors hidden in a drawer, but Katya made up a story. She was an adept shoplifter."

Alicia glanced toward the closed door, clearly nervous about her daughters overhearing anything.

"After Avery and I split up, he moved back to our house in Glass Town as our tenants were leaving. Well, it seems Katya is with him. If she's poking her head in your window, my guess is she's jealous of you and trying to scare you out of town."

Is that what this was all about? Jealousy?

Bad lady.

Horrible woman.

Leave this place!

"It's possible," Romy said, standing. "But when she first showed up, I'd only run into Avery in the grocery store. Plus, I was living with a guy. There was nothing to be jealous about."

"If he came home from the store talking about you, I wouldn't put it past her to get up in arms about it," she said, in a way that made it clear she'd had difficult times with Katya.

"Do you think she could be doing this to me without him knowing?"

Alicia sighed wearily. "Anything is possible with those two. At first—this is embarrassing—I tried to save our marriage. For the sake of Skylar and Savvie. But she —" She clenched her fists again, "wouldn't let go. Then I thought I needed to try to be accepting of it—again for the sake of our children. But she'd become enraged whenever he'd visit. Would even call and threaten me. Once she started that, I really had no doubt. No child has the ability to speak like that. So, he came over less and less. When the pandemic hit, it gave him the perfect excuse to stay away. Frankly, I'm fine with him staying away."

Romy couldn't see Alicia's mouth but could tell from the crinkles over the bridge of her nose that she was screwing it up distastefully.

"Honestly," she said, "it's sick to be involved with someone who looks like a twelve-year-old. It's bad enough he chose someone half my age—but who looks like a kid?" She shuddered.

"Did you call him recently when he was at my place? He wanted to see your daughters and you said no?"

"Me say no to him seeing the girls?" She snorted. "More like Katya won't let him around."

They decided wine was in order and returned to the patio with a bottle.

"This is the craziest story I've ever heard," Romy said. "You're absolutely positive she's an adult?"

"Positive as I can be unless there's an older girl who looks exactly like her. Not many people have eyes like hers. I've traced back news stories about her sprinting long enough that there's no way she's a child. I had to hire someone who spoke Serbian to do the research for me. From what Avery said, she had to prove she was legal before he'd start things up with her." She rolled her eyes. "Adultery was fine but he drew the line at child molestation."

Romy was still puzzled as to why the surveillance tape appeared to be on a loop but Katya sounded like the sort of person able to crack into Avery's phone, and then his camera app.

Staring in Romy's window in the middle of the night, hurling vague threats—it all seemed completely unhinged. But if Alicia's version of events was accurate, the girl—*woman*—*was* unhinged, or at least determined to keep hold of the man who'd allow her to live as her real age.

Romy had to ask herself if her own juvenile infatuation with Heath Asher had made her any less driven by irrational impulses. Sure, she'd been fourteen, basically a kid. But Katya, if she'd grown up in an orphanage without much direct care, could easily be emotionally stunted.

Along comes a man who represents everything she thinks of as safety—older, with a steady job or at least retirement plan, a nice house, a wife and kids—and who probably treated her well…

Who was to say that if Romy and Katya's fortunes were reversed, Romy may not be equally as unhinged?

But Avery must have known, or at least suspected, that the *little girl* Romy had described to him was his mistress. If so, that meant he could have sabotaged the camera footage on purpose. Was it to protect Katya?

We're dealing with something unknown.

Did he try to make Romy think the "little girl" was a ghost so she wouldn't ever call the police?

"I'm sorry this happened to you, Mrs. Sands," she said.

"Alicia, please. I'm sorry too, but mostly for the girls. They don't know about any of this." Her stare roved again to the second story windows. "Frankly, they're confused as to why Mom and Dad don't want to be together anymore. I'll tell them the truth someday but I can't now. I don't have the emotional strength. The couple next door—I think they wanted to keep a relationship with Katya, despite how she'd lied to them, and were prepared to help her get proper documentation. But she disappeared. I'll pass it along that she's probably with Avery but Katya doesn't tend to listen to anyone except him."

Despite herself, Romy began to feel a little sorry for Katya. Growing up in an orphanage with not one but *two* rare conditions couldn't have been easy. If she'd been willing to put on this ruse, she must have been ferociously determined to leave her home country.

And if Katya was hoping to terrorize Romy in an effort to push her out of town, then she also had deep mental health issues.

"Another question," Romy said. "This is going back a long time but do you ever recall Avery telling you one of his students was in an abusive relationship with her boyfriend?"

"Ohhh," Alicia said, chewing ruminatively on a thumbnail. "Well, there have been a few times over the years he's expressed something like that. Unfortunately."

"This would have been Misty Glass. The girl who drowned twelve years ago."

Alicia quickly snapped her gaze up. "Oh! Yes. I do remember that. Because after the tragedy, he and I discussed whether he should go to the police with his concerns. But we were both worried it would be the wrong move, given that the surveillance video exonerated her boyfriend—I've forgotten his name—so thoroughly."

She finished her glass of wine and made a gesture at Romy's nearly empty glass. "More?"

With an hour-long drive back to Glass Town, Romy declined, though she wished for nothing more than to imbibe until her mind was numb.

Chapter Thirty-Four

*B*ack at home, Mack was itching to go outside. Romy had stayed away longer than she'd intended—having a late lunch with Alicia to absorb the wine before her drive, then she'd hit traffic around the capital, though it wasn't nearly as bad as she imagined it was prepandemic.

"Sorry you were on the porch for so long, boy," Romy told Mack as she watched him let loose a long stream of urine on the far edge of the property, then picked up the rest of his bodily waste with a bag. She could have done without this part of dog care but at least he was well house-trained. She certainly wouldn't be able to hold her bladder for as long as he was able to hold his.

She grew somber thinking how Mack would soon be living with his proper owner but at least he'd be right next door. That is, if she moved back to Brooklyn permanently. Her grandmother's house deserved more than to sit abandoned, surrendered to rot and termites.

And she didn't have the energy or money to buy a car and all that entailed with insurance and parking (a nightmare in the city), so she could get to the house more frequently. She either had to clean the place out and sell it, rent it, or move in.

These past weeks had been some of the happiest in her life, but only because she'd been here with Heath, the man as she'd *known* him, not as Avery and Gillian had perceived him.

Not to mention she didn't know what to think about Avery anymore. She'd never imagined he was the type to cheat on his wife but wasn't naive enough to think cheating wasn't common. What truly disturbed her was how he'd lied about it, not only flipping the narrative so that Alicia was the cheater but going into elaborate detail, even apparently faking a phone call with his ex.

The significance of this—that her former mentor was not just a liar but a world-class, trophy-taking one, gnawed at her gut like acid.

On the porch, she stared glumly out into the woods, her heart dull and flat, because she knew that her time with Heath was nearing its end if it hadn't ended already. He was on the verge of a mental breakthrough in which he would remember something that put Romy at the scene of Misty's death.

Even if he wasn't, Romy determined she had to tell him. Preferably before he remembered it himself. In her fantasies, he would—perhaps in the future—realize she'd made a horrific mistake but that she'd been an immature and headstrong young girl who'd not meant any serious harm and had no inkling of what she was setting into motion.

Perhaps he could forgive her, eventually. But he certainly wasn't going to want to continue to make love to her, to live with her, to maybe start a family with her. Not knowing what he knew. What he *would* know.

Romy had also decided she was leaving tonight, going back to Brooklyn. She would wait until it was darker so there would be minimal traffic. She'd never driven inside of the city and was not looking forward to it. The later the better, she figured. There was no other way to get Mack back into the city except driving; she certainly couldn't bring him on a train.

She'd take her grandmother's Volvo as she doubted a rental car place would allow her to place Mack in one of their cars. Besides, it was almost five o'clock. She knew from past excursions that they all closed at five. Since her grandmother's car wasn't insured, it was another thing to worry about, but she wasn't going to stay in the house one more night with Avery's crazed young mistress on the warpath.

She mostly worried about her own reaction. Seeing Katya again might make Romy angry enough to let Mack loose on her. Even though the "little girl" was trespassing, Romy still didn't want to risk the dog getting in trouble if he bit her.

After packing, she texted Heath: "Hey, sorry to do this to you but I've decided to come back early. You can stay if you think you're unsafe at home. We'll figure out arrangements. By the way, we need to talk. It's important. See you soon."

She left what "arrangements" she was referring to open but damned if she was going to give up her entire apartment. She hoped like hell she wasn't going to walk in the door to find a dumbfounded, furious, or devastated Heath who knew Romy was responsible for Misty and his unborn child's drowning. That *plus* city driving for the first time was really too much for any human!

By eight p.m., it was getting darker, and she scoured the porch, trying to pick up all of Mack's slobber-smelling chew toys. She needed to keep him occupied on the drive.

Then she wrapped some things in old newspaper that she wanted to bring with her—hand-painted china, silver-plated utensils, and knickknacks, including Nana's collection of snow globes. Once, she'd asked Nana why snow globes, and Nana only replied, "They're pretty."

That was Nana for you, she didn't try to make a simple thing unnecessarily complex.

None of the items Romy wanted to take back to Brooklyn were valuable except to her heart, and she figured she was going to need all the heart-soothing she could get in the near future.

As she was packing her things into the back of the Volvo, preparing to get the very last things still inside the house—her travel bag with laptop and personal products, as well as Mack—she remembered something.

Do it later, she thought. *Do it when you get home.*

But she couldn't. Once the idea wormed into her brain, she had to know. There was no way she would be able to wait four hours or concentrate enough to navigate the city streets until she knew.

It wouldn't take long.

She went back inside and got her laptop out of her travel bag, and gave Mack a chew toy to keep him occupied in the living room. Habit made her head to the rollout desk in her grandmother's room, where she placed the laptop and logged back into her hot spot.

After what Alicia had told her about Avery and Katya, after hearing Avery's bald-faced lies about what had caused his marriage's breakdown, she no longer trusted him. And she had a sickening suspicion that he wasn't what she'd believed he was.

Not now.

Not *ever*.

She pulled up her email provider, then changed the address to Misty's.

In the password bar, she typed: "averysands."

When she got the familiar "incorrect password" message, she was relieved. But she kept going. She couldn't *not* keep going.

She typed: "AverySands."

Suddenly, the email was open. Misty's life spilled out before her.

Chapter Thirty-Five

*A*rtRomeo: You are beautiful. There's no denying that. I'd be a fool to try. But honestly, Misty, your exquisite face, your body Marilyn Monroe would envy, your sweet voice—doesn't interest me.

Misty: What does? <smiley face>

ArtRomeo: Your mind.

Misty: <laugh face>

ArtRomeo: Your heart.

Misty: <laugh face tears>

ArtRomeo: You don't believe me?

Misty: No.

ArtRomeo: Meet me after class. You know where. To talk.

Misty: <smiley face>

ArtRomeo: Is that a yes? I don't speak emoji. Save that for your football hero.

Misty: I know where.

. . .

ARTROMEO: Hello, beautiful.

Misty: Hello. <blush face>

ArtRomeo: How do you feel?

Misty: <blush face> <blush face> <happy face> <happy face>

ArtRomeo: I feel that way too. <blush face> I guess I need to learn emoji.

Misty: When can I see you again?

ArtRomeo: What about Mr. Football?

Misty: <vomit face>

ArtRomeo: Use your words, please.

Misty: I mean, I could break up with him. But it's not like we're really a couple. People think that but we're more like friends.

ArtRomeo: Oh? Do tell. Has he not tasted the goddess nectar?

Misty: No. LOL.

ArtRomeo: What a simpleton.

ARTROMEO: Good morning, beautiful. I thought about you all night long. Do you want to know the things I did when I thought of you?

Misty: Yes.

ArtRomeo: I'll tell you later. I'll show you later. I'll show you lots of things. I love to hear you sighing. I love to make you cry out in pleasure.

Misty: Oh my goodness. <blush face> <kissy face> I didn't know it could be like that.

ArtRomeo: It can and it is and it will be. With me.

· · ·

MISTY: Hi, Romeo. I can't stop thinking about you.

ArtRomeo: I'm happy to hear that, beautiful. The feeling is mutual, as you know.

Misty: I'm going to break up with Patrick. It's not fair to him or me.

ArtRomeo: Of course, I'm happy to hear that as well. But I'm in no position to make demands.

Misty: I know. I wasn't asking you to.

ArtRomeo: Maybe one day.

Misty: <happy face>

MISTY: Romeo?

ArtRomeo: Hello, beautiful.

Misty: I think something has happened.

ArtRomeo: Don't keep me in suspense.

Misty: I think we need to talk.

MISTY: Romeo?

ArtRomeo: I'm here, beautiful. Was busy. Did you want to meet at the usual place?

Misty: Yes, but I'm nervous.

ArtRomeo: Don't be nervous. You know how I feel. Same time, same place.

ARTROMEO: Hello, Misty Morning. How did it go?

Misty: Not so good.

ArtRomeo: What happened?

Misty: He wouldn't do anything. I tried. I tried so hard.

ArtRomeo: Hmm. He must be gay.

Misty: No. He loves Jesus more than me.

ArtRomeo: What a fool. I can't imagine why you were ever with him.

Misty: <vomit face> <laugh face> What do we do?

ArtRomeo: Beautiful, we find someone else. Do you mean to tell me there isn't one buffoon in the school who wouldn't want to ravish you?

Misty: Ravish?

ArtRomeo: Never mind. Who else, Misty? Who is single, stupid, and a walking erection?

Misty: There's a cute guy down at the country club pool. The lifeguard. I don't belong to it but my friend does. I've caught him looking at me sometimes.

ArtRomeo: Cute, eh? You been flirting with this guy?

Misty: LOL. No. Don't be jealous.

ArtRomeo: How could I not be jealous? Am I not made of flesh and blood? Tell me more about this loser. How old is he? We don't need any more problems!

Misty: He's a senior. Well, graduated.

ArtRomeo: Graduated. Name, please? No wait, tell me in person. But if he just graduated, we're in the clear. And he should be man enough to get the job done. Sounds perfect.

Misty: <smiley face> I'll try.

ArtRomeo: Do you have a white bikini?

Misty: No, a blue one.

ArtRomeo: Go get a white bikini. The skimpiest you

can find. If he's straight, he won't be able to resist for long. We got no time here, angel. NO TIME. Don't play coy with him.

Misty: Okay, but then what?

ArtRomeo: I'm thinking.

ArtRomeo: Well, beautiful? Are you home yet?

Misty: Success.

ArtRomeo: That stabbed me in the heart though I know it had to be done.

Misty: <sad face> I see him again tomorrow. He's very nice.

ArtRomeo: Don't tell me how nice he is. Tell all your friends. Go out and do things. Be seen around.

Misty: There's a problem though. He made us use a condom.

ArtRomeo: What?!!! You found the one horny teen in all of America who wants to use a condom?!!

Misty: It's okay though. Tomorrow I'm gonna tell him I'm allergic to latex and am on the pill.

ArtRomeo: Misty. You MUST make this work. If he doesn't go along, we need someone else. Pronto!!

ArtRomeo: Are you back yet???

Misty: Success!

ArtRomeo: No condom?!

Misty: No.

ArtRomeo: GREAT. Now get out there and be seen

with him. Introduce him to your parents. The whole deal.

ArtRomeo: How did it go, angel?

Misty: It was awful. I didn't like that part.

ArtRomeo: You said everything I told you to say?

Misty: Yes. He got really upset. He's a nice person.

ArtRomeo: But we're in a bind, angel. A serious, serious bind. You understand, right? Do you truly understand? You know what is going to happen to me?

Misty: Yes.

ArtRomeo: And he's happy to bang you. He's bragging to his buddies.

Misty: He doesn't seem the type.

ArtRomeo: All men his age are the type. We need him to be the type.

Misty: I don't know. He seems to really like me.

ArtRomeo: Stop being so charming. Oh wait, you can't help it. <kissy face> What about the nosy girl next door?

Misty: She definitely heard it because she came over and asked if I was okay.

ArtRomeo: GREAT! Better than we could have hoped.

Misty: I told her there are two of him. One nice, one not nice.

ArtRomeo: I like that. Like the three faces of Eve.

Misty: Who's Eve?

ArtRomeo: Forget it. See you tomorrow so I can take the picture.

. . .

ArtRomeo: Hello, Misty Morning. I told you-know-who I was concerned for you. We've got it covered.

ArtRomeo: Misty Morning? You're quiet today.

Misty: I'm here.

ArtRomeo: What's wrong?

Misty: I don't know. Not sure I can.

ArtRomeo: Angel, it's him or me. Him or me.

Misty: Why though? I'm sixteen. I'm the age of consent.

ArtRomeo: For fuck's sake, Misty! Delete this email! You want me in prison?

Misty: Hello?

ArtRomeo: Did you delete that other thread?

Misty: Yes.

ArtRomeo: Then go into the trash and delete again.

Misty: But here's the thing. What if I say it's his? To everyone?

ArtRomeo: We've gone over this. You can't say it's his then take off. He'll try to find you, hire a lawyer. And I take off too? How stupid do you think people are?

Misty: Then we don't take off.

ArtRomeo: What are you saying?! Are you going to marry this loser? Live with this guy?

Misty: For a while. Until you settle things.

ArtRomeo: You're cutting out my soul! What is going on? I thought you loved me.

Misty: You know I do.

ArtRomeo: And when the kid gets older and doesn't

look like him but looks like me? What about us? You sound like you've fallen for this guy.

Misty: Don't be stupid! I love YOU. But I feel bad. He's a nice guy, that's all.

ArtRomeo: You have to stay the course, beautiful.

ARTROMEO: You there, angel?

Misty: Yes.

ArtRomeo: You cracking under pressure? How are you going to hold up when you get questioned?

Misty: I'll hold up.

ArtRomeo: You know when to leave me the message? You know when to take his phone?

Misty: Yes.

ArtRomeo: We'll be in Alaska by next year. People don't nose around there. I need to cash out, leave with recommendations. Untangle myself.

Misty: I know.

ArtRomeo: You're devastated, you go first. I follow later. Then it's you, me, and the baby. A FAMILY. Little cabin in the mountains. You can see for miles up there. You don't sound excited.

Misty: I am. I just feel bad.

ArtRomeo: It's the way it is, angel. Delete this email. Then go into the trash and delete again.

ARTROMEO: Did you delete that thread?

Misty: Yes.

ArtRomeo: You sure?

Misty: Yes. I deleted.

* * *

ROMY SAT HUNCHED OVER, clasping her midsection, her blood cold with shock. She'd gone through dozens and dozens of email exchanges. Over a hundred. Watched how he'd masterfully swooped in, seduced Misty with talk of her mind, then quickly pivoted to her young, nubile body. Misty didn't stand a chance against a velvet-tongued, thirty-six-year-old man who knew his way around a woman's body.

Misty was probably unfamiliar with the machination of "love bombing," which adult Romy could clearly see Avery was doing to the teen, but which Romy had no doubt that, as a teen herself, she would not have been able to comprehend either. It simply seemed as if he was madly in love with Misty—Romeo and Juliet. Or in this case, "ArtRomeo."

The end of Misty's yearbook profile entry: AR&AJ
ArtRomeo and ArtJuliet.

As she could see from the email dates, the pair had begun sleeping together before the summer Misty died. They'd started that school year—the second semester. Misty was taking his Intermediate Drawing. The same class that Romy was in.

Her mind swam with repulsion to see her mentor in his full slimy splendor, to have the outward caring, sensitive, and above all, *honorable* Mr. Sands peeled back to reveal the beast he was.

They'd obviously set Heath up to take the fall for the

pregnancy. Misty was, as she'd noted, the age of consent. But as a quick search revealed, an adult over age twenty in a position of authority (such as a teacher) could still be charged with statutory rape despite the consent age.

Add in that his career and reputation would be over if the truth came out.

You're devastated, you go first. I follow later. Then it's you, me, and the baby.

At some point, Misty would run away. After enough time so the two occurrences wouldn't seem connected, Avery would follow. During that time, he would probably start arguments with Alicia, create a rift in the marriage, perhaps manage to get a divorce and take whatever assets he could. Up and leave her with two young children.

You're devastated.

Romy could hardly bring herself to think it. But she knew it. Her cold, nauseous gut knew it.

After setting it up so it looked like Heath was the father of Misty's baby, they planned to kill him. And they had a great excuse—self-defense, as they were framing him to look like an abuser.

Gillian had witnessed an argument that Misty had clearly provoked with sure-to-anger words provided by Avery.

"The picture" he'd mentioned must have been a picture of the bruise on Misty's wrist, which either she or Avery had caused, not Heath.

I've told you-know-who I'm concerned for you.

You-know-who was obviously Alicia, who could back

up that Avery had been concerned about Misty's "abusive" relationship. As Alicia hadn't mentioned seeing a picture of Misty's bruise, it must have been something he was going to spring on the police once Heath was dead and Avery—or Misty or both of them—was being questioned as the killer.

You know when to leave the message?

This pointed to Misty planning to leave her art teacher a voicemail about Heath's jealousy and her fear of him. More "proof" he was an abuser.

You know when to take his phone?

Romy's mind backtracked to what Heath had told her—and what she herself had witnessed that night— that he'd left Misty on the pool platform to go to the outdoor changing station when he heard his cell phone ring.

Misty had earlier taken his phone and planted it there. Avery must have called it from a blocked number. The call would act as a signal between the two of them, letting Misty know that Avery was in the woods and ready. They also wanted Heath to leave the area, so Misty could jump onto the tarp. She'd find the rip that she and Heath had avoided on earlier romps, and get halfway into it.

While she was in the water, her upper torso held up, Heath would rush out to save her.

Romy's stomach twisted as she pictured the scene, because she knew the next thing that would happen. They were going to kill Heath. How exactly, she didn't know.

According to the email trail that Misty hadn't bothered deleting, the teen was clearly conflicted about the plan but she stood no chance there either—she was sixteen, pregnant by her much older, married teacher, and under the full persuasion of a master manipulator.

What Romy *did* know was that when her fourteen-year-old-self had hurried down through the woods and sneaked out to unlatch the tarp, she had blown up their plan.

Romy may have killed Misty that night.

But she had saved Heath.

Chapter Thirty-Six

"*Alright, Mack Attack, let's go!*"

Romy finally had all her stuff in the Volvo, everything except Mack, who sat looking warily at the ancient car, not eager to jump into the back seat. Romy didn't dare have him in front where he may distract her while she drove.

She was jittery enough about driving in the city for the first time—and how she was going to navigate the streets with everything she'd just learned thundering through her mind like black storm clouds.

Maybe she should try to get a hotel somewhere. But it would be hard to find a decent place not crawling with the virus that would also take a dog. Besides, she should be back in Brooklyn in less than four hours.

How, how was she going to tell Heath everything she knew? Should she even tell him at all? Was it better to let him live with his rose-colored memories of Misty? But knowing the truth might alleviate the misplaced guilt he had about not having saved her.

Either way, Romy couldn't stick around here and brood on it. She knew too much about Avery Sands and didn't feel safe in this isolated house with him knowing she was here alone, and his crazy girlfriend knowing it, too.

Mack reluctantly hopped into the backseat, made a couple of spins, grunted, and hunkered down. Romy put his favorite blanket and toys in with him. Then she closed the door, went back to the house, and walked around it, checking that the front and porch doors were locked and all the windows closed.

It was now almost nine p.m. and nearly completely dark. Her heart thudded as she surveilled the house, worried for anything that might be hidden in the shadows or behind a bush or tree. Her grandmother's house was no longer a place of refuge. For that, she despised Avery Sands even more than she did as she'd read his grotesque emails to Misty.

Why Misty hadn't deleted this highly incriminating digital trail as Avery was consistently haranguing her to do, Romy didn't know. But she had a feeling it was the teen's way of starting to rebel against his control.

Romy imagined their life in Alaska—if they ever got that far—wasn't going to be as idyllic as Avery was counting on, and Misty wasn't going to be the malleable young woman of his dreams.

Inside the car, Romy looked at Mack through the rearview mirror. "Ready, buddy?"

He whine-grunted, and she turned the key. The engine whirred, whirred, whirred, then sighed into silence.

"Please, no," she pleaded, but the car sometimes didn't start right away. So she turned the key again, and this time the engine made only a few thin, feeble whirring sounds before sputtering out.

"Shit!" she shrieked. At this, Mack instantly stood at attention and poked his nose over the back seat, snuffling her neck.

"It's okay, boy," she said, reaching to pat his jowls.

Staring into her phone, she wondered why Heath hadn't returned her text message. It was unlike him. Had he finally exhumed whatever memory he'd repressed from that night and had gone into hiding from Romy? Should she leave him a voice message about what she'd discovered—and how was she supposed to break it to him that the girlfriend and baby he'd been mourning for over a decade were... not his?

She tried to start the car once more and when it made clicking noises, she gave up. In frustration, she began to cry, salty trickles down her cheeks, but they dried within thirty seconds. There was no time for this emotional indulgence. She had to figure out a way to get out of here.

Going into her chat app, she called Patrick, whom she remembered owned a car repair shop. After a few rings, she was hugely relieved when his ruddy face appeared on her phone.

"Heyyyy, Romy," he said, drowsily. She felt like she'd woken him from a nap.

"Hi, Patrick. I'm sorry to bother you but my car died and I really need to get back to the city. Is there anyone at your shop who could help me out? I'd pay, of course."

He rubbed his jaw. "Well, if your car died, we'd need a new engine. I'd have to order it. Coming out and looking at it won't make it start, I'm afraid."

"Can't you jump it or something?" She felt bad she sounded demanding, considering it was late at night and she hardly knew him, but she was becoming frantic.

"If the problem is the battery, that might work but my wife is out with the car. Had plans with her friend tonight. My mechanic quit soon as the pandemic started, decided to go back to the Dominican Republic and I haven't hired anyone else yet because of everything going on."

"Oh." She couldn't imagine the couple having only one car and wondered if he was fabricating an excuse to not come help, but she couldn't blame him.

"When my wife gets home, I can come out and take a look, see if it needs a jump," he added. "What's your address?"

Gushing with gratitude, she gave him the address as Mack started to whine, making antsy circles in the back seat.

"It would be really great if you could," she said. "I'm sorry to be so demanding, but it's kind of... well, it's a bit of an emergency."

"Sure thing, Romy. Is everything alright?"

"Oh. I can't get into all the details. I only need to get out of Glass Town."

"Gotcha," he said with that Yankee-spirit, *mind-your-own-business* reserve that guaranteed he wasn't going to pry further.

They hung up and she sat dejectedly staring into the

dark, empty road right off the dirt driveway. Could she call a car lift? Putting her destination into the app showed it would cost about five hundred dollars (without tip!) to get home, and she had no idea if a dog would be allowed in the car.

The last time she'd brought Mack in a lift was when she'd met Gillian at the winery, as she didn't want to drive after drinking. It had been a hassle, with both drivers sighing and rolling their eyes and acting none too happy about their canine passenger. How would she find one willing to drive two hundred miles with him? Not to mention all the things she wanted to bring with her.

Gillian was being extra diligent about quarantining, as her young son was asthmatic, so asking to stay over her place was out of the question.

There was only one thing Romy could think to do, and that was to call Heath. He had transportation. But between his possibly having remembered something about that night that would sever his relationship with Romy, as well as her recent coolness towards him, the odds of him obediently hopping in his Chevy and making the long drive on such short notice were virtually nil.

"Hi, Heath," she said into his voicemail, in a hopeful and slightly panicked tone. "I hope you got my text that I'm coming home tonight. The problem is my grandmother's car died."

She looked up nervously into the ever-darkening surroundings. Woods, woods, all she could see were woods, and a streetlamp-deprived, lonely stretch of road that, after dark, hardly saw any traffic. "I don't want to stay even one more night. If you're able to come and get Mack and me, I'd be eternally grateful. I'd pay your gas, give you money. Please let me know soon as you can."

She sat breathing a beat or two longer into her phone, as if that might give him a chance to pick up, then hung up. Mack, sensing the delay had gone on too long, stood and wriggled restlessly.

"Okay, boy, I guess we have no choice but to go back inside."

She got out, let him out, and as was the habit of a city-dweller, locked all four doors since her belongings were inside. She brought her tote with her computer and personal effects back to the house. Each step over the cracked cement pathway, in the shuttering-down dark, with the cicadas beginning to scream, put her nerves on edge.

Nana had never owned a garage. The Volvo had always sat outside in the dirt driveway, through every kind of weather, often getting buried under mounds of snow in the winter. Once her grandmother got too frail to dig the car out herself, Romy had done it, or her grandmother had hired local teens.

Romy's skin began to crawl ominously with the idea that Avery or Katya or both had sneaked into the yard and disabled the car. After all, it had been fine on the trip to and back from Saybrook.

But why? Avery couldn't have known that she'd visited his soon-to-be-ex-wife. There was no way Alicia would alert him to that. And Katya wanted Romy *out* of town, not stuck in it.

Inside the house, she locked the door behind her,

flipped on the biggest living room light and the kitchen light. Mack trotted in-step alongside her, on high alert.

Then she got a big, sharp carving knife out of a wooden block on the kitchen counter, went to the living room, and sat down primly with it clutched in both hands. Mack wandered over and sniffed the knife, gave her hand a lick, looked around for his pillow bed, and not finding it, lay down on the floor, his expressive brown eyes focused on her.

"Now what?" she asked him. He cocked his head, listening, then seemed to shrug and settled his head on his ham-paws.

After an hour of almost continually checking her phone, the knots in her chest and shoulders began to loosen, the familiar furniture, carpet, pictures on the walls, and smells of the home relaxing her senses. Mack was sound asleep, softly snoring.

She supposed she could stay here one more night. In the morning, she'd talk Patrick into coming out to help her or she'd take a lift to the capital to rent a car. Or maybe Heath will have appeared by then, though she doubted it. He'd now ignored both a text and a jittery-sounding voicemail.

Her stomach was nauseous with the idea that he'd never speak to her again, that he'd remembered seeing her that night. He was probably packing his things, leaving her apartment. Or had already left and was trying to decide how to confront her.

She'd started a relationship with him despite her knowing what she'd done. That was unforgivable. It hadn't been his baby that had died—hadn't even, really, been his girlfriend. But Romy hadn't known that until this very night.

If he never spoke to her again, so be it. If he reported her to the police, so be it. Anything was better than living in this cage of guilt and perpetual on-edge sense of being found out at any moment.

Mack got up from his nap and trotted expectedly over to her with that particular look in his eyes and a slight wiggle in his rear that meant he had to pee. She supposed there was no way to avoid going outside.

Rather than taking him for a walk, she stood right outside with him on his leash, the front steps light on, letting him pee and anxiously canvassing the yard and surrounding woods, willing him to hurry up with his business.

"Hi, Romy."

Romy let out a startled scream and Mack began barking and pulling on the leash.

"Woah, woah!"

The man stepped forward out of the shadows. It was Avery Sands. Romy's heart went into a full gallop.

"Woah, woah!" he said again. "I'm sorry. I tried to call you but you didn't pick up and I started to get worried."

"What?" she gasped. Mack kept barking and she was yanking on his leash.

"I've been calling you," he said, louder, trying to be heard over Mack's barks. "To see if you're okay. I can see I'm scaring the daylights out of you. Are you alright?"

"Mack!" she commanded. "Stop!"

Mack stopped barking and whine-growled but his tense body remained inclined towards Avery, who was walking towards them slowly.

"Is he okay? Mack, buddy, you don't remember me?"

"You better stay away," she said, the quaver in her voice betraying her fear. Why hadn't she brought out the knife? "He's in a really bad mood."

"Why? What's happening? Romy, are you alright?"

"Stay away!" she shrieked.

Her voice was shaking in earnest now. Why couldn't she move back into the house? She was frozen to the spot. Should she let Mack off his leash?

The thought kept clamoring in her mind that if Mack attacked him, he could press charges, get Mack put down. After all, Avery would say he'd only come to check on her, and wasn't any threat to her, and yet she'd allowed the dog to maul him.

Then his arm went straight out. At first, she thought he was putting his arm forward as a gesture of surrender, to show her and Mack he was only there with good intentions.

But then he said, very calmly, "Keep the dog on the leash or I'll blow it to pieces."

Chapter Thirty-Seven

*S*he began to tremble and couldn't speak, realizing he had a black gun pointed at her.

"I'll say the dog attacked me," he said, still with that calm voice, the voice she used to take so much comfort in as she sat in his office, telling him all her hopes for her future. "I'm a great shot. If you let it off the leash, it's dead."

Mack stretched the leash to its full length and began a low, steady growl. It was a growl she'd never heard from him before, a growl that clearly indicated he was prepared to tear out Avery's throat. If she let Mack off the leash and he got shot, which she had little doubt he would, that would doom her as well. No, she couldn't let Mack die. She'd gotten him into this mess.

"I can't control him with a gun in my face!" she managed to splutter, her voice quaking so much that she was ashamed.

"Into the house, then put him in a room, or he's got a bullet in his dumb head," Avery said.

She pulled the leash and pressed on the door handle but her hand was violently shaking, her mind tumbling this way and that. She clung to the idea of Patrick. Hadn't he said he would come over? Or had he said he *might* come over? Her insides were quivering so badly she thought she might lose control of her bladder.

"Mack! Come!" she snapped, her voice with more authority. He stopped straining at the leash and she somehow got the door open.

Avery followed her inside, the gun still gripped tight in his hand. She had never seen any guns except a few antique rifles her grandmother kept in a cupboard in the basement. Is there any way she could get to them? Would they even work?

"Put him in a room and close the door," Avery said. "I'm not going to hurt you, Romy. I only want to talk."

"With a gun?" In her mind, the question had been a forceful holler but it came out as nothing more than a puny-sounding whimper.

She pushed Mack into the spare bedroom and shut the door. He began furiously barking. Maybe one of the neighbors would hear him but it seemed impossible, given how far away they were and that she'd made sure to close all the windows.

Avery waved the gun, indicating she should return to the living room. How was it in the movies people could do karate chops and disarm villains? She could barely hear what he was saying, the rush of cold fear was thrumming loud in her ears.

"I just want to talk to you," he said. "I saw you give the finger to the camera. I saw your car leave this morning and come back in the late afternoon. Did you go see Alicia?"

"So the camera is working."

"For me, yes. For you, no. I put you on a different channel and ran the same tape."

"Okay, she told me about Katya," Romy said, her voice still tremulous. "I have no idea why she's coming around. And I don't care. I just want to go home. What you two do is your business."

Humiliatingly, she sounded on the verge of tears. Where was her strength? There is no strength with a gun on you.

"But that can't happen. I think you know why."

"I don't fucking know why!"

Hearing her voice rise, Mack's barks exploded to a furious crescendo. Then he quieted and she heard a deep, intermittent thumping on the door. She realized with awe that he was throwing his body against the door.

"Let's go on the porch," she said, calmly as she could manage. "Mack is going to hurt himself. I don't know what this is all about. I don't give a shit if you have a girlfriend!"

He shook his head, looking amused. Now she absorbed his cat burglar attire—all black. Black long-sleeved shirt, black hoodie, black pants. No wonder he'd been able to emerge from the dark with no warning. And she knew that he'd disabled the Volvo.

On the side table, her gaze rested on the knife she'd been clutching only minutes earlier and she considered trying to grab it. But the thought swiftly fled into the realm of impossible. She'd never be able to grab a knife, rush forward, and stab him faster than he'd be able to pull a trigger.

"Alright then, let's go," he said. "Watch your moves."

As she walked onto the porch, she had the ludicrous impulse to offer him a drink. Maybe she could talk him down, get on his good side. He couldn't possibly have known she'd cracked into Misty's old email account. Why was he here? What did he want?

On the dark porch, she flipped on the light. She couldn't see anything outside and knew the porch door was locked. Was there any way she could make a run for it? Could she get the damn door unlocked before a bullet drilled into her back?

Could she get across the long yard and down into the woods? She could run, and run fast. And she knew the woods; he didn't know them. She could easily get in those trees and hide.

But then he'd shoot Mack. She couldn't have that.

"I don't understand what you want, Mr. Sands," she said, deliberately saying his name the way she used to say it in hopes of jarring him back to a time when Romy was a child, no threat to him.

"Sit," he said, indicating a chair with his gun hand.

The last thing she wanted to do was sit but she had no choice and shakily lowered into the chair.

"For years, Romy, I've kept my eye on you, wondering what your game was. Were you a child frightened into silence? If so, what would happen when you grew up?"

She said nothing but began to get the queasy,

dizzying feeling he'd lost his mind. If so, that meant there would be no reasoning with him, no talking her way out of this situation.

"I—I don't understand."

"No, *I'm* the one who doesn't understand. Did you truly... did you really *forget*, Romy? Just completely forget? I've read about things like that but didn't think they were real."

She sat with her mouth hanging open, her fear intensifying as his words grew more baffling. "I—I don't know," was all she could stammer.

"In case you hadn't forgotten, I was as nice as nice could be to you. Helped you get into college. Helped you fill out all those damn forms for a loan. Helped you secure the scholarship. Gave you a glowing recommendation, beyond what you deserved, if I'm honest. You're not the talent I was telling everyone."

Easy to say with a gun on me, shithead, streaked through her mind.

"But I felt you'd somehow *forgotten...* blocked it out. The first day back at school, I was scared. I was prepared to tell you that you were imagining things, prepared to deny, deny, deny. After all, you were a troubled kid. Your parents had abandoned you..."

Again, she fought off the desire to talk back to him.

"But when I saw you again, I saw no evidence, no trace of it in your face, in your eyes. Heard nothing of it in your voice. Quite fascinating. Then years went by with no indication that you remembered. I started to let go. Truly, I did. You live your life, and I live mine."

"Yes," she nodded. She'd say whatever it took to

keep him from killing her. "Yes, exactly. No hard feelings."

His eyes darkened and she had the sickening feeling that she'd said the wrong thing.

"What do you mean *no hard feelings?*"

Her head shook, at a loss. "I don't know. I—Mr. Sands, you're scaring the shit out of me and I have no idea what you're talking about!"

"Misty!" It came out a hiss.

Oh God. He knew that she knew about their affair. How, how? Had he somehow planted spyware on her laptop?

"That was a long time ago," she said.

"Not that long. Twelve years. Every day hell for me, if you want to know the truth."

She remained silent.

"You know a man in his thirties, with a wife and two kids, a teacher of all things, isn't supposed to fall in love with a sixteen-year-old. But I did. Then what? I'm a monster. A predator. They'd put me in the news. I'd never work in education again, and that's the only thing I'm qualified to do. I would have treated her a hell of a lot better than any boys her age would have treated her but *I'm* the monster. What's a pimply-faced, binge-drinking asshole going to do with a girl like Misty? Give her bad sex and toss her aside, that's what. I would have treated her like a queen her entire life. But *I'm* the predator. *I'm* the monster."

Sounded like you were going to keep her knocked up in the middle of Nowhere, Alaska, is what Romy wanted to say but didn't dare. Whatever Avery had felt for Misty wasn't love. More like an obsession with a beautiful but inanimate object—a master painting or classical figurine. If he'd loved her, he would have let her grow up before doing what he did.

"So, we came up with a plan. Had to. No choice."

Mack was quiet. She hoped he hadn't rammed himself against the door so much that he'd passed out.

"I understand," she said. "It's unfair."

He squinted suspiciously at her. "Don't think you'll fool me by pretending you get it. Because you don't. Now you show up in town with that loser who was the last one to be with my Misty. The last one to kiss her, caress her, see her face. You show up here and want to play happy family in front of me?"

"No." She put her palms up in a calming gesture. "That's not what we were doing. We left because of the virus, that's it."

"I don't know, Romy," he smiled, eerily. "I think you came here to torture me. Rub my nose in it. Misty gone. Our baby gone. *All because of you.*"

Her heart lurched into her throat, beating erratically. She couldn't speak. How did he—

"I don't know if you don't remember or if you're only pretending not to remember. That's the thing. I don't know." He raised the gun, pointing it right at her face. "What kind of game are you playing with me?" he shouted.

As he raised the gun, it all flooded back. The gun right in her face, pressed up against her mouth so she could swear she tasted metal.

Chapter Thirty-Eight

The last thing she saw at the pool was Heath, sprinting from the changing station, *slap slap slapping* his bare feet on the platform pavement. Then she heard that dulled thump after he disappeared into the pool, and a muffled splashing.

Her stomach was icy and twisting. She knew something had gone catastrophically wrong but didn't know how to correct it. There was nothing at all she could do. She didn't have a phone, so she couldn't even call 911. She was not a good swimmer, and there was no way she would be able to help anything.

Pure panic took control. She scurried out from behind the wide tree trunk, turned, and tried to clamber up the hill, but forgot to take her flashlight out of her cut-offs' pocket, forgot to dig her feet in sideways, so she slipped and slipped back down, falling flat onto her stomach. The air got kicked out of her lungs and she lay trying to suck it back in.

At that moment, a stream of light wavered along the ground. When she looked up, she realized it was a flashlight and it was coming towards her. Instinctively, she rolled off the trail as the light got closer and closer, and she thought the light was right on top of her but it passed her. She lifted her head and saw the silhouette of a man's back.

He was standing looking out over the pool area.

Romy couldn't take in what was happening—in all her nights of coming up and down through the woods, she'd never once run into another human being. How could this man be in the woods?

She couldn't move and it felt like an eternity that she lay on the ground, with only her head held up, looking at the man as he looked at the pool.

"Oh my God," she heard him groan.

The voice struck her. It was a terribly familiar voice but she still couldn't piece together who it was or why he would be here in the woods.

"Get her out!" she heard the man say. "Get her the fuck out!"

That's when she recognized the voice.

"Mr. Sands!" she called.

The man instantly turned, the flashlight turning as well. The light stabbed straight into her eyes. She squeezed them shut and turned her face away, the back of her eyelids bursting with red hues.

"Who's there?" he hissed.

She didn't know why she had called him. Now she couldn't speak. Something inside of her told her this was all wrong, all wrong. Things were happening that were beyond her comprehension, yet she knew they were bad things. Things she had to get away from.

That's when she heard Heath's voice, loud, forceful, and barely holding down hysteria.

"Yes, I'm at the country club pool. A girl fell in. She can't swim. The—the tarp came off. It wasn't hooked. She got caught under it. Hurry! I'm giving her CPR but she's blue. No pulse. I can't bring her back! Country club pool. Hurry! Please. Hurry!"

"What the fuck is... what the *fuck*..." The voice of Mr. Sands, but not Mr. Sands. A Mr. Sands she'd never heard, never known.

Romy started to scramble up the hillside. She only wanted to get away, get back in her bed, back to her grandmother, back to not knowing about this dark adult world with its sex and treachery.

Then she heard the animal-like wails of Heath, the haunting cries that would assail her young mind for so many years. There was a glint of light beside her, and she heard the pounding of feet on the trail. He was right behind her.

She crashed into a prickly tree branch, and her feet fell out from underneath her. She slid back, clawing at the ground. He grabbed one ankle, pulled her, then somehow flipped her over. Shone the flashlight directly into her eyes.

"Romy, what the fuck are you doing out here?"

Face averted, eyes squeezed shut, she shivered with fear, unable to make a sound, her jaw trembling. Her wrist was grabbed, grabbed hard, and pushed down flat on the ground.

"Romy, did you do something to that goddamn tarp?"

"Just... p-playing," she stammered.

"*Playing*? Did you unhook it?"

He put his hand over her mouth, the beam of the flashlight no longer in her eyes. She opened them, stared up at Mr. Sands's face. The teacher with whom she'd spent so many hours in class, at art fairs, in his office. He was like her second father. Not this man on top of her, with his rough hand smothering her mouth.

"You did, didn't you? You unhooked the fucking tarp!" He was hiss-growling in her face, spittle spraying on her. "Why the hell did you do that, Romy?"

She could only try to shake her head. He lifted his hand from her mouth and bent farther into her face. "Why?" he demanded.

"I—I don't know. P-prank."

"You stupid little bitch." Then there was something in her face, something hard and black. A gun. "You killed my girlfriend. You killed my baby."

He brought a hand down on her neck.

"No," was the only thing she could say.

The hand began closing around her windpipe and she couldn't breathe, there was no air. *Help!* she screamed in her mind. *Help!*

Right then came a bright, blinding flash, it silently and brilliantly illuminated the entire forest. It flashed, flashed, flashed, then was gone. This made Avery unlatch his hand from her neck, and he turned to glance behind him. She hurled her fist up and hit as hard as she could on the bridge of his nose.

"Aargghh!"

She swung again, connecting with the sharpness of his cheekbone, then started kicking, kicking, kicking, maniacally, frantically.

His weight was gone and she began a mad scramble up the hill, digging her feet in sideways, up, up, up, panting, panting, panting, up, up, up, all the way up the hill.

Everything she'd experienced peeled away behind her, was shed like a dried-up, useless skin, because she had no room for it in her mind.

To hold it in her mind would mean a life she didn't want to live, a thing in her head that would push out all good things.

So she made it smaller and smaller and smaller with her mind, until it was only a blip, until she held it between her thumb and forefinger. And she extinguished it.

Chapter Thirty-Nine

"*Y*ou remember now," Avery said. "I can see it in your eyes."

"I don't know what you're talking about."

But when she reflexively darted her gaze away from him, she knew she might as well have announced, "I'm lying!"

"Alright, let's go," he said, jerking the gun towards the porch door.

"I'm not going anywhere, Mr. Sands. If you want to kill me, you're going to have to do it here."

The "Mr. Sands" was another effort to get him to remember that they used to have a cordial, even familial, relationship—that he used to be a human being. But like that other attempt, it was futile.

She was reaching for a version of him that she remembered, yet hadn't existed. Her memory of what he'd done to her in the woods proved that.

"I don't want to kill you," he said. "I want to show you something."

"Not leaving," she said, tensing her hold on the chair, shaking her head.

Whatever he wanted her to see, it wouldn't be any good. She was better off here where any minute Patrick might beep his horn or knock. Where there was a tiny hope Mack might succeed in beating down the door, for she now knew, with hideous clarity, that Mack had stood between her and death, had been her last hope, and locking him in a room may have saved him but it had doomed her.

Avery turned and looked outside. Romy followed his line of vision and saw a circular light bobbing in the darkness of the yard—a flashlight. It got closer and closer until it was right outside of the door. Hope soared as she imagined the arm directing the flashlight belonged to Patrick, or even a neighbor who'd heard Mack barking. Her lips popped open and she took a breath in anticipation of calling out.

But Avery's body language caused her stomach to drop back to sickening reality. Holding the gun in her direction, he moved sideways to the glass door, fumbled with the lock, then it was open.

The girl—*woman*—came up the porch's few crumbling steps and was inside. Katya.

Romy's insides gushed with fear because she felt on an instinctual level, by looking at her, that Katya was even crazier than Avery. And there was no history between the two women that Romy might appeal to and eventually succeed in tapping into.

Katya's white-blonde hair was pulled back, her all-black clothing offset her pale skin, round cheekbones, and brilliantly azure eyes. Romy was still struck by how childlike she appeared—not more than five feet tall with a slim, wiry build. Her bare arms were visible, ropy as those of a teen boy.

Despite outward appearances, it was now strikingly clear to Romy that she was no child. Not with that stone-cold look in her preternaturally blue eyes, a look that said she'd been around this planet for a while and found it lacking.

Avery flicked the gun towards Romy, said, "Go ahead," and Katya was coming at her with rope in her hands. Romy catapulted up from her chair, dashing into the kitchen. Katya was on her in a flash, bringing her down to the floor, sending chairs scudding and toppling across the linoleum.

On the floor, Romy thrashed and kicked but Katya was shockingly strong and easily slung Romy on her back and straddled her. Romy registered Mack's frenzied barking. If only she could get to the door and open it, he would tear them both to pieces.

Katya held Romy's midsection down with thighs of steel, and Avery was quickly over her. He must have put down the gun because he had both hands free to hold her arms straight while Katya expertly began wrapping the rope around her wrists.

Feeling herself becoming helpless, Romy spat at Katya several times but her mouth was so dry with terror that it only made an airy-sputter.

Within what seemed a matter of seconds, her wrists

were completely bound with rope, locked together as tightly as if they were sealed in a concrete block.

Romy was screaming nothing she recognized as words but she knew it was hopeless, there was no one around to hear her. All she was doing was making Mack agitated to the point where he'd probably injure himself trying to get through the door.

"Fuck you, fuck you, fuck you!!" she screamed, then went limp, drained from her pointless struggle, and filled with self-loathing that she'd wasted so much energy when she was so out-muscled. She should have used that energy to come up with a plan that relied on savvy, not strength.

"If you don't want your legs tied too, you'll start to cooperate," Avery said.

Her legs. Her legs were still free. This was the only thing that could save her. She stayed limp as a sign of surrender. Cautiously, Katya lifted off her pelvis and stood staring down with that creepily pale face. Avery grabbed Romy by her bound wrists and hauled her up until she was able to tilt towards him, get on one knee, and lever herself off the floor.

Then they marched her out the back door, through the yard, and down into the woods.

Chapter Forty

*S*he hadn't been in the woods since that night. But they were still keenly familiar to her—the tall, wraithlike birch trees, the thick, towering red maples, oaks and poplars, the musky-sweet scent of pine hanging thickly in the air.

It still felt like her territory, and her feet still knew their way around, planting sideways into the trail like they used to, with the glowing moon and lights of the capital half an hour's drive away bouncing up to the sky and back down into the woods, giving it an eerie, dim glow.

Thousands of fireflies hung suspended everywhere for a moment like fluorescent Spanish moss before dissolving their green and orange-hued lights. An exquisitely beautiful scene but for the horror of why she was here.

Katya and Avery had flashlights, and between their beams and the swollen moon, there was enough light to see maybe fifty feet in front of her before everything was swallowed into darkness.

At first, she imagined they were going to shoot her and bury her in the woods. But as they kept on the narrow but mysteriously still well-worn trail, the fear of being shot in the head and buried in a dirt grave gave way to an even greater, more singular fear that congealed around her heart like a frigid vise.

They were taking her to the pool.

"Why are you doing this, Mr. Sands?" she cried, but terror had her voice box in its grip, and her question came out nothing but a whimper. "I'm not going to tell anyone what I know. Haven't I kept it a secret all these years?"

"Shut up!" he snapped in an aggressive, low growl.

Katya, who wasn't that far ahead on the path, and who clearly had been spending time learning her way around the woods, stopped and turned. Avery's flashlight beam hit Katya's face and her expression communicated something to Romy—communicated it instantly. But whatever that wordless message was, it was diffuse.

"Keep your mouth shut, or I'll put a bullet in your brain, and go back and finish off the dog," he said.

They kept traipsing down the path until Romy grew so shaky with fright that her legs buckled. She collapsed to the ground like a sack of rocks, and lay on her side, blindly staring into a nearby tree trunk.

"For fuck's sake," Avery said. Katya doubled back, aiming the flashlight's beam right on Romy's face. Romy could only gaze into the tree's dark, rippled bark, hoping that death would mercifully come quickly.

She had no strength to fight them, physically nor mentally. She only wanted to use this remaining time to think about those she loved.

Her parents. She should have talked to them more, appreciated them more, and been more patient with their quirks. How would they feel knowing she'd been murdered and suffered greatly beforehand? Would they be able to live the life remaining to them with happiness? She didn't want them to live a miserable life, constantly bowed under the trauma of their daughter's murder.

Heath. She'd always loved him. Always. She didn't know why, didn't care why. It was a simple fact, and she couldn't question it or doubt it any more than she could question or doubt why a rose smelled pleasant.

She should have told him the truth about what happened that night. Maybe he would have understood. Even if he hadn't, he'd deserved the truth. How she would miss him.

But wait, she wouldn't miss anyone, would she? Where was she going? What happened after this life? Was it all a void of nothingness?

Now she knew why she'd been summoned to the pool, why the idea of unhooking the tarp had drummed persistently away inside of her tender young brain, the drumbeat escalating until she was forced out of her bedroom and down to the pool.

Because something had intervened. She'd been the conduit for a spiritual force that connected her and Heath. This power had told her he was about to die, and she needed to do something about it.

Did this mean there was an afterlife, guardian angels, perhaps? And if guardian angels existed, where was her angel right now?

Please, if you exist, help me. Don't abandon me.

"Hold this," she heard Avery say. He grabbed her bound wrists and hoisted her up from the ground. "Keep walking, Romy."

His voice was smooth, almost friendly, the familiar voice of her mentor, not this unreachable monster. "I'm not going to hurt you," he said. "I want to show you something and I knew you wouldn't come if I asked politely."

He's lying, her brain screamed. *He's lying!*

"Katya, give me the gun," he said.

Katya handed it to him, and she looked at Romy in a way that was... not how she'd been looking when she first came onto the porch. Looking... dare Romy grasp onto hope that there was pity in her strange, hard eyes?

"Run up ahead and..." Avery broke into a stream of another language. To Romy's untrained ear, it sounded like Russian. But from what Alicia had said, it was likely Serbian. He must have learned enough to communicate with Katya on a basic level.

Katya gave Romy another lingering look, then darted down the path like quicksilver, her alabaster ponytail and arms and black clothing giving her the appearance of a disembodied specter. She moved breathtakingly fast—there one second, then simply gone.

"Keep walking. Now we can talk a little," Avery said, still with his voice so calm and paternal that it dissolved

278

a bit of the cold, tingly fear gripping her chest. Maybe there was still a way out.

"Tell me why you're doing this," she said, her lips trembling as if it was the depths of winter. She hated how terrified she was, wanted to turn and punch him in the face, kick him in the groin, get away from him like she'd managed to get away from him once before.

But that night, her youthful ignorance had worked in her favor. She'd reacted like a trapped animal, all instinct. Back then, she hadn't given a half-second's thought to a bullet that could have pierced her small back. Now, she was too aware of the odds stacked against her, about death and how real it was, how it came to young and old, good and bad, sick and healthy alike.

"Romy, you're going to tell that moron what you know. You have to. Because you love him and you want him to stop mourning. And what will that mean for me?"

"I won't tell."

"Of course you will. And I can't have it. I'm in enough trouble with the whole Katya thing. If Alicia, my girls—everyone—knows about Misty, that would be one scandal too many, I'm afraid. Alicia and I are still negotiating the divorce. Maybe Misty's parents sue me. Or I'm belatedly charged with a crime. Who knows! Besides, you and that moron—I can't say his name—don't get to have what you denied to Misty and me."

"We're not even together."

"You will be. Once you come clean with him, he'll forgive you. I saw the way he looked at you in the grocery store. I saw the look of 'She's the one I want to spend my life with.' Maybe you couldn't see it but I could."

"What was the plan?" she surprised herself by asking. It seemed pointless to need to know all the specifics when she was going to die but she did. "You were setting him up to look like he'd gotten Misty pregnant and was abusive. But how did you plan to get rid of him?"

Several moments passed in which she could only hear their feet crunching softly on the trail's thick carpet of pine needles, and she didn't think he would answer her. She might die never knowing exactly what she'd interrupted that night, and for some reason, this was unbearable for her. But then he began speaking in a monotone.

"She'd once told me about a rip in the tarp that she'd stuck one leg through by accident, how much it had scared her. That got me thinking. If she went halfway in, being a lifeguard, he should have no problem getting her out. Of course, you fucked that up. She went completely under."

"I know all that. Tell me how you were going to kill him."

More soft crunching of pressed pine needles, the occasional chirp-warble of a bird, and the sounds of small animals scattering in the brush. If she got lucky, they'd traipse upon a bear den and an enraged mother would surprise them.

"She left me a voice message that she was meeting him down at the pool to tell him she was expecting," he said. "She asked me to come and secretly watch them because she was worried about his reaction. Knowing his history of violence, having seen and taken a photo of her bruise, I took a licensed gun with me. When I got there, I was supposed to see them in the pool—him trying to drown her. Then I'd rush down like a super-hero and…" He stopped speaking but he didn't need to say anything else.

He was going to shoot Heath and claim he'd done it to save Misty. Both Heath and Misty would be wet from the rip in the tarp, and cops could very well buy the entire story. At any rate, it would be Avery and Misty's word against a dead man.

"Why would you even bother telling him about the pregnancy if you were going to kill him anyway?"

"Romy, Romy," he clucked. "So many questions. I suppose we hoped he might react badly. That would have made our jobs a lot easier. Imagine if he'd even gone so far as to hit her. That would have been a jackpot."

She wanted to tell him not only had Heath not reacted badly but he'd asked Misty to marry him—and she'd said yes so swiftly and excitedly that perhaps she wasn't as in love with Avery as he imagined. But Romy knew that would mean a bullet in the head.

"What about the surveillance camera?" she asked.

He laughed in a slow, short clap of *heh heh heh* that didn't sound like he found anything amusing.

"We didn't know about it. He never mentioned a camera to Misty. Think of that. You not only killed Misty and saved the moron's ass but you saved mine too

—from a murder charge. Though I might have gotten away with justifiable homicide if I could have proven I had legitimate reasons, made in good faith, to believe that he was trying to drown her, not save her."

He sighed loudly, as if it was a bother that his murder plans had been unfairly thwarted. Romy desperately wanted to point out to him how his faulty plan sounded unlikely to succeed, and he should take some responsibility for Misty's death—but she knew he'd only ever been pretending to be the type of person who believes in accountability.

He'd convinced himself that Romy was the one thing that stood between him and utopia with a teen beauty in the Alaskan wilderness. He'd spent more than a decade crafting this chimera, and there would be no dismantling it here in the woods.

"Now I belong to the club," he said. "Why would I want to be where Misty died? This is *why* I want to be here, the last place she was. There's no tarp anymore. The club decided it was a liability. It never installed more cameras. But what's the best part?"

His silence stretched on until Romy realized he expected her to come up with an answer. She finally said, "I have no fucking idea."

"The best part is, we're in a pandemic. Members got an email that the pool will be closed all summer. Everything is shut down. Including the one camera. I know for sure because I asked the president if he could check the footage for a puppy that was last seen near the pool, could have slipped through the gate. He helpfully informed me about the camera being off while the pool is closed."

Romy saw the woods opening up, saw the dark pool area through the thinning scrim of trees. As they were headed for where Misty died, she guessed he would find it poetic justice to kill her in the same way his teenage love had been killed.

Drowning.

Her hands were tied, and he was going to fling her in the water. If he kept her feet untied, she might be able to kick to the top.

But she'd spent too much of her youth idly sitting outside of the water, reading, drawing, or fantasizing about Heath, when she should have been inside of it, swimming her ass off in preparation for the day her maniac art teacher was going to try to drown her.

"Does Katya know what this is all about?" she asked.

When he didn't answer, she had her answer.

Katya was going along with this for another reason. That's why he'd gotten so angry when Romy had alluded to his past with Misty. Why he'd told Katya to run ahead before he would speak.

What he'd said to convince Katya to haunt Romy's windows, help tie her up and march her to a pool, and then throw her in, she couldn't imagine, but it must be a doozy.

She tried to think of what Katya was most scared about. Losing Avery? Had he told Katya that he and Romy were lovers?

"What was the point of all this? Sending Katya to my window?"

The question seemed to take Avery by surprise, because the soft crunch of his shoes on the pine needles came to a halt. She turned to look at him. His flashlight went down and it was too dark to see his expression but she could feel it.

He was contemplating her question, as if the answer was a mystery.

"I suppose, Romy, it was to torture you," he said.

Chapter Forty-One

*a*t the bottom of the woods, the pool area was in full view. It looked exactly as it had twelve years ago. But because it was closed, none of its platform lights were on.

Avery indicated that Romy should walk to the left, exactly where she knew he would tell her to go.

The gate was open and Katya was standing at its mouth. Romy realized that Katya had slipped through the same bent metal bars that Romy used to slip through as a teenager. Then she'd merely walked to the locked gate and opened it from the inside.

The underwater perimeter lights that normally gave the pool an aqua shimmer were turned off, leaving a gulf of darkness.

But the powerful chemical smell of chlorine made it terrifyingly clear the pool was still filled. The scent instantaneously retrieved her youth—the long, lazy, humid summer before her sophomore year, her painful yearning for Heath Asher, her profound pleasure when they'd talk, her dreams for a future career in art and leaving Glass Town. It was all there in the chlorine's molecules, fossilized as if in amber.

As Avery pointed her through the gate, Romy's heart was spasming so hard against her ribcage she thought there was a realistic chance she might die of a heart attack before he threw her in the water. This would be merciful. In fact, she was considering begging him to shoot her in the head. Anything but toss her into that water.

She weighed screaming as loud as possible. There were homes along the hillside. As she used to hear voices floating up from the pool, someone could hear her. But she knew the second any loud noise left her mouth, he was going to bum-rush her, or Katya would do it, and she'd be in the water.

A scream wouldn't do much good anyway—people would think it was someone horsing around or, if she got lucky and someone called police, it would take them a while to figure out where the scream had originated from. More time than she had left.

She had to think, think. She stood no chance with Avery. But Katya… hadn't Romy detected a hint…

Think, think.

Katya was a woman. A woman in love with this man. Why, why? What was the thing she loved about him?

The way Alicia had sourly said, "Anything is possible with those two." It sounded like their relationship was volatile. Maybe Katya wasn't as manageable as Avery would like. Maybe she had a mind of her own.

Suddenly, Romy yelled out, "He got a sixteen-year-old girl pregnant, Katya!"

"Shut up!" he growled, moving towards her.

"Is this your hero? He got a sixteen-year-old pregnant while he was her teacher! I've got proof!"

Sharp pain smashed into the side of her face, so forcefully she thought her left eye had popped out of her skull, and she was down on the pavement. He'd hit her with his fist.

"You're going in, bitch."

He started dragging her with one arm by the rope binding her wrists. She wildly kicked, screaming, "Katya! Help me!"

Katya yelped in her reedy, childish voice, "What she say? Pregnant girl?"

He let out a stream of foreign language as he kept dragging Romy towards the pool while she futilely kicked.

"She deport me, no?"

Romy latched onto the word "deport" as if it was the one thing between her and death, which it very well might be.

"No, Katya! I won't deport you! I can't deport you! He lies! Help me!"

"What she say?" Katya shrilled in her high-pitched, girlish voice. "She not deport me?"

"She wants to deport you. She's working with Alicia. I told you."

"Lies!!! Lies, Katya!!!"

Katya ran over to him and pulled on his hands. That little body was supernaturally strong and she managed to pry his fingers off the rope, sending Romy's arms plummeting to the pavement.

"Why she say lies?" she demanded. "You lying, pig?"

"I'm not lying. *She's* lying."

"Katya, he got his student pregnant," Romy yelled breathlessly, trying to roll on her side. "I know all about it so he wants me dead. I wouldn't deport you. I'm just a designer!" She tried for a word sure to be understood by someone who may not be English fluent. "Artist!"

She realized Katya and Avery were physically tussling and this was her chance.

"Tell me what she saying, pig!" Katya spat, grappling with his hands.

Romy thrust her body to the side, got on her elbows, and began the awkward process of trying to stand. She teetered up and staggered towards the gate but within twenty feet, pitched sideways and capsized, slamming down onto the platform.

"Help!!!" she screamed, her voice raw and hoarse.

Avery was on top of her and shoving something into her mouth, some kind of cloth.

The cloth went deep to the back of her throat, smothering her. Then he was dragging her by the wrists again. Her loose pants had been pulled down in back from the dragging, her bare back scraping along the cement, but there was no pain. There was too much adrenaline for pain. She kept kicking her feet, hoping to loosen his grasp, but he was so strong and fast.

"Katya!" he whisper-bellowed. "Get back here!"

Romy didn't see Katya anywhere. Had she left? Oh God, she'd left. Her last chance. No!

At the edge of the pool, he sat his full weight on her thighs to keep her from kicking, then leaned into her face. His expression was startlingly calm and blank.

He grabbed the bound rope with one hand and held it steady as she desperately tried to pump her feet, hoping to dislodge him off her thighs. Then he reached into one of his hoodie front pockets and took out something. She saw his other arm rise up and fiddle quickly with the rope but she was blind with panic, unable to take in what he was doing.

"There's a GPS tracker under your boyfriend's truck. He's half an hour away. When he gets to your place, I'll be waiting for him with this untraceable gun. He wanted you to die where the mother of his baby died. You were a fool who confessed to him. Then he took his own life. Murder-suicide."

She tried to scream but the cloth only worked its way farther down her throat. If she didn't drown, she was going to choke to death.

He was off her and rolled her to the edge of the pool. Then he plucked the cloth from her mouth and rolled her once more.

"This is for Misty."

Chapter Forty-Two

*S*he hit the water face first. It rushed up her nose, harsh and stinging and cold. Her lips were pressed tight but her heart was banging so spasmodically against her ribcage that she knew it would only be several seconds before she'd have to draw a breath that would instantly kill her.

This was the way she was going to die. A flood of water into her lungs and like a bullet to her brain. Here it was, all around her, undeniable, absolute, all-encompassing, death held back by a thin, permeable membrane, by one breath, yet the soul clings so resolutely to life, there was still a large part of her that refused to believe it. She'd wake up from it. It couldn't be real.

She started madly kicking, trying to get velocity under her legs so she could paddle upwards. Her bound wrists went up, down, up, down in frantic, helpless strokes, but she instantly realized the movements were burning energy that she needed to store to keep her breath held.

She felt herself sinking, sinking. If she let go and allowed herself to rise, the air in her lungs might offer enough buoyancy to float her to the top but she would have to take a breath before then.

She wasn't ready to die. Too young. Too much to do. Not her time, not her time. Her soul cried out the one and only thing it could. The one and only thing before being wiped out, plunged into the vast unknown.

God, help me!

But there was no God here. It occurred to her to go out gracefully. To not die in stark terror. In her last seconds, fractions of seconds, to have... dignity.

She opened her eyes and all around her was inky blue bleariness, as if she was in a womb. She heard her heart thump-thumping in her ears, and that's all she could hear.

To open her mouth and take one quick, sharp, final breath so she could die without suffering. Die with dignity. It was all she had, all she had.

The words came, quite clearly, inside her skull.

I'm with you.

I'm with you.

I'm with you.

A feeling unlike any she'd ever felt or imagined enveloped her. Peace. Utter and complete peace, serenity and oneness with everything.

It saturated her, a sensation of belonging to the water, to its atoms, to the universe, and all beyond the universe. The water inside of her pores, flowing through her veins, passing along her neurons.

She was rising. Being lifted.

I'm here for you.

The words were inside of her head, being spoken very plainly, in a voice she would never forget. A voice from her youth, a time when all possibilities lay before her, everything wide and open and welcoming, dreams obtainable, future golden.

Why?

I know you didn't mean for it to happen.

Black strands of hair fanned and floated in her vision like underwater reeds, and she turned her head enough to see the sky-blue eyes of her youth, the face she'd once thought to be the most beautiful face she'd ever seen, in fact, the most beautiful one in existence— because in that face shone the reflection of the love of the young man she herself loved.

If you hadn't done it, he'd be dead. I was young and stupid and in love. What I thought was love.

Do you forgive me?

Of course. I always forgave you.

Are you happy here?

Oh, very. We don't suffer anything.

The stinging cold was loosening its grip on her lungs, the feeling of weightlessness coming to gravity. She was almost near the air, near the surface.

Misty?

Yes?

I'm sorry.

And she burst forth.

Chapter Forty-Three

*S*he gasped loudly, pulling a deep funnel of air into her starved lungs, the sweetest, sweetest, most exquisite feeling.

Harsh water drizzled out of her nose as she rolled to her left side, paddling her arms as if she was in a canoe, again and again, forceful one-sided stroking in a rhythm that wasn't perfect but kept her moving towards the edge of the pool.

The moon glowed bright enough that she could see the glint of the silver pool ladder's handles. Pumping her tied arms to one side was taking too much chest power, she had to grunt with each paddle, and she worried the noise would alert Avery that she was still alive and he'd return and finish her off. She tried pumping her arms up and down in front of her but that was strenuous and hardly moving her.

So she rolled on her back and went into a frog kick that she remembered from childhood swimming lessons, keeping her tied hands pulled close to her chest. This slushed her forward through the water but with nothing that could be described as speed.

When she sensed she was close to the ledge, she turned her face and was about a foot from the ladder. Beaten with exhaustion, she grasped the top step with her fingers, pool water drooling from her nose and mouth. She bobbed there, not knowing what to do if he came back and pointed the gun at her.

She lay her head wearily on the top step, breathing hard, her lungs still grateful for air, still worried it might be taken away from her any moment, floating up and down with the slight undulation of the water.

A crack-pop split the air and she jerked her head up, adrenaline shooting through her body again. The sound hadn't been very loud but it seared her soul, penetrated straight into her heart. For she knew what it was—the gun going off.

Avery had reached her house, and when Heath arrived, he'd been shot. The "murder-suicide" for which Avery planned to frame Heath. The sound of the gun had ricocheted down through the forest.

Heath, she cried out silently. *Heath. I couldn't save you this time.*

She sank her head back to the top step, breath coming raggedly, salty tears spilling out of her eyes, and she tried to wail, to give voice to her grief but nothing came out of her mouth. This was the sadness Heath had experienced that night. The grief she'd always, shamefully, been grateful had not been hers to carry.

"Romy!"

Her bleary, stinging eyes went wide and she stared straight ahead down the length of the pool, not sure what was real and what wasn't.

"Romy!"

It was Heath. It was *Heath*. But Avery had killed him. She was hearing him like she'd heard Misty. He was a spirit now, a vapor.

"Are you down here? Romy!"

Weakly, she turned her head and tried to see up over the ledge. She bent her right leg and fumbled her foot in the water until it found the bottom step of the short ladder. But with tied hands and unbearable hollowness, she didn't have the strength or maneuverability to climb it.

"Huhhhhh…" The word came out foggy and desolate, like the last utterance of a dying person. He had a name that formed not on the tongue but almost solely inside the lungs, exactly where she had no power.

"Romy! Where are you?"

"Heeeeeeee…" she croaked as loud as she could, triggering a coughing fit that was louder than she could call. She kept coughing and hacking, watery phlegm jarring and rattling inside her chest.

"Oh my God, Romy!" One arm was grabbed, then the other. "I got you." He was pulling and she was pushing her leg down, or at least trying to, and within a few seconds, he'd hauled her to the platform. "Stay on your side," he said, propping her.

Chlorine-tasting water spurted out of her lungs and

onto the platform. Keeping her on her side, Heath reached around and began working the knot on the rope. It came loose and he unwound it, sliding it off her wrists.

Then he wrapped his shirt around her chest, pulling it up close to her neck. That's when she began to shiver, her teeth clacking so hard she worried she'd crack them.

"Yes, I need an ambulance," Heath said authoritatively. She couldn't see him but assumed he was speaking into his phone. "We're at the country club pool on Country Club Lane. There's been a near-drowning. ... Yes, she's breathing. Romy, can you speak?"

"Uhhhh..." she groaned.

"Yes, she can speak. Barely. Hurry. Okay, thank you."

She tried to tip forward but he wouldn't let her. "Stay on your side."

"Maaaahhh..." she groaned, as close as she could get to "Mack."

"I came to the house and all I could hear was Mack barking, barking. I found him in a room and let him out. He was crazed and had a leash on. Went tearing around the house. You weren't anywhere. I saw your phone. He tore out to the porch and was scratching at the door. He dragged me around the yard. That's when I heard you screaming. I thought you were in the woods."

"Uhhhh..." she groaned.

"I started down with him straining at the leash. I was about halfway down when I saw this—this *figure* coming up the path. A man. Mack went berserk. The guy's flashlight went in my eyes. I—I let the leash go. Mack shot off and the guy screamed. Last I saw, Mack was on top of him. But I had to keep looking for you. Was—was that a gunshot? What was that?"

"Aaaavvv-errrr… he… he... try… k-kill… *kill*…"

"Aver?"

"Saaaannnn… Saaaands…"

"Jesus Christ, the art teacher? Romy, what the hell happened?" He tightened his arms around her and her shivering subsided for a moment. All she could think was Avery had a gun and would return for them any second.

He must have killed Mack. Oh my God. Mack.

"He… cuh-come… guh-guh…"

"Okay, can you stand?"

She nodded. Heath stood and was pulling her up but her feet felt as if they wouldn't work, only slabs of numb flesh. Leaning heavily on each other, they started slowly hobbling.

"Guhh," she croaked. "Guh-guhn. Caaaall. Hellllp."

"Hello, we need the police. There's a guy with a gun in the woods. Avery Sands. The art teacher at Glass Town High. For some reason, he's trying to kill my girl-friend. … Country Club Lane. We're at the pool. I just called for an ambulance. I'm trying to get us out of here. … Yes, she says he has a gun. … No, I didn't see it but I heard it. He's going to come for us. … Uh, Caucasian. Forty-something. Dark hair. About five foot ten. … I don't know what he's wearing. If they see a pittie, he's our dog. Tell them don't shoot the dog, okay? Don't shoot the dog!"

They faltered through the open gate and haltingly

walked towards the road, dimly lit with a smattering of streetlamps.

"We're on the road," Heath said. "We're coming up the road. If they see the dog, tell them not to shoot the dog, okay? Don't shoot the dog!"

"Maaa…" she groaned. While Heath seemed convinced Mack was alive, Romy knew he wasn't. Avery had kept threatening to kill him, and he'd done it. Oh God, what would she tell Bill?

The wail of an ambulance was getting louder and closer.

"Okay, I hear the ambulance," Heath said into the phone. "Are the cops coming? … Okay. Oh shit! Holy shit!"

Romy followed his line of vision. At first, she thought the stooped, four-legged creature was a raccoon. But then she realized it was Mack, trotting out of the trees circling the pool's perimeter. He appeared to be out for a casual stroll, his leash dragging behind him.

"Maaaa…" she cried, but it came out a croaking warble.

Heath whistled an ear-splitting whistle and Mack snapped his head in their direction. "Mack! Here, boy!"

Panting, Mack started towards them but the screech of the siren was growing louder and louder. Worried he would get startled and run, Romy drew all her breath up with every ounce of strength her lungs could muster, and rasped out, "Maaaack! Come herrrrre!"

She squatted and opened her arms. He trotted faster and faster until she had him in them, her head on his comforting, muscly body, inhaling his earthy scent.

She stayed on the ground with him, shivering, and holding him tight.

Chapter Forty-Four

*I*t had been at least four or five hours since she'd tremblingly climbed into the ambulance and an EMT strapped her sitting up into the gurney.

The last time she'd seen Heath, despite one of the EMTs returning his shirt, he'd stood bare-chested and holding onto Mack's leash. The gun must have gone off but hadn't hit Mack, who didn't have a scratch on him. Heath peered despondently at her as one EMT put an oxygen mask over her face and the other closed the doors.

At the hospital, various doctors and nurses in full protective gear came in, listening to her chest, taking her blood, and giving her a chest X-ray. Mostly they listened to her chest, wanting to make sure she wasn't going to suffer an awful-sounding thing called "dry drowning." She was wrapped in a white puffy blanket through which pumped warm air.

She had several stitches sewn into her left cheek,

where Avery had slammed her with his fist. Fortunately, he'd missed her eye, and managed not to break her jaw.

After a few hours, a masked policeman entered. He took what statement she could manage to give him, not having the strength to speak at length.

About an hour after he left, he came back and told her they'd found Avery, hiding in the woods, half of his shirt ripped off his back but otherwise with no severe injuries. She was disappointed that Mack had let him live—and with all his limbs intact, no less.

As she didn't have a phone nor anyone's phone number memorized, she lay there waiting to see if Heath would call. Because technicians kept listening to her chest, they didn't want her on pain medication, which would knock her out. She didn't want to sleep anyway, terrified of what dreams might take hold.

At around three in the morning, her bedside phone rang.

She was now unbearably tired but still unable to sleep. Each time she shut her eyes, she could only see Avery's face, his last blank look before he casually tipped her into the water, as if she was not human, only a piece of trash.

All she heard were his last words to her: "This is for Misty."

Then her mind would spin downwards to her time in the water, how defenseless she was, nothing but neurons silently screaming with the sickening terror of sinking and the harrowing, excruciating certainty she was about to die.

Until she heard Misty's voice inside of her head. Until Misty guided her to the top.

She had no doubt what had happened was real. Misty had come to her rescue. But Romy knew everyone would tell her she'd had an end-of-life hallucination.

People who survived near-death experiences universally reported seeing the dead, they'd say. The brain is flooded with dopamine right before death, causing a sense of peace, triggering tranquilizing, calming hallucinations.

But Romy knew the truth.

"They won't let me inside the hospital because of the virus," Heath said on the phone. "How are you feeling?"

"Better. I'm pretty sure I can leave tomorrow." Her voice was stronger, the pain in her cheek continually throbbing.

"Cops have the house cordoned off but let me get your phone. I got a hotel that would take a dog. I think they're desperate now with no one traveling. Do you want me to call your parents?"

"No, no. I'll tell them once I'm out of here. I don't have the strength to talk to them tonight and deal with their reaction."

She lay on her side with the large, white, plastic landline under her head, on her good cheek. They were both silent for several moments before she said, "I didn't know you were coming."

"Yeah, sorry about that. I decided to come down to talk and didn't realize my phone was dead. When I hit a rest stop, I gave it juice but didn't check my messages.

The whole time I was driving, I felt like I needed to rush. It—it was the strangest thing. Once I got to Route 2, I gunned the truck. Ran red lights. Like I knew. Knew I had to get to you."

Eyes closed, she couldn't help thinking about what would have happened if Heath hadn't rushed, hadn't run red lights. He would have given Avery enough time to get back to the house and kill him.

"Heath," she said quietly, her lips pressed all the way up against the mouthpiece. "I told the detective everything. Now I have to tell you everything. I don't know how you're going to feel about it but I have to tell you and I have no idea how to do it. So here goes. Um. Heath... I'm the one who unhooked the tarp that night. It—it was supposed to be a prank. I panicked and ran and I couldn't bring myself to tell anyone. I feel sick about it. I don't blame you if you hate me. But there it is and there's nothing I can do about it."

Silence. Silence during which she only heard continual beeping and muffled voices from the hallway.

"Yeah, Romy..." he finally said in that low, slow drawl. That voice she loved hearing so much but which she now anticipated was going to slice her to shreds before hanging up on her. "You know I've been sleepwalking. A couple of nights ago, I sleepwalked right into your dresser. It was the first time I woke up in the middle of a dream."

She absently listened, bewildered as to why he'd choose this moment to bring up his sleepwalking.

"But... I started to believe it wasn't a dream. It was the memory I'd been blocking." He paused. "After the ambulance took Misty that night, it left me there. There were no cops involved, not at that point. I went back into the main building to look at the surveillance video. I wanted to see what the hell had happened, because it was all so jumbled in my head."

He paused again, and she listened to his breathing, the world suspended in time.

"Romy… I saw you. I saw your back and your hand. I knew it was you. I saw what you did. I knew why you'd done it. Because you liked me and were messing around."

"Oh my God…" They were quiet for a long time. Finally, she whispered, "You didn't remember?"

"No, not until two nights ago."

If what she'd done was on the surveillance video, why hadn't police come to get her? Why hadn't she been arrested or sent to a juvenile detention facility?

"I don't understand," she moaned. "Cops must have seen me."

"Romy…" he said. "Is anyone in the room with you?"

She turned to peer around the room, because sometimes a nurse would come in and stand silently by her. But no one was there. The door was open, she could hear the same muffled voices and ceaseless beeping.

"No," she said, under her breath. "No one's here."

He was silent for several seconds, then said, "I erased it. That part of the tape. It was only about five seconds. I was used to erasing the tape, did it every morning when I got into work to cover up Misty and me being there at night. It was stupid, cops could have figured it out but I guess they never bothered to look back that far. Once they saw her jump and go under, and me giving her CPR, it was open and shut."

"Jesus," she said, but wasn't sure she had said it aloud.

"Then I guess I blocked out what I'd done. Which also blocked out seeing you."

They were quiet again, and Romy heard what she recognized as Mack whining in the background. He clearly had to go outside.

"I'm so sorry for everything," she said.

"I know. It was an accident. But…" He paused and the silence was charged. She strained her ears for whatever he was about to say next. "You were fourteen. What you did was unintentional. I was eighteen. What I did—erasing the tape—wasn't." He paused again. "Do you understand what I'm saying?"

"Yes. Yes, I get it."

So now it was Heath who had a secret to protect. She might not be charged with anything but he could very well be.

"The detective advised me to get a lawyer," she said. "Like a fool, I'd told him the whole story before he mentioned that. Even if I'm not charged, everyone in town, especially Misty's family, should know the truth."

"If it's any consolation, I'm here for you, Romy. If it helps at all."

She began to cry, immensely relieved and touched that not only Misty, but Heath, had forgiven her.

"There are other things that are going to come out," she sobbed. "About Misty and you…"

"Yeah, I've kind of been piecing together why Avery Sands got involved. It was his baby, wasn't it?"

She nodded into the phone and, realizing he couldn't see that, stammered out, "Yeaahhhh."

"Romy... were they... were they planning something that night for me?"

"Yeeahhh..." she croaked.

"Was it... to kill me?"

She nodded but again realizing he couldn't see that, went on, "Y-yes. But don't—don't blame her. She—she —was... under Avery's control."

Misty saving her from the water was still so clear in her mind. Romy had to do what she could to defend her.

A long, resigned sigh came through the phone as Heath's mental portrait of the pure, kind-hearted Misty he'd loved for so long slipped away and was replaced by this new, more complex, much more gray-area Misty.

"I don't blame her," he said. "She was so young."

Romy huffed and sniffled, trying to rein in her tears and maneuver her emotions to a degree of stability. She'd been getting oxygen on and off for the past several hours and it had made her loopy.

"You called me your girlfriend," she said.

"I—sorry, I did what?"

"On the phone with 911. You called me your girlfriend."

"Oh." Pause. "I guess I didn't have time to... well, okay. Maybe I did." Longer pause. "What do you think about that?"

Then because when the end was imminent, when

she needed to take a breath that would kill her, there was one big regret that had haunted her mind. Something else she should have said but had not. She would say it now, no matter the result.

She told Heath she loved him.

Chapter Forty-Five

One Week Later

"I'll see you tomorrow," Heath said, looking down from the driver's seat of his Chevy. "You're sure you're okay to stay here for the night?"

"Yep. PD asked me not to leave town yet, so I'm not leaving town. Not even for the night."

She'd told Heath how the "little girl in the window" was actually Avery's twenty-year-old mistress, and who knew where she was now.

But despite Romy's determination to keep on the right side of the truth these days, she couldn't bring herself to tell police about Katya's involvement in her attempted murder.

Yes, Katya had disappeared in the middle of it. But Romy knew that the young woman, like Misty, had been under the full sway of Avery. And as Katya appeared to think she could be deported because she'd entered the country with false documents, had taken off somewhere.

Romy could only hope that as Katya was free from Avery's manipulations, she would go on to have a decent life.

Romy's lawyer (a woman recommended by her mother's former business attorney) said Avery and his lawyer weren't saying much yet but appeared to be hatching some kind of "the pandemic made me go crazy" defense.

He currently sat in jail, charged with a litany of criminal offenses, and denied bail.

Romy and Heath met in the middle, her on her tiptoes, him leaning down through the driver's window, and kissed. Mack, in the passenger seat, put up with it for several long moments before making a loud *let's get going* yowl.

Bill was feeling much better and yearning to have his companion with him. Heath would clean out his room at his apartment and move his belongings to Romy's, then return to Glass Town until the police cleared her to leave.

Romy had decided she was a city gal. The action, the culture, the magnified view of humanity, both good and bad, is what she craved—not sitting here watching the woods.

Positive cases had come down significantly in the city, and though there was talk of a "third wave" that would hit in a few months, Romy wanted to be in her city.

There were many small but impactful things she

could do to help out—ask a neighbor if they needed errands run, walk dogs from a shelter, patronize local businesses that must be struggling.

Besides, Glass Town had turned out to be a bit too crazy for her tastes.

But it was nice to get away occasionally, and Nana's house was the perfect place for that. For both her and Heath.

"Mack Attack," Romy said, stroking his soft, gargantuan head through the passenger window. "You be good. I'll see you soon, okay?"

Mack eagerly stood, letting out a playful yelp, thinking she was going to open the door for him. "No, you go with Heath. Your Daddy Bill is well enough for you to go live with him. But we'll be right next door." He gave an eager bark, then reluctantly settled down on the seat.

Heath tapped his bottom lip, and Romy came back around to give him another kiss. "Drive careful, okay?" she said.

"Will do, Golden-Eye. Wait, did I say that out loud?" He smiled mischievously.

She gaped at him for several long seconds, then burst out laughing. "Oh my God. How did you figure that one out?"

"Took me a while," he said, pointing at his temple. "I went through my emails with Golden-Eye. There were a few times she used expressions that were, let's say, old-timey. Once, she said, 'right as rain.' Another time, she apologized for being a little late by saying she was 'losing her marbles.' You lived with your grandmother. I put it together."

"Um," she said, squirming. "Sorry."

"And your eyes. They're golden."

"They're brown, kind of hazel in the sun."

"Golden."

She tried not to smile, but couldn't help it.

"All I want to know is if that's the last thing?" he asked. "Or is more coming?"

"No. That's it. I swear on Nana's ashes."

"Then come here."

He leaned down, and they kissed for several more moments until Mack gave an exasperated yowl.

"By the way," Heath said. "Loretta asked if we'd like to go to her wedding. Because of the pandemic, it's going to be online."

"Wedding?"

"Yeah, her and her girlfriend." He grinned. "I didn't know either."

"Sure," Romy said, adding Loretta's supposed crush on Heath to her mental list of things she'd been stunningly wrong about.

She and Heath waved to each other and she watched as his truck disappeared down the curve of the hill, a giddy grin plastered to her face.

Chapter Forty-Six

*A*bout an hour later, she was cleaning out her old bedroom, piling things aside that she wanted to bring back with her to Brooklyn, including the musty braided area rug, when the doorbell rang.

She grabbed her favorite cloth mask hanging on the nearby wall pegs. The pegs used to be for keys, hats, umbrellas, and the like. Now they were filled with various masks she'd ordered online, ninety percent of which were too uncomfortable or itchy to be worn for long periods.

At the door was the lead detective on her case, Detective Jarrod Bourbeau. Even behind his black mask, he appeared young enough to have graduated from the police academy in the past week or so.

The district attorney had not yet made a decision as to whether Romy would face criminal charges for what she'd done as a juvenile. Many factors would be taken into consideration, including Misty's parents' wishes.

But Romy's lawyer believed prison time was highly

unlikely; at most, she would receive community service and probation.

But there was always the chance that Misty's family could bring a civil case against her. Because of this, Romy's lawyer insisted that she not try to speak with Misty's parents herself, though it was the thing she wanted to do most.

Her lawyer had also informed her that Misty's parents had long been aware of the possibility that Heath may not have been the father of Misty's child. Heath's timeline of when the pair began having sex and the coroner's estimation of the fetus's age did not match up.

But, at the time, Misty's parents had assumed Heath was lying about the couple's date of first copulation to avoid admitting that Misty had cheated on Patrick, junior prom king and star quarterback.

As Heath was never charged with a crime, the business of Misty's remains was solely the purview of her parents. They had chosen, for whatever reason, not to share this tidbit with Heath. Perhaps, grieving as they were, and given the press's preoccupation with their daughter's death, they didn't want to open up the possibility of the press then becoming obsessed with the question of Misty's sex life.

Now that Misty's parents knew the truth of the baby's paternity, Romy's lawyer said they were gunning for Avery Sands, and may even be willing to work with Romy in order to get him the maximum in his attempted murder case.

"Hi, detective," Romy said.

"Sorry to bother you. Mind if I come in for a few?"

"Sure thing." She opened the door and let him in. He was so tall that his head, like Heath's, nearly grazed the popcorn ceiling.

"I wanted to show you something we managed to get," he said.

Romy indicated he should sit on the couch and she sat next to him. He had a leather case hooked to his belt and he unsnapped it, then took out a mini-tablet.

"I wanted to ascertain again how you believe you got out of the pool," he said.

"Well, I don't remember much of it. I kept kicking, and I suppose I managed to float to the top."

"Miss Renskler, we believe the ten-pound weight found in the pool was hooked to the rope around your hands."

She didn't know why he was pressing her on this. She'd been asked all kinds of questions, but the majority of them had to do with what Avery had said and done inside of her home, and what he'd said and done as he'd marched her through the woods and down to the pool.

Detective Bourbeau had numerous times returned to how Avery had been able to tie her hands, and she'd said he had a gun and she'd thought it best not to test whether or not he'd use it. So she'd put her wrists together and allowed him to bind them.

But she couldn't bury the feeling that the young officer suspected that Avery had had help that night, and for whatever reason, Romy wasn't revealing this to him.

"The weight must have come off," she told him.

Then, a bit exasperated, "All I could think about was I was going to die. I don't know how I got to the surface."

She certainly wasn't going to tell him the truth—that Misty's spirit had saved her.

"I understand," he said. "I know this is difficult for you, we're just trying to figure out what happened."

Bourbeau tapped around his tablet, and Romy's heart beat faster as she realized there was every chance that the pool's surveillance camera—which he'd earlier confirmed had been turned off—had been turned on after all and the camera had caught all three of them: Romy, Avery, and Katya.

She still hoped to keep Katya out of everything—didn't want to be responsible for the young woman being sent back to whatever she was trying to avoid in her home country.

It's not that she forgave Katya for helping Avery, or even how she'd run off after changing her mind about being a co-murderer but that Romy knew how it felt to be under Avery's spell. Knew how good he was at weaving it, and that Katya, given her impoverished background, had had even less chance of not falling under it than either Romy or Misty had.

Add in that Avery wielded Katya's real fear of deportation as a way to control her, and Romy felt Katya must have been practically brainwashed.

"Turns out the club had another camera, and it was turned on," Bourbeau said. "They forgot about it."

"Oh!" was all she could say as her heart rate ticked upward.

"They installed it a few years ago—inside of the pool."

"In—inside? The pool area?"

"No, inside the pool itself."

Romy was clawing at her leg but couldn't stop. "Okay," she said.

"We believe what the camera caught is very important," he said. "But I don't know how you feel about seeing yourself. Seeing yourself... in the position you're in."

There was an enormous, stone-hard lump in her throat. She could hardly take in what he was saying. "You mean it... sees me? Under the water?"

"Yes." He nodded soberly, sympathy in his eyes over his mask. "I do believe you should see what's on here, Miss Renskler. But I want you to be prepared for it. Would you prefer to view it with your lawyer present? Or a social worker? A friend or parent?"

What a sly thing he was. He must have known that by showing up with no warning, bringing the tablet and having it sitting mere inches away was going to be too tempting for her to delay the viewing until she could find emotional support.

"No," she said, gnawing on her thumb knuckle through her cloth mask. "I should see it."

He made another tap on the tablet, then shifted it towards her. She saw the square box of a video; it was dark and blurry.

"You're ready?" he asked. "If at any time you prefer to stop, say so. Just say 'stop.'"

She nodded and he pressed the cursor button.

The video was very dark, with only a shaft of wide, diffused light slicing through the middle of the screen, what she imagined must be moonlight.

When something hit the water, all she saw were millions of tiny bubbles. When those cleared, she could see herself, or the silhouette of herself, fanned-out hair obscuring her face, her bound hands floating ahead of her, slightly weighed down by her chest, her legs akimbo.

She happened to be wearing light pants that night—loose cotton pants, as the temperature had risen, and she'd wanted a comfortable drive back into the city. The pants ballooned out from her splayed legs.

She looked utterly helpless, like a fetus in a womb. Then she watched as she began to twist and impotently kick her legs like a beetle flipped on its back.

Everything in her dropped to the pit of her stomach, watching herself like that, and remembering the torturous feeling of being completely powerless and doomed, with her brain racing downwards to its final forever quiet.

Bourbeau's finger was on the screen.

"This is what we're looking at, here," he said, as a stream of bubbles cascaded into the left corner of the screen.

Romy's mouth hung half-open as she realized that what had saved her—what she was absolutely certain was Misty's spirit—was going to appear in some form on the video.

The thick funnel of bubbles started to break apart and fly away upwards to the top of the screen.

Through the shadowy gloom came the silhouette of

an arm, and another arm, and two hands, looking so graceful, like an underwater ballerina.

The two hands went around Romy's bound wrists and a small dark circle—the ten-pound weight—fell away and sank out of camera range. One hand stayed on Romy's wrists, the other arm floated upward, and slight legs and balletic-pointed feet began to kick. The two silhouettes started to ascend.

As Romy's floating hair fanned and thinned out, a large split appeared, and in that space, something else appeared. The detective stopped the video. He put his finger directly over the space created by Romy's freeze-framed swaying tendrils.

It took her a long moment to process what appeared inside of the tendrils was a face. The face was blurry and shadowy, but the more Romy stared at it, the more it began to crystallize into an image she dimly knew.

"This," the detective said. "Someone jumped in and brought you out. Do you know this person?"

Romy sat staring, staring, for this wasn't what she'd expected. This wasn't what she'd heard or experienced.

"I don't," she said, shaking her head.

"You're sure? It appears this person removed the weight. Saved your life."

She made a quick calculation. Bourbeau seemed like a nice young gentleman. Should she be straight with him? Tell him what she feared?

She couldn't, because she herself didn't know exactly why she was doing what she was doing. She'd gone so many years protecting her own secret, and now she had no secrets but she'd become the protector of not one, not two, but three people with secrets of their own. Bill, Heath, and now…

Yes, "this person" had saved Romy's life. Therefore, Romy must protect her, must save her back.

"I don't remember," she said, looking away from the screen, towards the window, in which she half-expected to see Katya, grinning with that strange, otherworldly mouth, staring with those luminous, aquamarine orbs.

Katya, the woman who'd found the strength to defy the man she'd thought was her chance at a new life to come back and rescue the life of a woman she didn't know.

Romy had not been wrong about her. On the trail in the woods, she'd sworn she'd seen compassion flickering in Katya's mesmerizing but hardened eyes. This made Romy turn her efforts from trying to sway Avery back to humanity and using instead what little time she had left to sway Katya.

She'd chosen correctly.

While in that dark, sealed, watery tomb, Romy had not heard, seen, or felt Katya. She'd heard, seen, and felt Misty. Perhaps her brain, sputtering to its demise from lack of oxygen, had made a last-ditch effort to absolve herself from her guilt and conjured the form of Misty for her absolution.

She'd believed while in her terror in the woods, when her soul had begged for a guardian angel, Misty had responded.

But it had been Katya. Katya was her guardian angel.

"Miss Renskler?" the detective asked. "Look closely."

"Sorry," she told him, defiantly folding her arms and flopping back on the couch. "I don't know her."

In a way, this was the truth. Whoever Katya truly was, whatever or whomever she was running from, Romy didn't know. Would probably never know.

For the rest of her life, when she'd think of Katya, as she often did, Romy would see her as she looked with that thin, underdeveloped body, that pale, almost glowing-white skin, and those extraordinarily blue-blue eyes.

She would see her as she stood outside Romy's window, looking just like a little girl.

FOR MORE THRILLERS by C.G. Twiles, please sign up for her newsletter at CGTwiles.com or keep reading.

If you enjoyed this book, it would be much appreciated if you leave a review. Reviews are the life-blood of an author and often determine whether or not books are carried at retailers. Thank you for reading *The Little Girl in the Window*.

More Thrillers by C.G. Twiles

Please request my books at your **local library** or **bookstore**. See CGTwiles.com or my Instagram page for all retailers.

Brooklyn Gothic*: A Modern Gothic Romantic Thriller*

While working in a Gothic mansion, an idealistic young reporter begins to suspect her multimillionaire boss—and lover—is keeping dark secrets.

The Neighbors in Apartment 3D*: A Domestic Suspense Novel*

Cintra suspects her new neighbors have kidnapped a child. But who will believe a compulsive liar?

The Last Star Standing*: A Psychological Thriller*

A forgotten talent show winner has a second chance at success. But first, she'll have to murder the runner-up.

About the Author

C.G. Twiles is the pseudonym for a longtime writer and reporter who has written for some of the world's largest magazines and newspapers.

She enjoys traveling, animals, old houses, ancient history, and cemeteries. She lives in Brooklyn.

Please find her on social media, she'd love to connect!

facebook.com/cgtwiles

instagram.com/cgtwiles

goodreads.com/cgtwiles

bookbub.com/profile/c-g-twiles

Acknowledgments

As always, much gratitude to my readers, for without you, there are no books.

A major debt to Liz Alterman, my buddy and compatriot in publishing. Thank you to my astute beta reader, Megan Easley-Walsh, and to Polly Kahl for dialogue help.

Much gratitude to Bookstagram for your support and warm welcome.

To the first responders and essential workers: While Romy and Heath left Brooklyn, I did not, and I'm in awe of your strength and perseverance during the pandemic.

Thank you so much to my online support network: Wide for the Win, Trauma Fiction, Cops and Writers, Vellum Users.